Wood You Marry Me?

Lovewell Lumberjacks Book 2

Daphne Elliot

Copyright © 2023 Daphne Elliot. All Rights Reserved

No part of this book may be reproduced in any form or by any electronic or mechanical means, including information storage and retrieval systems, without prior written permission from the publisher.

This book is a work of fiction. The names, characters, places, and events in this book are the product of the author's imagination, and any resemblance to actual events or places or persons, living or dead, is entirely coincidental.

Published by Melody Publishing, LLC

Editing by Beth Lawton at VB Proofreads

Cover design by Elora Sperber

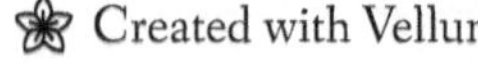 Created with Vellum

Chapter 1
Hazel

I always envisioned my wedding day... differently.

Granted, I was fairly certain I would never *get* married. So right away, things were not going according to plan. But if I did, I would do it right. Not because I was a particularly traditional person, but because I wanted to experience every special moment.

I imagined laughter and happy tears and an overabundance of hugs from friends. I did not imagine crippling nausea. However, that may have had more to do with my inflamed gallbladder than my impending nuptials.

Regardless, this was *not* the happiest or most romantic day of my life.

The strangest? Absolutely.

The most confusing? Without a doubt.

I would deny it with my last breath, but deep down, I wanted a wedding. More so than the ceremony, I wanted the dress and the flowers and cake. And the party. I did enjoy a good party.

Growing up the way I had, poor and with a mother who drifted in and out of my life, meant there hadn't been many parties. No birthdays, no family dinners, no celebrations. Not of my own, at least.

Though I'd told myself I didn't need it, and I was doing just fine without it, that desire remained. The longing to have a special moment that was just for me and my groom. The first dance, cutting the cake, a dress fitting with my best friend where we laughed and cried and drank champagne.

I secretly wanted it all.

But instead, I got a municipal building in Bangor, Maine, on a chilly Tuesday morning.

I got stained drop-ceiling tiles and industrial carpet instead of votive candles and chandeliers.

As I stood in the reception area, waiting for them to call our names, my stomach churned.

Relationships had never been on my to-do list. And I was a hell of a list maker. But I had learned early on that men were nothing but trouble. So I'd had fun. I dated. I slept around a bit in my early twenties. And I was content with that.

My mom was a young college student when she discovered she was pregnant. She dropped out of school, and in no time at all, she had two kids under two and was stuck in a trailer park in Northern Maine while my dad disappeared on benders for weeks at a time.

When I was really little, before she started using, she would tuck me in at night and make me promise to go to college and get a good education and a good job. She made me promise that I wouldn't give up my dreams for anyone.

And every night, I would look into my mom's haunting gray eyes and swear it.

Though none of that meant I was a nun.

Dates weren't hard to come by in the city. Especially in academia. In data science, the men outnumbered the women five to one.

I dated casually, had flings now and again, and some one-night stands. I liked sex, and I was pretty comfortable with my body. But I always used protection and never let feelings get involved.

Because I had come too far to get derailed now. That doctorate was so close.

To most, it was nothing more than a couple of letters added to the end of my name and a piece of paper. But to me, it meant everything. That diploma would signify that I'd done the most I could for my career.

And in seeking that degree, I had learned valuable skills.

I wasn't a waste.

I wouldn't have to rely on welfare like my mom.

I wouldn't have to accept charity ever again.

Those letters meant I had taken our shitty family history and turned it around.

I needed it. And I wouldn't let anything stand in my way.

If only my fucking gallbladder had gotten the memo.

So here I was, on my wedding day, questioning so many of my recent choices. But it was too late to back out now. The vows were just a formality. I knew that. So I sat, arms crossed, certain I was making a huge mistake.

But what other choice did I have?

Girls like me, we didn't get the princess weddings. I was

a trailer-park kid. And although I had come a long way from Mountain Meadows, deep down, I was still the girl who hustled every single day just to get by. The kid who wore too small shoes and ate expired food.

And I had never stopped hustling. All the way through college and grad school. And right now, I was killing myself to finish my PhD. I may not have been a princess, but I was making something of myself.

Life had taught me, though, that hard work was never enough. A person needed luck too. And I had recently run out of it.

So here I was. Ready to get married. Because it made sense. It was a good plan.

As we waited, he took my cold, clammy hand in his warm, rough one. His grip was tight, as if he was afraid I'd run away. It was strangely comforting to know that he was nervous too.

I could feel the heat radiating off his body as we sat, shoulder to shoulder, on the wooden bench. He was perfectly still, a tell if I'd ever seen one, since he was always in motion. Had been for the decades I had known him.

I shifted in my seat and looked into his dark eyes, noticing for the first time faint flecks of gold. He smiled at me. Not his usual gregarious grin, but a small, shy smile.

Oh, Remy Gagnon.

Star of all my teenage fantasies. My would-be shaggy haired knight in shining armor. For years, I'd convinced myself he would show up in his beat-up old truck and we would ride off into the sunset together.

The lanky boy with the dimples and ripped jeans. Who

shared his lunch with me when I had none. Who never made fun of me for being brainy and intense.

Looking at his kind face helped calm my heart rate. This was the right choice.

I repeated the mantra for the hundredth time since he'd picked me up this morning. *He's a good man. We have a solid plan. This will work.*

I could do worse than fake marrying my brother's best friend.

Chapter 2
Remy

One week earlier...

My phone rang as I headed down Main Street toward the diner. I had thirty minutes to pick up lunch for myself and my siblings before I had to be back at the office. Just another day of paying penance for my bad behavior. After my fiancé revealed she'd been cheating on me and dumped me, I went a little off the rails, and my family has not let me forget it.

I was lucky to have a job. Hell, I was lucky to be alive.

And my brother. I'd never forgive myself for what happened to him. I was the family fuck-up. No doubt about it. So I was on office duty—and coffee duty and lunch duty—indefinitely. Hoping to win back their trust by being a boring, responsible adult for as long as it took.

I dug my phone out of my pocket, and my stomach dropped at the name lit up on the screen.

"Remy. What's new?" Tim was a fast-talking sports agent from Boston who wore sleek suits and drove a Porsche

SUV. He was old enough to be my dad but looked thirty-five and did Ironman triathlons for fun.

He represented, in his words, "alternative athletes." Martial artists, dancers, a few skiers, and skateboarders. And me. We met a couple of years ago in Portland at a festival where I placed first in an axe-throwing competition. After, he bought me a beer and talked up the growing popularity of timbersports.

He encouraged me to get on social media, build a brand, and aim higher. I kept his card in my wallet for more than a year before I finally reached out. And after I placed third in the Maine state championships last year and set a regional record for speed climbing, he started talking sponsorships.

But it had been a long, lonely winter. I had focused all my attention on working and trying to make amends to my family and our employees. My behavior last fall had been appalling, and I was still plagued by shame over how I'd fallen apart.

And all that guilt and shame was wrapped up in the endless questions around my dad's death. What we'd thought had been a tragic accident, we'd recently discovered, was foul play. Despite working with law enforcement and the state inspectors, we still hadn't gotten answers. And I was beginning to doubt we ever would.

"Competition season is around the corner. I got an email from my guy at Stihl. He's still interested in you. Said he and his kids and grandkids are coming to the northeast regionals to see you. Hopes you can set another climbing record."

I winced. Climbing required strength, focus, and precision. Three things I lacked at the moment.

I blew out a breath. How did I tell my agent that my

fiancé had cheated on me and fucked up my life? That I barely had the motivation to atone for my wrongdoings, let alone impress sponsors with my dedication to training and sparkling personality?

"Ramp up your social media again. Post training videos on Instagram. Play up the small-town family-man story. Show off your wife and your workouts and footage of you climbing trees. Got it?"

My eye twitched. I should tell him Crystal was fucking other dudes behind my back. Tell him she left me for Cedric LeBlanc.

That asshole used to be my friend. His family was also in the logging business. We'd grown up in neighboring towns, but we'd played on the same peewee hockey team and had run into each other regularly over the years. Especially when we both got into timbersports. We usually grabbed a beer after competitions and shot the shit. He was an easygoing guy, and I'd enjoyed catching up with him often.

According to Crystal, they had been hooking up for months. Months. Behind my back. And he was in law school at UMaine and "*so* smart and *so* ambitious."

Her words. Not mine.

And he wasn't the only guy she'd been seeing. She rubbed it in my face. All the others. The weekends she spent in Portland with her friends, or when she visited her parents in Florida during the winter while I was working from sunup to sundown, logging in the freezing, frigid cold to keep a roof over her ungrateful, bleach-blond head.

Every time I thought about it, nausea rolled in my gut and humiliation almost brought me to my knees all over again. How could I have been so dumb? So trusting of a woman I could now see had never earned it? How could I have fallen for someone so cold and evil?

"I mean it." Tim droned on about branding and synergy, though I had zoned out. "Signing with Stihl would open a lot of doors for you. And I'm talking to Racine."

That got my attention. Racine Trading Company was one of the largest manufactures of workwear in the country. Most of my crew wore Racine clothes day in and day out. Working with them would be a dream come true.

"Their models are all real, working people. They would go crazy for you. Small-town lumberjack from Maine, married to a hometown girl. All you need is a cute dog, and this shit will sell itself."

Racine would be a game changer. They advertised during the Super Bowl, for Christ's sake. This was the kind of sponsor I had to land if I wanted to leave my day job and be a full-time athlete.

"They're hosting a fun charity event this year. It's adorable. Wife carrying. Apparently, it's a big deal in Finland. Man runs an obstacle course carrying his wife. Looking for competitors to volunteer. I'll sign you up. Text me your girl's name."

"I'm not married," I muttered, biting my lip. I would do anything to get Racine's attention, but I couldn't carry an imaginary woman through the woods.

"Doesn't matter. Fiancé. Girlfriend. Whatever. It'll be cute, and it's for charity. Your followers will eat that shit up." He chuckled. "I'll sign you up."

I swallowed past the lump in my throat, deliberately not correcting him. "I'll think about it."

Tim sighed. I had a feeling he spent a lot of his time

giving pep talks to athletes. "Just stay focused. You've got talent, and this is a growing sport with an international audience. Opportunities are coming."

"You think so?" This was all so foreign to me. I was just a guy from Maine who cut down trees for a living. I'd been competing my entire life, sure. Most people up here did it for fun. But the past couple of years had opened my eyes to the possibility of making this my career.

"You are on the cusp, dude. Keep training hard and get ready to go pro."

Again, I said nothing. As of late, I'd only done the bare minimum to stay in shape. I needed more pushups and less pizza if I was going to qualify for nationals.

"And you gotta get back on the Gram, dude. Daily training videos. Showcase your life in rural Maine, the work you do in the field. Wear more plaid."

I laughed at that, though the sound was foreign these days. While my brother Henri was a Paul Bunyan knockoff with a thick beard, thick shoulders, and the requisite flannel shirts, I was more of a jeans and T-shirt type.

"I'm serious. Focus on branding. We talked about this."

"I know. I know. I'm on it," I replied. "I'll be ready. Sponsorship would be a dream come true. I want it." The last thing I wanted to do was broadcast my life on social media. Crystal had loved that shit. Always seeking the validation of strangers. A few times, she posted videos of me chopping wood, and they had gone viral. Which was beyond embarrassing. All the guys at worked teased me mercilessly about it. I had accounts, but I never bothered to update, even before I had lost my motivation.

"I've worked with a lot of athletes over the years. And everyone wants to make it, but few have the grit to get there."

"I'll get there," I vowed. I wasn't sure how. But I wanted something different. Something more. And I was going to get past this mental roadblock. I had to.

"Good man. Now take some photos with the wife, go for a run, and climb. I'll see you in a few weeks."

I stuffed my phone in my pocket and pushed the door open, the bell above me chiming. As I crossed the threshold, I plastered on a big smile and greeted the friendly faces around the diner. Behind what I hoped was an easygoing look, though, I was panicking. Why hadn't I just told Tim that Crystal and I had broken up? It should have been easy. But shame about my mistakes, about Crystal, and about my own lack of motivation these days choked me.

Wallowing over a slice of pie seemed like a superb idea after that conversation. Strictly speaking, pie was off-limits while I was training, but I'd been half-assing it pretty spectacularly for months. If not for my brothers forcing me to train with them and Dylan showing up at my door for occasional runs, I'd be a wreck.

My bare-minimum activity was not going to be enough if I really wanted to compete at the highest levels in a few months. But one more slice of blueberry wouldn't kill me. And there was a good chance it would make sitting behind a desk for the next few hours bearable.

"Hello, Mrs. Kenny," I said to one of my mom's knitting friends. She'd no doubt tell the entire town I stopped by today, so I had to be extra friendly, lest I get a verbal ass kicking from Mama Gagnon.

Thank God I'd moved into the small cabin on Henri's

property outside of town. A few months of living with my mother at almost thirty years old was more than enough for me.

I was waving at the Lowerys and checking my phone when a small shriek sounded behind me. I spun and instantly collided with the source of the noise. And before I could get my bearings, I felt it.

Warm, sticky, and sweet, all over my face and neck.

"What the hell?"

My vision was blurred purple as I held my breath so I didn't inhale the goopy mess clogging my nostrils. I used a sleeve to wipe my eyes, and when the violet haze had been cleared, a small woman in front of me came into focus.

"I didn't see you. I'm so, so, so sorry," she cried, looking utterly terrified as she frantically scanned the mess oozing down my shirt.

I recognized that voice. Taking a napkin that Mrs. Kenny offered, I worked at the remnants of what appeared to be fresh blueberry pie still adhered to my face so I could get a good look.

"Pip?" I studied her face, streaked with pie filling, and smiled. Hazel Markey was the last person I expected to see. Yes, she was one of my oldest friends—we'd known each other since childhood—but she had lived in Boston for years and only came around during the holidays. The girl was destined for great things.

"Hi, Remy." She peeked up at my face, then focused on my shirt again with a grimace.

"What are you doing here?" I asked, following her line of sight, and winced. My shirt was deep purple, and pie filling dripped down the front of my favorite jeans.

"I was taking these pies to the counter for Bernice before you crashed into me." She'd also become a victim of the blueberry pie. The filling was sliding down her collarbones and all over her white T-shirt. There was a smudge across one lens of her glasses and a glob on her cheek. And it was just so absurd. All of it.

The phone call from Tim, the bullshit at work. And now pie. Fucking pie in my nostrils.

So I laughed. Because there was no other way to react to taking a motherfucking pie to the face on a Tuesday.

And I couldn't stop. The laughs came from deep in my gut, and pretty soon Hazel joined in. Tears rolled down her face, the tracks tinted purple. It wasn't just funny. It was the kind of thing that could only happen to me.

The entire diner disappeared as we laughed. Hazel was doubled over now, an arm banded around her middle. I hadn't seen her giggle like this since we were kids. There would no doubt be photo evidence of this moment. This town had a long memory. I'd be long dead before people in this diner stopped talking about the day hotshot athlete Remy Gagnon took a pie to the face.

"Jesus, Mary, and Joseph," a familiar voice boomed. "What is going on in my diner?"

Bernice emerged from the kitchen, massive tray in one hand and coffeepot in the other, looking horrified.

"I give you two pies to carry to the counter. Was the task really so difficult?" She glared at Hazel, who was wiping tears from her eyes, still chuckling.

"And you?" she said, turning that death stare on me, still balancing a tray full of tuna melts and fries. "I know she's small, but use your damn eyes. You could have hurt someone." She huffed a breath and slipped past us. "Go get your-selves cleaned up. Then grab the mop and deal with this mess. I've got tables."

Still laughing, I headed to the bathroom, Hazel behind me.

I popped the top on the paper towel dispenser and handed the roll of coarse brown paper to Hazel, who tore off a long strip and got to work wiping at her neck.

"What are you doing here?" I asked again, rubbing at the pie clinging to my hair.

"I'm back. Got here yesterday, actually. Staying with Dylan."

Hmm. Dylan hadn't said a word. Hazel and I kept in touch mostly through Dylan, who was constantly telling me about her life as a graduate student in Boston—the classes she took, what she was studying, the unique spin she put on the subjects she wrote about. He was so proud of his little sister.

"It's a shame," she said, wiping a glop of blueberry off her cheek with a finger. When she brought it to her mouth and licked it, the bathroom suddenly felt way too small, and I was way too warm. "Such a good pie." She tilted forward awkwardly in the cramped space so she could rinse her hands in the sink.

Hazel had always been like my little sister. The kid who tagged along with Dylan and me. And when she wasn't trying to keep up with us, she had her nose stuck in a book. She was the unlikely third musketeer of my childhood, the one who would shake her head with scorn when Dylan and I got into trouble. The smart, precocious child who would help me with my homework and come up with genius pranks to play on my older siblings. We had always been friendly, but life had taken us in vastly different directions. She'd ended up in the city, and I remained in the woods.

"Jesus. You're a mess. You got the worst of it." She unwrapped another long piece of paper towel and used it to wipe the pie filling off my shoulders. With her free hand, she plucked chunks of crust from where they were drying to my shirt and tossed them into the trash bin.

Then she was wiping my shirt. She moved in from my shoulders and across my pecs, then lower again. And I froze, holding my breath and unable to form the words to tell her she could stop.

But did I flex my abs? Yes.

Was I proud of that fact? Absolutely. Not.

But a man could only be knocked down so many times. And a pretty girl who smelled like blueberry pie was rubbing her hands all over me. I was only human, after all.

"I think that's good, Pip," I finally uttered, my voice strained.

She peeked up at me and froze, like she finally realized the position she was in. Awkward didn't begin to explain the proximity of her face to my belt.

Her eyes widened comically behind her glasses and her face turned beet red as she backed away from me, tripping over her feet in the process.

Deftly, I snagged her elbow before she hit the wall.

"Thanks. Sorry. Thanks." She dropped her chin and studied her feet.

"My gym bag is in my truck." I hiked a thumb over my shoulder. "I can change before heading back to the office." Ugh. I hated the sound of that. *The office.* I was not the kind of guy who wanted to be tied to a desk. But since my semi-public meltdown last fall, Henri, who was the CEO of our family's fourth-generation lumber company, had relegated me to office duty.

I missed being outdoors, missed the crews and the long days spent in a crane or hauling logs down the Golden Road from the Northern Maine wilderness. But Henri did what was best for the company, so I'd do my time and work to earn the trust of my family members again while I was there.

She backed away, and I dropped her elbow. Her face was still flaming and her attention was still fixed on the floor. "Sorry," she repeated, pushing up her glasses. "About this whole thing."

"It was my fault. You had your hands full, and I wasn't looking. I deserved it."

"No one deserves a pie in the face." She giggled again, spurring me to join in. She tilted her head and finally peered up at me, an adorable smattering of freckles across the bridge of her nose visible now that her face wasn't coated in blueberry pie filling.

I ran my hands through my sticky hair. "I sort of do. I walked in here feeling sorry for myself and got a pie in the face. Trust me, things can only get better from here."

Hazel patted my arm and gave me a genuine smile. "Good to see you, Remy. I'll mop up the rest of the mess. Bernice promised to feed me, so it's the least I can do. You go back to work."

I headed back to my truck, still sticky and laughing. The town rumor mill was inevitably going crazy with this one already, and it was only a matter of time before the texts rolled in. If my nephew Tucker got a hold of a photo, he'd have dozens of memes created by the end of the day, and I'd probably go viral for all the wrong reasons. That kid was too smart for his own good.

I jumped in my truck with our takeout containers and headed back to the office feeling surprisingly lighter. Even covered in pie. Yes, I was stuck in the office and my motivation had up and disappeared, but there were good things to come.

As I drove, the smell of blueberry pie filling my truck, Tim's words swirled around in my brain. Competition season was coming up. And I wanted this. I had spent so many years striving to make it to the next level.

And letting Crystal ruin me like this? It was giving her too much power.

I wanted so badly to be more. To do more. If I could go pro, get sponsors, and make a living pursuing my passions, I could support my mom and honor my dad, who'd spent his life in the forest and had taught me to swing an axe.

Tim made it sound easy. Training, branding, sponsors. But it still felt so far away. I could go for a run tonight. Head up to Henri's and chop for a bit. I had to start somewhere, right?

Seeing Hazel—laughing adorably with blueberry streaked across her face had pulled me out of my funk. Just thinking about her made me smile.

Maybe things weren't totally shit after all.

Chapter 3
Hazel

My first full day back in Lovewell was certainly eventful.

I hadn't factored in time to shower, but I ran back to Dylan's and scrubbed the pie out of my hair before I had to be at the bar.

Poor Remy. He had gotten the worst of it. And I felt like such an idiot. I wasn't a klutz, but when a big, broad-shouldered wall of lumberjack bumped into me, staying upright while also saving the pies was impossible.

Oh, Remy Gagnon. My older brother's best friend and my first crush. The middle schooler inside me was mortified that I'd pied the cool, hot dude in the face. The adult woman inside me was also mortified, but I was forcing myself to move past it. I probably wouldn't see him much, anyway. He worked a lot and was constantly training for those lumberjack competitions. A lot of people up here, men and women, competed locally and even regionally, but Remy was the real deal. He'd been winning events since high school and was talented enough to move up to the pro circuit.

But I wasn't here to think about Remy Gagnon. I was on a mission. One I would not give up on. I had come a long way since my Mountain Meadows days. I'd worked tirelessly to put myself through college and grad school—there was no luck involved there; only grit and humility—though now I'd boomeranged back to my hometown.

But only for a little while.

And I needed a job.

Duck Duck Moose was part dive bar, part pool hall and the town's preferred gathering space. There were other bars and restaurants nearby. Most with better food, drinks, and service. But locals loved the Moose.

The inside was perpetually dark. Oak paneling, a lacquered wooden bar top, and dim lighting added to the mystique. But it was clean and had the best waffle fries in Maine.

Jim Tremblay, one of the grouchiest men ever to inhabit Planet Earth, and his wife had bought the place thirty years ago. They had run it together for decades before she passed from cancer when I was in high school.

Without his beloved wife, Jim had nothing to do but serve drinks and scowl, but owning the busiest bar in town meant he needed help on the weekends. And I had dealt with my fair share of difficult personalities over the years, and the tips would be worth it.

So I showed up early, with a smile and a can-do attitude.

"You're a little thing," he remarked, side-eyeing me while drying glasses. The bar was spotless, as usual, and Led Zeppelin played softly in the background.

I shrugged. "Hasn't stopped me yet."

Yes. I was only five foot two, but I was battle tested. A person doesn't go from trailer park to Ivy League without a thick skin and pointy elbows.

As an introvert who didn't drink, bartending didn't seem like a natural fit for my skill set. But I could do it on weekends, and the tips were good. This job would give me the two things I needed most at the moment: money and time to work on my dissertation.

Plus, I was a scientist, a born observer. It was one of the benefits of growing up an outsider. We got really good at watching closely.

The Moose would give me great insight into the community, the fabric of this place. As well as the gossip. And I hoped it could help me forge connections for my research. The opioid epidemic was personal to me, and to most people who lived in this community. So it was no surprise that I'd chosen public health and opioids specifically in grad school. I wanted, no needed, to understand how this happened and how we could fix it. And there was no better place to remind me of the stakes.

So far, the governor's office had not been returning my calls. So I'd start smaller, more local. The Maine Department of Public Health had been generous. They'd supplied thousands of pages of documents and data sets to go through. But I needed to understand how things were going on the ground. Data and statistics could only tell me so much about how a public health crisis like the one I was studying played out in ordinary towns like Lovewell. And how the people in charge, the people with the money and power and access, planned to help them.

Jim scrutinized me, busying himself with bar tasks but watching me as he did so. It was chilly for May, but it was the start of the busy season up here, and Bernice at the diner had told me that he was looking for help.

After a long silence I'm sure he used as a tactic to unnerve those he thought too weak—but one that didn't faze me in the least; not after the years I'd spent outside this town—he nodded at me. "You back for good?"

I rounded the counter and washed my hands, then snagged the basket of limes and a cutting board. If there was one thing a guy like Jim respected, it was hard work.

"No," I said, slicing the first lime. "I'm here to conduct research and write my dissertation. Then I'll go wherever I can find a decent job."

"Good." He grunted, grabbing another rack of glassware from the kitchen. "How long will you be here?" he asked when he returned.

"About a year." It was a hard pill to swallow. But I was a realist. I had spent the last decade pushing myself harder than I ever thought possible. And the finish line was in sight.

But my mind and body were exhausted. Not to mention my finances. I couldn't afford Boston rent, and I needed to settle in a place where I could get my research done. And given the scope of my ambitions, I needed to plan accordingly.

So it was back to Maine. Back to this complicated town and its expectations and realities, things I had never quite been able to shake, despite a decade away.

"You can change a keg." It wasn't a question.

I nodded without looking up from my work.

"And you'll cut people off when they've had too many? Can't have a timid little girl working my bar."

I paused and turned to him, knife still in hand. "Wouldn't be my first time. I can handle it."

"The job's yours for six months. And then you get your ass outa this shit town. You hear?"

I rolled my eyes. "Shit town? You've lived here your entire life."

He cocked a brow, clearly going for nonplussed, but he couldn't hide the hint of a lip quirk. Maybe old Jim was capable of smiling after all. "Exactly. That makes me a goddamn expert in just how shitty this place is. Everyone knows you're destined for great things. You're a good kid, but you're not a bartender. You're better than that."

I shook my head. It was the refrain I'd heard my whole life. Everyone here expected a lot, and I was doing my damndest to make it happen. "I just need work. Preferably on nights and weekends so I can finish my PhD."

He nodded. "Don't get distracted. Do your research and then get the hell out."

I smiled.

"Fine, you're hired," he said with a deep sigh. "But don't talk too much. I hate that. And don't try to reorganize things or brighten the place up. I don't want to have to fire you for that shit."

I nodded, biting back my excitement.

"I mean it. The menu, the decor, it was all designed by my Janie, and I'm not changing a damn thing."

"I wouldn't dream of it," I assured him.

"You start tomorrow. Four to close."

I wanted to hug him, but I had no doubt he'd fire me on the spot.

"Thank you," I said, my attention on the limes again.

He nodded, heading back toward the kitchen. "Do the lemons before you leave."

Chapter 4
Hazel

Nothing had changed. Bernice's bouffant was just as voluminous as ever, despite the deeper wrinkles around her eyes. And the diner was spotless but worn. The rips in the vinyl booths had been patched with tape, and the black and white checkerboard floor tiles had been chipped over the years.

This place was a lot like Lovewell. Proud but tired.

I was camped out here with my laptop. It had only been three days, but I was already losing it. I needed space to work, to spread out, and to think. And distance from my big brother. I had a big mountain to climb, and I hadn't even made it to base camp yet.

Dylan's apartment above the bank on Main Street was small. But the brick building had large windows that overlooked the town, and the rent was cheap. He had moved in after he graduated from college, and for a tiny bachelor pad, it was always scrupulously clean.

Though he was less than two years older than me, Dylan

had raised me. Our dad split when I was a baby, and Mom battled depression and addiction for years. We had nothing but one another and our shitty single-wide trailer on the wrong side of town. And we were only fortunate enough to have that because our grandma had left it to us when she died.

He taught me to read and to tie my shoelaces. And he used the money from his paper route to buy me a bike for my thirteenth birthday.

I still woke up every day knowing just how much I owed him.

So we were close. We had to be. It was the only way we'd survived. When I was identified as gifted in kindergarten, he never let me skip a day of school and helped me study for every single test, often learning right alongside me. When I was in high school, he attended community college while working nights at the sawmill, but he was still there, standing over my shoulder each night, making sure I studied for the SAT.

When I graduated as valedictorian, no one was prouder. He shouted and cheered, and we celebrated with pie at the diner. When I got a scholarship to Brown University, he drove me to Providence, Rhode Island, in his ancient truck, unpacked my dorm room, and gave me money for books. Never mind that he was a student himself, studying education while still living in that trailer and working two jobs.

So there was no time for slacking. Dylan hadn't pushed me this far for me to get distracted now. This dissertation would not only be produced in record time, but it would blow the socks off my advisors and result in what I hoped was an abundance of job offers.

Public health wasn't a particularly lucrative field, but a prestigious research grant or a placement at an Ivy League university would certainly pad the resume and get me to the next stage of my career.

So I'd returned home, ready to work. Not just to level myself up, but to do something for the community that had taken Dylan and me in and championed us since childhood.

"Hazel, darling. Are you only using me for my Wi-Fi? Or do you plan to visit with me?" Bernice asked. While she mostly scowled at everyone else, she gave me a bright smile that juxtaposed her reputation around town. My mom had worked here for a bit when I was a kid. She was a terrible waitress, but Bernice and Louie had taken pity on her. Naturally, she flaked out, but they had always had a soft spot for Dylan and me. They fed us when we needed it and gave me a quiet place to do my homework. They were the surrogate grandparents we so desperately needed.

"I'm teasing. Gossiping with old ladies won't help you become a doctor."

I sighed and fought a smile. "I'm not going to be a medical doctor. Just a PhD." This was a common misconception in town. Since I'd left for Brown when I was eighteen, the legend had grown and evolved. This small-town rumor mill was notorious for its exaggerative misconstruction. If random townspeople were surveyed, the results of what I was doing with my life now would vary from being the current secretary of state to a NASA astronaut inhabiting the International Space Station. At least doctor wasn't too far off.

"*Just* a PhD?" she scoffed. "Louie, did you hear that? *Just.*" She waved her hands at me dismissively and turned to the kitchen window, where her husband Louie was visible as he worked the grill.

"Smartest person to ever come from Lovewell, that's for damn sure," he hollered.

"We're proud of you, sweetie." She shuffled over and kissed my cheek.

My heart clenched. The words made my skin itch. I hadn't earned them. The research was barely started, and I had an enormous mountain to climb. Moments like this reminded me of how much was riding on my dissertation. How much I owed the people who'd looked after me for years, not because they had to, but because they'd chosen to.

I couldn't screw it up.

Being the pride of Lovewell was a blessing, sure.

This place helped me realize my potential, and the people here had rallied behind me when I needed it.

They embraced me, the kid with the thrift store clothes and the broken glasses, and they protected me. Even took up a collection to help pay for my books after that first year at Brown and worked out a care package schedule so I was never without homemade treats, knit scarves, and cans of moxie.

I loved this place. And I wanted to make the town proud. We had been through so much, and so much of our regional identity had been lost in recent years.

This town and my brother were all I had.

So here I was, twenty-eight and broke, overeducated and underemployed.

I eyed the plate of fries Bernice delivered to the table next to me. *No.* My poor GI tract was angry enough as it was. The stress I was under had graduated from manifesting in emotional ways to physical discomfort lately. Thankfully, before I caved and begged Bernice for my own order, Lydia slid into the booth across from me.

"You're late," I said, though I couldn't stop the smile that spread across my face at the sight of my friend.

She shrugged. "I ran into Mrs. Peters on the sidewalk. She went on for ten minutes about Walter."

I raised a brow. "Her son, right?"

"Yup. He's fifty-one and still lives at home."

"Oh shit." I tossed my head back and laughed so hard my stomach ached.

She ran her hands through her long red hair. "Yup. Everywhere I go, people are trying to fix me up with the single men in their lives. It's a nightmare."

"That's what you get for being the most eligible bachelorette in Lovewell."

"You say it like it's an achievement." She glared. "It's more like a life sentence."

"So get a boyfriend." I shrugged. Lydia was quick-witted and had a level head, but she was clueless when it came to my brother. To the rest of the town, it was obvious that Dylan had been pining for Lydia for years. But he had never made a move, and I would never betray his trust and mention it to her.

It wasn't how we operated. We didn't keep secrets, and we always had each other's backs.

Despite his feelings, they remained good friends and coworkers, both teaching at the local school.

"I wish it was that easy. A couple of weeks ago, I went on a date with a guy I matched with on Bumble. Met him at a restaurant in Orono. Before we could even order, he was telling me I had 'pretty teeth' and asked if I was 'fertile.' I went to the bathroom and never came back."

I winced. "The odds are good..." I said.

"But the goods are odd," she finished, and we dissolved into giggles at the popular Lovewell catchphrase. The men outnumbered the women by at least two to one, but very few were actually datable.

Lydia had graduated a year ahead of me. She was the youngest of four, and her parents rarely minded having a fifth in tow, so I had spent many nights tagging along to family dinners and sleeping over.

She had deep red hair and long legs that made me irrationally jealous.

For the last five years or so, she'd taught at Lovewell Community, and she was an incredible skier. She'd even started a free ski clinic for underprivileged kids at one of the local mountains not long ago. She was loud and pretty and didn't take any shit—the best kind of friend.

After coffee, we walked through downtown, remarking on all the ways Main Street had changed.

"Is that a salon?" I asked, craning my neck to get a peek at the sign across the street.

"Yup. And it's a good one. You should stop by. Becca's super cool. She's relatively new to town; her daughter is in my class."

Even a salon in a place like Lovewell was outside my budget these days, but I was intrigued. My dark brown hair was way too long and spent most days scraped back into a ponytail.

I hummed noncommittally, not wanting to get into why I wouldn't be scheduling an appointment soon, and took off again, ready to change the subject. But then I was doubling over as a sharp pain ripped through my abdomen. Instantly, I broke out in a sweat, despite the cool temperature, and my heart rate skyrocketed.

The searing pain under my ribs was so intense that my legs shook.

"Hazel!" Lydia shouted, grabbing me by the elbow. "Are you okay?"

I couldn't answer. It took everything in me to stay on my feet and force air into my lungs.

Thankfully, Lydia threw my arm around her shoulder and led me to a bench in front of the post office.

She helped me sit and pushed the hair out of my face. "Should I call 911?"

I shook my head. That was the last thing I needed—to be billed for an ambulance. Not to mention a hospital visit.

"Hazel, you're scaring me."

I winced. "It's fine. I've got a gallbladder thing. No big deal."

Lydia rubbed my arm and examined me, a frown marring her face. "Seems like a big deal to me."

I gagged, nausea threatening to overwhelm me. "I need to get home. I have supplements that help it."

She helped me up again and led me back to Dylan's apartment only a block away. Once she'd settled me on the couch, she rooted through my backpack until she found my magnesium supplements.

When she held a glass of room temperature water out, I took it gratefully and downed the magnesium. I squeezed my eyes shut and sucked in long, slow breaths, desperate for relief from the pain. It would pass. It always did.

Lately, these attacks had been happening more frequently and lasting longer.

I gagged. The nausea was so bad I considered just giving in and vomiting my brains out in hopes that it would bring me relief.

Lydia was on the phone, and it took me a moment to clear my mind and focus on her end of the conversation. She must have called Dylan.

Of course she had. He was my person. And now he would fuss and worry and try to talk me into having surgery.

But that was the last thing I needed right now.

I needed to work at the bar and get my damn dissertation finished.

My fucking gallbladder would just have to learn to behave.

Eventually, Dylan returned home. I was curled up on the couch, thankfully feeling a bit better. He and Lydia were speaking quietly in the kitchen. Then a third voice chimed in. *Shit.* I lifted my head, regretting the sudden movement immediately. It was Remy Gagnon. One more witness to my utter humiliation.

After our encounter at the diner on Tuesday, where I accidentally hit him with not one, but two of Bernice's award-winning blueberry pies and then accidentally groped him in the bathroom, I hoped I could avoid him for the next year, if not for the rest of my life.

Awkward, neurotic me had inadvertently copped a feel of my brother's best friend. And what a feel it was. Remy was muscular and built and broad and, damn, my face was flushing again.

I buried my head in the throw pillow, wanting nothing more than to suffer in peace.

"Good to see you again, Pip," he said softly as I picked my head up. The sound of the familiar nickname made me smile. His father, Frank, had given it to me as a kid. I was so tiny, the entire family had taken to calling me "Pipsqueak," which was eventually shortened to pip. My heart clenched for Remy and his family. His father had been a wonderful man. He'd always been kind, loving, and devoted to this town.

I looked up at his son. The man was tall and handsome and more than capable of carrying on his legacy. "Good to see you too, Remy."

Chapter 5
Remy

She looked so small and frail curled up on the couch. I attempted a joke to cheer her up. "Thanks to you, I still smell like blueberry pie. I think it worked its way into my sinuses."

"You're welcome," she groused, sitting up and crossing her arms over her chest. "That's a big improvement for you." There was the Hazel I knew.

"Very funny." I chuckled, though an unexpected wave of insecurity rushed through me. Did Hazel think I smelled bad? And why did I care so much if she did?

"Can I get you anything?" I asked, pushing my ridiculous thoughts away. She was clearly sick. I should be helpful, not mentally beating myself up over whether I should switch deodorants.

She shook her head, craning her neck like she was trying to eavesdrop on the conversation Dylan and Lydia were having by the door.

"I'm sorry you had to come all the way over here," she

said, pulling her legs to her chest and hiking an old blanket up to her chin.

I sat next to her and shrugged. "No problem. We were headed out for a burger, but it's fine. You know your brother."

She sighed. "He's way too overprotective."

Before I could respond, Lydia was leaving and Dylan was stalking toward the couch, his face red and his fists clenched.

Dylan was my best friend. The Robin to my Batman. Nah, he wasn't the sidekick type. More like the Donatello to my Michelangelo. Yeah, that worked. Especially since we'd spent the majority of our childhood playing Ninja Turtles in my backyard.

He was serious and careful and thoughtful. Never forgot his homework or left his coat at school. He had to be—taking care of not only himself but his little sister. While I was the wild child of my family.

I forced him to loosen up and be a kid, and he helped me tone down my antics just enough so that I could graduate and become a productive member of society.

Not that I had been particularly productive as of late. No, these days, I spent a lot of my time lying on his couch, beer in hand, complaining about Crystal.

He wasn't overly tall. Not that I could talk. As the shortest Gagnon brother, I was constantly teased about it. At six feet, I was relatively tall compared to most, but my two older brothers were massive.

And while I was lean, Dylan was sturdy and strong. He was also one of the most capable and thoughtful people I'd ever known. Not to mention an extremely overprotective big brother.

"Jesus, Hazel," he said, pacing the living room while running his hands through his wavy hair. "You scared me half to death. No more messing around. I'm taking you to the doctor tomorrow, and you're scheduling that surgery."

Hazel sat up, her dark eyes flashing with anger. "You're overreacting, as usual. It was just a small gallbladder attack. Nothing to go crazy over."

Dylan stopped his pacing and looked from me to his sister, his brows furrowed and his jaw clenched. "The situation is only going to get worse, and there could be serious long-term consequences."

At those words, I examined his little sister, who was now sitting next to me on the threadbare couch, wearing a calm expression.

"I have cholecystitis," Hazel explained when she noticed me studying her. "It's just my gallbladder."

"Not just," Dylan interrupted, his voice quivering with anger. "It's severe inflammation."

Hazel ignored him, still turned toward me. "I need to have my gallbladder removed eventually."

"Immediately, actually. And if she doesn't, she will die."

"It's not that dire. Eventually, yes, it could be bad. But right now, I'm weighing my options."

There was something they weren't telling me. Every muscle in Dylan's body was taut, and Hazel was avoiding making eye contact with him. I was no stranger to sibling tension. As the youngest of four, I was used to it. Especially because we all worked together. Usually I'd crack a joke to defuse things. But this felt different.

I shifted on the couch, taking in the dark circles under Hazel's eyes and the general air of exhaustion around her. "How can I help?"

She looked at her brother and then at me. They were a cohesive unit. They'd worked together, just the two of them, their whole lives. No parents, no supervision. They were responsible for themselves and each other.

Finally, after a long silence, Hazel spoke. "I don't have health insurance." She dropped her chin and picked a piece of invisible lint off the blanket draped over her knees. "And the little bit of savings I had went toward the tests. There were so many just to get a diagnosis."

That information hit me like a punch to the gut. Gagnon Lumber had always offered excellent benefits to its employees and their families, so I'd been covered every day of my life. Sure, I had heard stories about people going bankrupt from medical bills, but I had never seen it up close.

In moments like this, I felt the distance between us. The privileges I had enjoyed in childhood—loving parents, a warm bed, healthy meals—were still paying dividends in my adult life. Where Dylan and Hazel were still scraping by, still crawling themselves out of the hole their parents had pushed them into.

"Let me pay for it," Dylan pleaded.

"You don't have that kind of money."

"I can take out a loan. I've got a good job."

"I can't ask you for that. It'll be like fifty thousand dollars without insurance. You've worked so hard for so long."

Dylan went back to pacing from one end of the room to the other, and I racked my brain for ways to help while I watched him. His small apartment was nice but sparse. The only thing on the wall was a framed black and white photo of the siblings at Hazel's high school graduation, huge smiles on both of their faces. Dylan had only been a kid, probably nineteen or twenty, but he was bursting with pride.

"I'm sorry," I uttered softly. And I was. "I take it for granted, that I have good health insurance through work."

"You have to," Hazel said. "You have one of the most dangerous jobs in the world. You need it."

I winced at the reminder. Over the years, I had seen so many injuries. And then there was Henri's accident last fall. After coming up to camp because I lost my mind and couldn't do my job, he'd hopped behind the wheel to deliver a load of lumber to the mill.

He'd lost control of the truck and had to jump out of the cab on a steep mountain road. Adele was certain his brakes had been tampered with and had the evidence to prove it, but we still had no definite answers. The incident haunted our family and our business. Because we'd lost Dad the same way two years ago. There were so many questions and no definite answers. But there was one certainty. Life was precious and often way too short.

That mentality was common in our industry. The men and women who did this work knew the risks and took them willingly. Not that I was doing anything strenuous these days. Nope, these days I was riding a desk, doing grunt work for my older brothers, and dreaming about climbing trees. No more heavy machinery for me. The only thing I was trusted with was the damn printer, and most of the time, I had to call my nephew Tucker to fix it when I inevitably jammed it up.

One more reminder of what a fuck-up I was. Screwing up left and right. No good for anyone, least of all myself.

Dylan perched on the coffee table, elbows on his knees, and dropped his head in his hands. The three of us sat in silence, the tension radiating throughout the room. "What's the fastest way to get health coverage? Marriage, right?"

Hazel nodded. "Probably."

Then Dylan sat up straight and let out a small chuckle. "If only you could marry Remy. He's got the good insurance."

Hazel burst out laughing, pushing her glasses up her nose and turning to me. "He's officially out of his mind," she said with a shake of her head.

I sat up straighter, trying not to feel insulted that the idea of marrying me was so preposterous to her. Maybe it was all my Crystal baggage, but it stung a bit. We'd been friends forever. We'd seen it all, and we'd built up a type of trust that could only be born out of childhood scrapes and teen shenanigans. Who else *would* she marry? There was nothing romantic or sexual here, just years of friendship. I would never, could never, go there. Not just out of respect for my friendship with Dylan, but out of respect for my friendship with Hazel too. But I could help. I knew it.

"I mean it," Dylan urged. "People get married for health insurance all the time. And," he said, nodding in my direction, "it would help with your problems too."

Hazel contemplated me, her head tilted and her expression thoughtful. "Remy? You have problems?" she asked, as if it were absurd that anything could go wrong in my life.

I narrowed my eyes at her. "I've got plenty of problems." The last thing I wanted was to dissect them with her.

Because *I need to get my head out of my ass and actually chase my dreams instead of sitting around feeling bad about myself* felt indulgent when compared to the need for life-saving surgery. But her reaction was so typical of what I had experienced my entire life. Carefree Remy, the jokester. People assumed I had no concerns, no problems. That I was immune to the force of life's blows because of my easygoing personality.

"You need to get healthy so you can finish your dissertation. You've been working so hard for so long," Dylan mused.

I zoned out while they argued, my mind spinning with this new possibility. I couldn't marry Hazel. She wasn't... I wasn't... We weren't that way. It would be wrong. Weird and very, very wrong.

But in the dark recesses of my brain, I considered it. She was sick and needed help. And the thought of protecting her, of providing for her, it flipped a switch in the caveman part of my mind.

Henri was the dependable one. Not me. I was glib, not taken seriously, always up for a good time. But maybe, for once, I could offer more than just fun. Maybe I could be the person she depended on, the person she needed.

Dad had always done what he could to lend a hand. He overextended himself constantly to help others. Since we were kids, both my parents had drilled into us a sense of responsibility for our community and neighbors.

In this moment, I couldn't shake the thought of my dad. If he were here, he'd be rolling up his sleeves and finding a way to help Hazel, his little Pipsqueak. He always had such a soft spot for her, stepping up when she needed a father figure or a male role model. In eighth grade, she made the finals of the state science fair, and my dad took the day off work to drive her and then took her out to celebrate her second-place trophy. The thought made me smile. Dad wouldn't let Hazel suffer because of a treatable medical condition. And neither could I.

I lifted my eyes and met hers. For a moment, we said nothing. I had spent millions of minutes with her over the past few decades, but never had I stopped to really *look* at her. I took in the contours of her face, the wide brown eyes and lips that were, admittedly, more than a little kissable. "I'll marry you, Pip," I said softly, as if Dylan wasn't in the room.

She threw her arms up in frustration. "You guys do not need to solve my problems for me! Why do you even need a wife?" she asked, scrunching up her forehead and pulling me out of my thought spiral.

Dylan butted in before I could respond. "Because vile Crystal screwed him up. He hasn't been training, he hasn't been posting on social media, and he's not right in the head."

"Hey!" I protested. Though he wasn't wrong.

"You could go pro! This is your year, dude. You won state's last year." To Hazel, he went on. "If he places in the top five at regionals, he'll qualify for the National Championship. And if he does that, he could land sponsorship deals."

"It's not that simple," I protested, although I guessed it kind of was.

"His agent thinks he has a great chance. And he needs to get his ass back to training."

I instantly regretted telling Dylan everything. It was just

like him to apply logic and reason to my life and make me feel like a spoiled fool in the process.

He turned to me and shook his head in disgust. "If you quit now, then that devil woman wins."

Hazel looked at me, wide-eyed. Then she turned to her brother. "Leave him alone, Dylan. If he's got a broken heart, that's his business."

My face went hot at that comment. That wasn't it. I had just lost my motivation. Between my dad's death, Crystal's cheating, and all the trouble I'd caused for the family business, I'd lost myself. Carefree Remy was gone. The guy who never took things too seriously started fading when we lost my father to a horrific accident. That disappearance only accelerated with the hurt Crystal caused. And the recent knowledge that my dad's death may not have been an accident was the nail in the coffin.

I wasn't sure anything would get me out of this rut. Especially not a sham marriage to my best friend's little sister.

"Sounds like you need a therapist, not a wife," she quipped, making me chuckle.

"You're not wrong," Dylan added, "but sponsors and fans love a devoted family man. A wife could help his image."

"That is some straight-up sexist bullshit," Hazel said. "You need a pathetic, doting little woman cheering for you to make you a viable asset for a sponsor? Fuck that noise."

"Amen," I said. "It's so backward and unnecessary these days." I swallowed thickly. "But Dylan's right about the other stuff. I do need to train harder. And be more focused..." God, I was a mess. My dream was finally within reach, and I was sabotaging my chances. And that had never been clearer than it was sitting here with my two oldest friends, who had done far more with their lives with far less than I had been given.

Thankfully, before I could drone on about my woes, Hazel stood and threw the blanket onto the back of the couch. "I gotta go shower. I'm bartending tonight."

"You can't work. You're sick," Dylan protested.

She spun around and put her hands on her hips. She was tiny but carried herself like a warrior. "It's bad enough I'm broke and sleeping on your couch. I gotta work."

And with that, she strode out of the room.

And I would be lying if I said I didn't notice the sway of her hips or the curve of her ass in her oversized sweats.

When did that happen?

Chapter 6
Hazel

I poured pint after pint, catching up with locals and explaining—repeatedly—what I was doing back in town. The work was hard, but the hours flew by. Mostly, I just had to smile and make drinks. Plus, it saved me hours of talking to people at the diner, since every single bit of Lovewell news and gossip was on display at the Moose tonight.

I was no stranger to manual labor. I had endured every type of job since I'd started working at fourteen. House cleaner, dog sitter, barista, camp counselor, car wash attendant and ghostwriter, to name a few. But I always came back to food service. The chaos of a busy bar or restaurant always helped me detach from the constant stressors in my life. The frenzy allowed me to turn off my brain for a few hours and focus on the task in front of me.

Counting my tips at the end of the night, even now, gave me a thrill. Honest money for honest work. Uncomplicated. And exactly what I needed right now. If I stopped moving, I risked letting the overwhelming thoughts that constantly swirled take over. The pressure, the expectations, the decade I'd spent in school. It all hung on the next year and whether I could pull off my dissertation.

The passion was there. The opioid crisis was personal for me and millions of other Americans. I had seen firsthand how opiates could ravage rural communities like Lovewell. And I had spent years digging into the science and data surrounding it, working on ways to fix it.

The point of this research wasn't just to add those three little letters to the end of my name. My goal was to help further the dialogue about this deadly problem and offer solutions to communities in danger.

So I had to buckle down. Get more sleep. Better sleep. Could I fit a twin-size mattress in Dylan's living room? How mad would he be if I did? My back ached after only a few nights, and the crick in my neck intensified every day. I'd need to find a quiet place to work, maybe the town library, and get cracking.

Everything else would have to wait.

A shadow fell over the bar top I was wiping down, pulling me from my thoughts. And there, across the bar, was a familiar pair of dark eyes.

"Henri." I would have hugged him, but I was way too short to reach him from across the bar.

The gruff eldest Gagnon brother gave me a small smile. "Good to see you, Pipsqueak. Loraine says you're back for a while. That true?"

I nodded. "It's cheaper up here than in Boston, and I've got a lot of work to get done."

"We're real proud of you," he said, cramming a twenty into my tip jar and making me blush. "A doctor..."

"Not yet," I trilled, "and it's a PhD."

"Same difference. My mom will be calling you Doctor Pip at Thanksgiving for the rest of your life. Get used to it."

He gestured to a knockout blonde beside him. "You remember Alice?"

I nodded. We met at Thanksgiving. She had impressed me with her kind heart and her ability to keep the eldest Gagnon in line. That was no easy feat. Mainers were stubborn and contrary on a good day, and Henri was no exception. Especially after the injury that put him out of commission for a while. If he was a cranky bear before, he'd morphed into a grizzly for a while, from what Dylan had told me.

She gave me a small wave, her eyes bright. "Our kids will be so happy you're back." Henri and Alice were in the process of adopting two kids from foster care. It warmed my heart to know Tucker and Goldie would have such incredible parents. Their lives so far had been even harder than what my brother and I had gone through.

I fixed their drinks and promised to come over for dinner. Then they slipped away, returning to a large group that included the other Gagnon siblings and several people from around town.

Of course Remy was there, the sight of him now bringing back a tinge of the embarrassment that had hit me when Dylan told him about my gallbladder and lack of insurance.

Remy Gagnon was larger than life. He was funny and charming and always moving. As a kid, he'd charmed his way into extra cookies from the lunch ladies and extensions on papers from our high school teachers.

He didn't take himself too seriously either, despite his good looks and athletic talents.

Though recently, his charmed life had fallen apart. And this Remy was a shadow of the man I'd known for most of my life.

His charisma had been tempered, his dark eyes swimming in pain. And if he wasn't training? Things had to be bad. The guy who needed to be in the woods twenty hours a day and never stopped moving? I had always assumed he'd be on the cover of a Wheaties box by now. But instead, he was hanging around Dylan's apartment moping? As far as I knew, he'd never moped a day in his life until now.

If I ever laid eyes on Crystal LaVoie again, I was going to punch her so hard she'd need a second nose job. She had always been a selfish brat, but openly cheating on Remy? He was a good person. Loyal and faithful, and although his taste in girlfriends had clearly been lacking, he would have given her a beautiful life.

Sure, I was small, but I was scrappy. And although I generally hated violence, I would make an exception for that hell beast any day of the week and twice on Sundays.

I dried a rack of glassware while covertly watching Remy across the bar. The way he moved around the pool table was positively feral. He was all long limbs and quiet grace. His brothers were big, beefy types, but not Remy.

He was lean and graceful and looked like a natural athlete, even holding a pool cue. Even from here it was obvious he was absolutely decimating his brother Pascal, who wore a crisp tailored dress shirt and his usual scowl.

Remy was all man, yet his boyish qualities lingered. Maybe it was the stubble? Or the dimples? Or the messy hair in need of a trim?

When his group had ordered drinks, he'd asked for a water, though he'd always been a one-beer kind of guy. I didn't want to pry, so I made another crack about his blueberry pie cologne.

He scoffed. "You're giving me a complex, Pip. Time to try a new brand of deodorant, I guess."

Despite my teasing, Remy actually smelled like pine forest and testosterone, not that I had noticed or anything.

And I definitely hadn't been keeping track of just how good he smelled since I hit puberty. Nope. Because it was Remy. His smell was immaterial. Unimportant.

And my brother had no sense. Dylan was positively out of his gourd for suggesting we get married. Yes, it would solve my health care problem, but it could potentially cause many others. But then again, Remy hadn't seemed offended by the suggestion. And it was probably wishful thinking, but I thought I caught a spark of curiosity in those dark irises when my brother brought it up.

Nah, it wasn't possible, no matter how much teenage Hazel would have loved it.

It was natural, required even, to have a teeny, tiny crush on one's older brother's best friend. And when said brother's best friend was Remy Gagnon, resistance was futile.

He was the subject of every one of my teen romantic fantasies. The cute older boy who understood my tortured soul and saw the real me.

In reality, he had looked at me like an annoying kid sister and had spent years of his life lusting after Crystal LaVoie, the queen bee of Lovewell. Blond and tall with a rich dad, no one in their right mind could compete with her. Thankfully, I was long gone when they started dating. Though it was inevitable. The charming, handsome athlete and the pretty blond princess. Every generation in every small town had that couple. And although they didn't connect until after high school, people like that? They were magnets for one another.

Eventually, Remy would recover and magically find another gorgeous woman with the perfect body and a bubbly personality, but hopefully she'd understand how wonderful he was. Then I would see them every Thanksgiving and smile. As long as he was happy, I'd be happy too.

"Bartender!" Bernice hollered over the crowd. She put an arm in the air and made a circular motion, gesturing for another round. I gave her a thumbs-up over the bar and got to work. She sat in one of the large booths in the back, surrounded by a group of older ladies. For as long as I could remember, they came in every Friday for girls' night, as they had been calling it, though Jim refused to even consider themed nights.

I grabbed a cold bottle of pinot grigio from the cooler, thankful it was a twist top, and scurried over.

"Amen," cried Jodie Martin, lifting her glass as I poured. She was my sixth-grade math teacher and used to stay late a few days a week to teach me algebra. I gave her a big smile. Yet another person in Lovewell I owed.

"Can you ask Jim to send over another basket of fries?" Steph Dumas asked, batting her exaggeratedly long false eyelashes at me. She and her husband Steve had run the bakery in town for decades before their son took over a few years back.

I nodded. "Not a problem. Can I get you ladies anything else?"

They shook their heads. "Girls' night!" Bernice shouted, and they all raised their glasses.

"You know, we've been doing this for over thirty years," Bernice said. "Every week, rain or shine."

"Or blizzard," Steph added.

"Shit! Remember '96?"

"That was the year Erica put on her snowshoes and hoofed it over here."

That brought on a round of cackles from the whole table.

Erica, who had been the first woman foreman at the mill, raised her glass. "It was a great workout. We're Maine girls. A little snow won't keep us from wine and gossip."

I bused a few tables as I made my way back to the bar, watching them laugh with one another and wondering, not for the first time, whether things would have been different if my mom had had friends. If there had been anyone nearby to support her. But I put a stop to my musings quickly. It was a dangerous train of thought. She was gone. Dead the year I went off to college. And no amount of what-ifs would bring her back.

Nope. Best to put my head down and keep working, keep moving.

Just like I'd always done.

After last call, as patrons filtered out, I was stacking the final load of glasses in the dishwasher rack. Once the stragglers had left, I could mop up and leave.

Remy's boots thudded on the hardwood as he

approached. The music was turned down low, and the murmurs around the room were muted.

"More water?" I asked when he stepped up to the bar.

He shook his head.

"Always thought you were more of a beer guy."

He winced, the action making my stomach sink. I knew better than to say something like that.

"It's not good for me. Water's good for me."

I had heard the gossip, and I'd gotten bits of the truth from Dylan. Last fall, Remy had gone through a hard time after Crystal left him. He was skipping work and drinking too much and had caused some problems for the family business. I suspected there was a lot more to the story.

I had known Remy for almost three decades, and I had never seen him like this. Serious, quiet, and almost defeated. He was carrying some baggage. A concept I was all too familiar with. I gave my old friend a smile, wanting him to know I understood.

"It's all good," I said. "You know me. Don't drink and never have." It was a silly cliché, a bartender who didn't drink. But being raised by an addict had scared me off any type of controlled substances for life.

Rag in hand, I wiped off the section of the bar in front of me. He gave me a nod of understanding.

Remy and his family had had the pleasure of front-row seats to the train wreck that was my mom. She loved us fiercely, but the disease took her from us, and we never got her back. Watching how it ate away at my mother, eroded every aspect of her personhood, convinced me early that the risks outweighed any kind of benefits. And I respected the hell out of Remy for making hard choices and putting his health first.

"Plus," I said, hoping to lighten the mood, "alcohol is expensive and makes accomplishing things harder. I wouldn't have graduated summa cum laude if I made a habit of coming to class hungover."

He smiled. "You never disappoint. Always my favorite nerd."

He gave me one of his flirty winks, and I hated myself for the way my heart rate sped up and how heat pooled low in my belly. It was like I was thirteen years old all over again and dreaming about him giving me my first kiss. But I had never, ever been on his radar. To him, I wasn't a girl, or at least a possibility. Sadly, his nobility and loyalty to his friendships only made him more attractive.

He was known to most as the fun, carefree guy, but there was so much more beneath the surface. It was what had always attracted me to him. He felt deeply and thought deeply. He empathized with others, and he'd always treated everyone, even in high school, with kindness.

Sure, he was a tall, broad, muscular lumberjack with big hands and a sexy, scruffy beard, but under that disturbingly attractive exterior was a man with a massive heart. Which made the cavewoman part of my brain light up when Dylan had mentioned marriage.

Because a teeny tiny part of me would always be just a little in love with Remy Gagnon.

Chapter 7
Remy

Hazel had always been... around. The little sister. Wearing her brother's hand-me-downs and asking endless questions, she was a daily fixture during my childhood.

She was introspective and bookish but never shy. Nope, we always knew where we stood with Hazel. She was known for outsmarting teachers and once, during the Christmas Eve Vigil, corrected Father Marcel's Latin pronunciation in front of the congregation.

Didn't matter that she was tiny or that she was dirt poor. Hazel was a force to be reckoned with in her own observant, brilliant way.

And now I was here, asking her to marry me.

"Hey," she said, holding open the door and waving me in. "Dylan's at the gym, and then I think he's headed to Bangor to hit the Target."

Just inside the doorway, I stopped. I couldn't keep my eyes from wandering. This was Hazel. I'd never looked at her body. But tonight felt different. She was wearing yoga pants and the smallest, tightest tank top I had ever seen. My eyes roamed hungrily over her neck, her collarbones, and her full breasts. Distracting. And bad. Some switch had been flipped in my brain, and suddenly, she wasn't Pip, Dylan's kid sister and my old friend, but Hazel, a woman who was smart and beautiful and needed my help.

Hazel was right. I did need therapy.

Stuffing my hands in my pockets, I blew out a breath as subtly as I could, trying to get control over my hormones. I needed to get these words out. I had spent the morning rehearsing and psyching myself up for this.

It was time for me to step up. To man up. It's what my dad would have done. She needed help, and I was going to help her. Because I hadn't been able to think about anything else for the past few days.

"I'm not here to see Dylan," I said softly.

She closed the door and looked up at me, head tilted, and waited.

"I, uh," I stammered, mustering the tiny bit of courage I could find, "wanted to talk to you about getting married."

She pushed her glasses up her nose and gaped at me, her eyes widening. "Nope. No way. Not happening." With that, she turned and hustled to the tiny kitchen. She busied herself with filling the kettle and putting it on the stove, going about it like I wasn't here.

I stood still, watching her as she busied herself. This conversation wasn't over. If she wanted to freeze me out, I'd wait.

"If that's the only reason you came here, you can go now. I'm not discussing this lunacy any further." She popped up on her tiptoes and reached for a mug in the cabinet.

I stalked toward her, angry and frustrated and feeling a strange tension in my chest. The patience I'd felt moments ago had disappeared in a cloud of smoke. Hazel was on the quiet side but had a bossy streak a mile wide. With anyone else, it would be hot. But with her, it was more of an annoyance.

"Think about it," I growled, splaying my hands on the countertop across from her.

"You also laughed when Dylan suggested it. And yes," she brought a hand to her heart, "that hurt a little. But you were right. I'm sorry he pressured you to help me. I promise I'll be fine."

Dammit, the urge to help her, to protect her, had intensified more every day since then. I couldn't live with the thought of her not receiving the medical care she needed. Yes, getting married was extreme, but we certainly wouldn't be the first couple to do it for this reason.

And I needed to help her understand that this could really work. Of course it was crazy. Totally bananas, really. But my good sense had gone out the window the minute I heard she needed help. Or maybe it had left me that night at the bar when I watched her bust her ass with a smile on her face. Or maybe that tiny tank top had driven me over the edge, and these were the last gasps of my sanity. Didn't matter.

"Then let me help you pay for the surgery. Between Dylan and me, we can swing it."

She narrowed her eyes, her dark irises flickering with heated anger. "I don't want your charity."

I tried to open my mouth to calm her or backtrack or to defend myself—something—but her low growl and the death stare had me frozen in place.

"My brother has been taking care of me my entire life. Every choice he's ever made has been in service of my needs. I will not let him drain his savings. He has dreams, and I won't stand in his way."

"I know you wouldn't. But your health is precious."

She slapped a tiny hand on the countertop. "You think I don't know that? You think I want to be doubled over in pain every day?"

She angled forward, giving me a tantalizing view down her tank top that I tried *so hard* not to home in on. "The last thing I need is another overprotective man telling me what to do with my body."

I took a step back, hands up. Shit, I should have known my usual charm would never work on Hazel. She was too smart and too tough to be easily talked into anything. And she was right. I couldn't come in here and demand she fake marry me, even if it was for her own good. This was Hazel Markey, the smartest and most determined person I had ever met.

But maybe she would agree... if it was for *my* own good? I changed tactics, wandered over to a tower of small moving boxes stacked in the corner of the room. Lazily, I tugged on one flap of the top box. Neatly stacked books, large and small. So Hazel.

She couldn't sleep on Dylan's couch long term, and I could help her. I just had to get her to accept it. She couldn't let something so easily fixable derail her dreams. And I would know, as someone struggling to reach my dreams too.

So I shuffled back into the kitchen wordlessly and poured myself a mug of tea. I plopped onto the couch and sipped it quietly, letting my silence communicate how serious I was.

Eventually, she made her way into the room and stood over me, examining me, a crease between her brows. Hazel had distractingly thick eyelashes. They framed her chocolate brown eyes perfectly, along with her chunky glasses.

They were intense eyes. Not sweet or sensual, but deep pools of brown with hints of gray, hiding all sorts of secrets in their murky depths.

She was short and curvy and always wore Chucks. As a kid, she had been a tomboy, but now that look had morphed into something different. Womanly but cool. The tank she wore clung to her waist, ending just above the top of her leggings. As she paced, still watching me with every turn, it slid up a bit, giving me a glimpse of the pale skin hiding beneath.

I chose my moment, forcing myself to look away from her bare flesh and focus on her face once again. "This is hard for me to admit, okay?" I ran my hand through my shaggy hair. "But I need your help. I'm a mess. I need someone to kick my ass and help me find my motivation again."

Finally, she stopped. She placed her mug next to mine on the coffee table, then she crossed her arms and regarded me with pursed lips and a skeptical arch of one brow. "I'm not a cheerleader, Remy."

Fuck, she was always right. Just another reason she'd made an excellent short-term wife. I needed to change tactics. How could I get her to accept my help?

"I know that. And I'm not asking for you to be a doting,

simpering wifey who'll build me up and cheer me on. I'm trying to change. To be more focused. And..." I paused, not wanting to say the next bit out loud. "And I worry that seeing Crystal and Cedric at competitions will derail me again."

I watched her face soften. *Jackpot.*

"The truth is, I'm a mess. Being a pro athlete—that's been my dream since I was a kid. And I'm finally in a place where it's possible. But I know once the competition season starts up, I will see her." I ran my hands through my hair. "And it would be a lot easier with you by my side."

It wasn't a lie. Seeing Crystal and Cedric would be shitty and probably not help my mental game going into competition season. Not because I was still in love with her, but because it would bring up all the guilt, shame, and frustration I felt after she left me. The anger at myself and the shame of what I put my family through. And I knew I probably wasn't strong enough to stay focused, to stay on track.

Having Hazel by my side, it would help. I wasn't exactly sure why. But in this moment, she felt essential. Her presence through all the ups and downs of training and competition would make a difference. I knew it.

"We've known each other forever, and we'll make a good team."

She eased onto the couch next to me, silently regarding me with curiosity, the wheels turning in her super-genius brain.

Though on the outside, what I was proposing was transactional—I'd help her, and she'd help me, and then we'd part ways—my heart was racing, and my hands were clenched. I wanted this. Marriage, Hazel, something different. Though I couldn't be sure why. But my mind was going a hundred miles per hour, and I didn't have time to stop and analyze it.

With a sigh, she covered my hand with hers. A tremor of excitement shot through me at her proximity. And the scent of her shampoo, citrusy and clean, along with the smoothness of her small hand, brought a wave of calm immediately after.

"You are talented. Have been since we were kids. Don't waste it because you're stubborn and heartbroken."

I huffed a laugh. "You're annoyingly logical, you know that?"

She shrugged.

"But this is why this crazy marriage makes sense. You get surgery. I mentally get my shit together. As individuals, we're hot messes. Together, as a team? We can do better."

She dropped back against the couch, crossing her arms and depriving me of her touch. "I hate to admit it, but you're kind of making sense. I need to get this fucking gallbladder out without bankrupting myself or my brother. Or dying of sepsis. Though marrying for health care isn't exactly the stuff of romantic fantasies."

"We've known each other our entire lives. We trust and respect each other. We can make a short-term marriage work."

"People will say you're on the rebound."

"I don't care. And neither should you. I see it as upgrading to someone brilliant and gorgeous. And everyone else will see that too."

She dipped her chin and blushed in response. And I liked it. I felt a small thrill that my words affected her. That I could have a small impact on how she felt.

But the satisfaction I got from that blush was dangerous.

The big, noisy elephant in the room trumpeted, telling me to proceed with caution.

Because as I sat on this couch next to her, I began to realize that Hazel wasn't just cute. She wasn't just Dylan's kid sister anymore. She had grown and evolved into something far more dangerous. Something I couldn't risk. This would take a lot of willpower and discipline, but I'd handle it. For her.

She regarded me for a few minutes, those lips pressed into a straight line, before standing and pacing again. Finally, she stopped in front of me and put her hands on her hips. "I need to think about this. Between you and me, I'm terrified, and I need this surgery. But I just want to buckle down, do my research, and then get my dream job far away from this town."

"Let's work together," I offered. "A team."

"Okay." She gave me a clipped nod. "I'm gonna order dinner. We can't get fake engaged on empty stomachs."

"No sex," she said, picking a mushroom off her slice. "Never ever—"

"Of course," I agreed, interrupting her. In no version of this marriage would I ever consider sex. Okay, maybe that wasn't quite the truth. But obviously, we would never go there. We weren't attracted to each other like that.

I took another bite to buy myself some time. It was a logical and useful rule to establish. And every single neuron in my brain knew that I could never, ever cross that line with

Hazel. Out of respect for her and for Dylan. This could only work if we kept it friendly.

So why did hearing her say it bother me so much? It was like the moment she said it out loud, I couldn't stop myself from thinking about it. I imagined slowly sliding the strap of her tank top down her delicate shoulder and kissing the spot at the base of her neck. Then I shook myself out of my stupor and chugged my ice water. These were the exact kinds of thoughts I'd have to learn to control if I wanted this to work.

"That's the most important thing. To keep things platonic," she continued. "Let's not do anything stupid."

"Totally platonic," I said, nodding a little too vigorously.

She pulled a threadbare blanket around her shoulders and shifted to face me, crossing her legs in front of her. "Okay, let's think this through for real. We get married next week."

"And I'll add you to my insurance the next day. Our policies kick in immediately. Then you schedule your surgery."

"It'll probably be a few weeks before they can get me in at the surgery center, and then I've got to recover."

I drop what's left of my crust onto my plate and wipe my hands on a napkin. "Competition season starts in late June and goes through early fall. You'll have plenty of time to work on your dissertation while I train. And when I travel, you come with me, help me handle Crystal and Cedric, and make me look responsible to potential sponsors. Hopefully, I can qualify for nationals, which will take everything to the next level."

She tapped her chin. "So we need to stay married for what? Six months? A year?"

"You decide. How long will it take to finish your dissertation and land a job with good health benefits?"

She shrugged. "Probably a year. That's too long…"

A year of being married to Hazel. Not something I would have ever thought would happen, but it didn't sound so bad. I had no interest in women after the Crystal debacle, and Hazel's focus and work ethic were bound to rub off on me. "Nope. Works for me. And you can get follow-up care. Anything you need—physical therapy, a dietitian, medicine. I mean it. I want you to take care of yourself." Glass of water in hand, I gave her my most serious look. One that didn't make appearances very often.

She leaned forward, pushing her glasses up.

It took Herculean willpower not to sneak a peek at her cleavage in the process.

"I have one, um, request." She looked down at her hands, which were shredding a takeout napkin.

"Anything."

"Can we not tell everyone it's, you know, fake?" She stood and started pacing around the room. "Lovewell has always supported me and believed in me. And I want to make this place proud. But I'm embarrassed. And taking charity from you—"

"It's not charity," I interrupted, standing as well. "It's a mutually beneficial arrangement to benefit your health."

"Sure. But I feel pathetic. The trailer park orphan can't even take care of herself at twenty-eight. You know how people talk."

"Yes. I know how people talk. You should hear the things they've been saying about me for the past six months. And no one is going to look down on you for needing health insurance."

She winced.

"But I respect that. We'll come up with a story for the town gossip mill. We won't tell anyone but Dylan."

"And Lydia."

"Sure. And Lydia."

She dropped her shoulders in acquiescence. "So I have a year to get healthy, and you have a year to become a professional lumberjack?"

"Sounds like a solid plan."

We spent the next hour making up our cover story. It probably wouldn't have taken so long, but we spent most of that time laughing as I offered one crazy suggestion after the next. I loved making Hazel laugh.

"Witness protection?"

She rolled her eyes and threw herself against the back of the worn couch. "No!"

"We were abducted by aliens together, and the experience bonded us deeply."

"Too crazy, even for Lovewell."

I shifted on the couch, noticing for the first time what a nice laugh she had. "Okay. We'll just say we've been friends forever, and one day, I woke up and realized I couldn't live without you."

She put her hand over her heart. "And we know we're moving fast, but when you know—"

"You know," I said, giving her a wink while finishing her sentence.

She bit her bottom lip and scanned the room, then

brought that intense gaze back to me. "Okay. That will work." She held out a tiny hand.

I slid my palm against hers, sealing the deal. The little thing sitting next to me had a surprisingly strong grip. She'd probably be a great tree climber.

"You know," she mused. "I planned to never get married."

I gave her my best gentlemanly bow. "Then I am honored to be your first and only husband."

Chapter 8
Hazel

My wedding day started like every other day. Waking up on Dylan's couch with a backache to the sounds of him humming as he made coffee in the galley kitchen.

It was only as I stretched and rearranged the messy bun on top of my head that I recognized the tune. "Here Comes the Bride." Fitting.

Bleary-eyed, I stumbled to the kitchen. I'd never understood how he could be such a morning person. We shared DNA, for God's sake, and I couldn't function before nine.

Before I could ask him to pour me a cup, he slid one into my hand and raised one eyebrow.

"You okay?" He was awake and chipper and dressed for the day in his requisite teacher attire—pressed khakis and button-down shirt.

I nodded silently. Words were impossible before the coffee kicked in.

"Are you really going to go through with this?"

We had spent the last few days arguing over my impending nuptials. Though he had been the one to suggest it, he'd quickly changed stances on the matter when I told him we were actually going through with it. But the bottom line was, I felt good. I was at peace with the decision.

I took a sip and let the bitterness spread across my tongue, the familiar sensation clearing away the first layer of my morning brain fog.

I shrugged. "Too late now."

Dylan set his cup on the laminate countertop and scowled. "You haven't even gotten the license yet. It's the perfect time to back out."

"I'm not backing out," I insisted, huffing a breath. "Remy and I made a deal. It'll benefit us both. I'm not a kid anymore, Dyl. I'm just trying to make my life work right now."

He continued to watch me, the skepticism in his expression exasperating. Yes, this was a bit insane, but being an adult meant making hard choices sometimes. And if all went as planned, it would help both Remy and me in the long run.

"You're coming to meet us after, right?" Despite the unaffected façade I was hiding behind, and regardless of my mile-wide independent streak, I needed my brother there on my fake wedding day.

He cracked a smile. "Of course. Lydia is going to cover my last period study hall so I can head out early."

When I called Bangor City Hall, I jumped on the first available appointment, and since they were only open Monday Through Friday, Remy was taking the day off so we could get everything accomplished.

But Dylan couldn't join us until after the ceremony since he hadn't found a sub on such short notice.

I hadn't been to many weddings, and I doubted this would be like anything I'd seen on TV. Googling only gave me the basic requirements, so I still couldn't wrap my mind around how it would feel to say vows, to sign a document legally binding me to another human being.

And it was silly to create expectations at all. This was all for convenience. A business transaction rather than a romantic moment.

But still, Lydia and I had taken a trip to my favorite thrift shop in Orono yesterday, where I found the perfect lilac dress. It wasn't bridal, but it was vintage, sleeveless, and had a flared skirt that swished around my knees. It made my waist look tiny, and just putting it on made me feel confident.

Confident enough to marry my brother's best friend so I could get health insurance, at least.

I took a long shower, shaving and moisturizing everything, even though we had explicitly agreed never to consummate this marriage. But it felt necessary to mark the occasion. I even put on makeup and carefully blew out my hair, pulling half back and securing it with a pretty vintage barrette that I had found at a thrift shop in Boston.

It was the kind of thing I liked to pretend I'd inherited from my great-grandmother. In my mind, she was a society girl from Beacon Hill who'd rejected every suitor her parents found for her because she was too smart and too opinionated to marry for anything but love. Silly, I knew. But when a young girl didn't have her own family history, when there were no special memories or keepsakes from her past, she got really good at making things up. And those indulgent stories had stayed with me.

But I couldn't let my brain run away with romantic fantasies today.

The only way to make this work was to stay focused on the goals we'd spelled out. My health, his career, maintaining our friendship. Nothing more.

We would remain married for one year, and then quietly and amicably divorce. Preferably after I had defended my dissertation and was accepting a glamorous job offer far away from Lovewell.

Visualizing made it easier to grasp. Repeating the reasons helped obliterate any sneaky romantic notions of what a marriage should be that crept in when I let my guard down. Because I knew all too well that most marriages were disasters. But we'd make this one a smashing success. We were going in with our eyes wide open and, at my insistence, had set very specific parameters.

Plus, I had Dylan. He was, by far, the most uncomfortable with this arrangement.

And if anything went wrong, it would devastate him. Remy's friendship was one of the most precious things in Dylan's life, and I would never, ever get in the way of that. My brother had already sacrificed so much for me.

And Remy. He thought he needed me, but in reality, everything he wanted was within his grasp. If only he understood that. Still, his willingness to help and his generosity were so endearing they made me want to help him in return. Get him back on his feet and ready to compete. Taking the next step as an athlete would get him out of his Crystal funk. And if the confidence he found once he made it didn't, the women who would inevitably throw themselves at him once he made it to the pro competition circuit would surely help him move on from her.

The thought made my stomachache. But I had to face facts.

After our divorce, he would go on to marry again. He'd find a beautiful girl—preferably someone far sweeter than Crystal—who would give him babies and laugh at his goofy jokes. She'd be easygoing and fun, and they would grow old in Lovewell together, then simultaneously die from old age in their sleep while holding hands.

Though it hurt to think about, I wanted that for him. He deserved it. I, on the other hand, was destined for different things. Marriage and babies were never going to be part of my journey. That part of me, the trusting, hopeful, optimistic part, was long gone. Or maybe it had never existed at all.

I didn't trust guys enough to make it to a third date, never mind the rest of my life and a mortgage.

I'd have to rely on Dylan to give me nieces and nephews to spoil. I'd be okay being known as the cool aunt.

Because I knew what I wanted. And today was just the first step in getting there.

***

Though we hadn't gone into detail, Remy and I had briefly discussed our attire. Dressing up and taking a few photos for social media was necessary to make this all feel legitimate and give us something to remember this wild marriage by. We'd decided to take a few at city hall, and then pose in front of the Paul Bunyan statue in downtown Bangor in our wedding finery. His agent would be thrilled when Remy posted them to his Instagram page, and they were the type of lumberjack-y stuff potential sponsors would eat up.

In some corner of my mind, though I tried to keep myself from accessing it, I understood that he would look good in a suit. Remy was handsome. More than handsome, really. Rugged and masculine but still playful. The bastard could probably smolder in a tutu.

So when he arrived to pick me up, I expected him to look decent.

But in no way had I counted on Remy in a vest.

No, sir. When I carefully planned this day, there were no vests involved.

Especially not one made of soft gray wool that emphasized his broad shoulders and narrow waist. Or that he would get out of the truck with his sleeves rolled up and his hair pushed back while holding a professionally arranged bouquet of flowers.

Nope. My careful planning did not account for these variables.

I wobbled on my heels and my cheeks flamed.

"Ready to get hitched?" he asked, wearing a lopsided grin and holding the bouquet out.

"Where did you get these?"

"Mrs. Laurent."

Of course. When we were kids, Laurents' flower shop created amazing arrangements for every wedding, funeral, and graduation in this town. But after the mill and the inn closed and so many families left the area, there hadn't been enough demand to keep them in business, and they'd closed their doors.

"But they've been closed for years."

He shook his head. "My brothers and I helped paint the new salon on Main Street a few months back. Her daughter-in-law Becca owns it. So she owed me a favor. Her greenhouses are full, and she spends all her time out there now anyway. So she's happy to part with some of her flowers on occasion. She sends her congratulations, by the way."

All I could do was drop my chin and shake my head. It was so Remy. Everyone loved him and everyone owed him favors. Of course Mrs. Laurent was happy to come out of retirement for him.

They were gorgeous flowers too. All shades of white, cream, and purple.

"How did you know I liked purple?" I asked, running a hand over the skirt of my lilac dress.

He looked down and kicked the sidewalk with his dress shoe. "You always picked the purple popsicles. And you put purple streaks in your hair in high school. And you took that purple backpack with you everywhere. I always assumed it was your favorite color."

I inspected him for a moment, and not just because I couldn't get enough of dressed-up Remy. He had been noticing little things about me for so long. It wasn't a secret that my favorite color was purple, but it still shook me to the core that as a teenage boy who had so many other things holding his attention, he had noticed something so simple. And that years later, he'd remembered and considered it when buying my wedding flowers. What else had he noticed about me?

My cheeks heated and my stomach fluttered at the notion.

But I refused to analyze that reaction.

Jeez. If simple deductive reasoning was giving me shivers, how was I going to survive being married to this guy for a whole year?

"You look beautiful," he said softly, jamming his hands into his pockets. He was staring at me, drinking in the sight of me. His darkened gaze landed on my lips, putting my body on high alert. My pulse hammered as we stared at one another, and an intense desire to kiss him washed over me. And not because of the flowers or the compliment. But because of the way he regarded me. It was different from anything I'd ever felt before. His eyes were hungry, and he'd sunk his teeth into his bottom lip.

I turned toward the truck, desperate to stop the heat coursing through my body. "I guess it's time." I said lamely, rounding the hood to the passenger side of the truck.

Without a word, he rushed past me to open the door.

As we set off toward Bangor, I stared out the window, wondering what the hell I was getting myself into. Because while the marriage would be fake, the desire I was feeling for my husband was painfully real.

Chapter 9
Remy

TV makes getting married look easy and beautiful and romantic. But in reality, there's a lot of standing around in dingy government buildings and paperwork involved.

Not to mention I was having a difficult time keeping my eyes off my bride. I had almost tripped over my own feet when I picked her up. She was wearing a dress. One with a swishy skirt that hugged her curves and showed a tantalizing glimpse of her collarbones. I had never given any thought to collarbones until that day we collided and hers were covered in pie. But now I found myself wondering if I could get away with licking them.

I had stared like an idiot. But everything felt different. She looked different. Feminine and sensual. My brain struggled to process the sudden realization that Hazel was a gorgeous woman who would be my wife very shortly. Though that didn't scare me nearly as much as it should have.

Looking at her in her pretty dress, holding fresh flowers, I felt the kind of want, this longing, that I'd never experienced before. Her plump lips, all glossy and kissable, were messing with my head.

And her hair. It was down her back, pinned with some fancy thing that made her look regal. Her cheeks were rosy and her lips pink and her thick eyelashes fluttered every time she peered up at me.

Our plan was probably insane. But she needed surgery, and I was in a position to help her. And I knew, deep down, that being married to Hazel, even for a short time, would change me. I was ready for it. When I looked over at her, where she was chatting politely with the clerk, it didn't feel crazy. Strangely, it made sense.

When she returned to where I was standing against the back wall, I draped my arm over her shoulders, enjoying how she had to crane her neck to look up at me, even in heels. "You don't have to do this if you don't want to."

She watched me for a long moment, giving me the chance to study just how rich her chocolate brown irises were. Then she cocked one brow. "Getting cold feet?"

I shook my head. "No, ma'am. Just wanted to be a gentleman and offer you one last chance to escape."

Taking my hand in hers, she squeezed, her small, smooth hand fitting perfectly in my larger, callused one. "I'm all in," she said softly.

I returned the squeeze. "Me too. Let's get hitched."

"So the JP started coughing?" Dylan asked over his bottle of beer. He had met us in Bangor, where we were celebrating with happy hour drinks—alcoholic for him; nonalcoholic for us—and pretzels.

Hazel giggled. "Not just coughing. He was hacking. Bent at the waist, hands on his knees to brace himself, coughing. I was patting his back and Remy rushed out in search of water."

"Gross."

"He didn't cover his mouth or anything. It was disturbing."

Dylan took a sip of his beer. "I'm sorry I missed it, guys."

"I'm glad you're here to celebrate with us."

"As the joint best man and man of honor, I'd like to propose a toast." Dylan raised his glass.

I froze, worried my best friend was about to embarrass me.

"I thought hell would freeze over before I allowed my best friend to marry my little sister. But I was wrong. You're good people in challenging situations, and I want what's best for you, which I guess means this insane fake marriage."

I gave him a tight smile, trying to ignore the hell freezing over comment and the slice of pain I felt when he said it.

"So. To Mr. and Mrs. Gagnon. May you both get what you want and then get amicably divorced."

We clinked glasses, and Hazel threw her head back in laughter. And I joined her, because it was impossible not to when she looked so happy. This day was strange and wonderful, and we were having a good time. It was too late to turn back, so we might as well embrace the married life.

"Are you ready for photos? We've got to convince the world you're in love."

We spent the rest of the afternoon traipsing around Bangor, taking cheesy photos and laughing with Dylan. Not the most traditional wedding day, but we could have done a lot worse.

After frozen yogurt at Giffords in lieu of wedding cake, we ended up at a candlepin bowling alley.

The ugly bowling shoes looked adorable with Hazel's fancy dress. Her hair was back up in its usual ponytail now, and she wore a permanent smile. The look made my heart squeeze. It was a drastic change from her often serious, worried demeanor.

"How did you get so good at this?" I asked after losing another set to her.

She shrugged. "There was an ancient bowling alley in the basement of my dorm at Brown. You had to stack the pins yourself, but it was free. I used to go down there to blow off steam."

I shook my head. "My wife is full of surprises."

"If you think I'm good at bowling, never challenge me to a game of scrabble." She gave me a saucy wink and then sauntered off to the ladies' room.

Before I could relish that wink, Dylan appeared next to me, his face serious.

"We should probably talk."

I gestured for him to sit on the bench, but he remained standing. "When I first suggested you two get married, I was joking. But it's done now, and I'm man enough to admit it's a good thing. She needs insurance. She needs to get healthy. And I know you're doing this for her. You've got nothing to gain here, and I am so grateful for your generosity." He worked his jaw from side to side and glanced over to where Hazel had disappeared. "But. I need to be able to trust you with her." Dylan wasn't just protective of Hazel. It was so much more than that. Their parents, their childhood trauma. He became responsible for her at such a young age. And he never stopped looking out for her.

I was close to my siblings, hell we worked together every day, but the connection between them ran so much deeper.

"Of course you can." I smiled, trying to assure him while attempting to mentally extinguish the flame of attraction that I'd started to feel for my bride. It was going to be difficult, but I respected Dylan. As a friend and as a brother. And I would never do anything to violate his trust. There was a lot he would tolerate. And trust me, I had pushed those boundaries a few times. But not with hazel. Never with hazel.

He didn't seem amused. "I'm only going to say this once. Hazel is my baby sister. She's smart and ambitious and too good for this place and this life. She's always looked up to you. Even had a little crush when we were kids."

That was news to me. And also irrelevant. We were adults and had entered into this marriage with clear intentions.

"Do not hold her back," he continued. "Do not make her compromise her dreams like my mom did. Do this stupid marriage thing and then let her go."

"It's not like that," I protested. "It's not real."

"You say that. But you care about her, and she cares about you."

"Yes. As lifelong friends."

"Keep it that way. If you really care about my sister, help

her get healthy so she can write her dissertation and get the fuck out of here."

Dylan was trusting me to do the right thing and be a good man. And I was not going to let him or Hazel down.

I held out my hand.

"You have my word."

Chapter 10
Hazel

Remy shoved his hands into his pockets and kicked the dirt. "This is it."

I gasped when I got a good look at the home before me. It was beautiful. So much more than he had described. I rarely ventured out of town and had never been up here. The trees were enormous, and the air was crisp and clean.

"This is the little cabin?" I turned to him with my hands on my hips. The trailer I grew up in could fit on the front porch.

"Henri built it. He lives up there now with Alice and their kids." He pointed up the hill to a massive timber-style home that looked like it had been cut out of a magazine and pasted into the Maine landscape.

He dug his phone out of his pocket and held out his arm, snapping a picture of us with the cabin in the background.

"Come take a look. Then we can grab your stuff." And with that, he was heading toward the front porch.

My feet were rooted to the dirt driveway. Entering this home—the one we were going to share—behind my *husband* felt too intimate. This was inevitable, of course, since we were married. But other than my college roommates and Dylan, I had never lived with anyone before. Definitely not a guy.

My husband.

Saying the words and sharing a chaste kiss, those parts were easy. But this? It felt like too much.

"Oh." He spun on his heel and, wearing a grin, smacked his forehead. It was disarming and pretty adorable. "I forgot."

Before I knew what was happening, Remy rushed for me and swept me off my feet, then strode for the door.

I was momentarily shocked by the feeling of his hands on my body and the effortless way he scooped me up into his arms. If I was a Victorian noblewoman, I would have properly swooned.

When I pulled myself out of my stupor, I threw my arms around his neck, holding on for dear life while protesting loudly. "What the hell are you doing?"

"Carrying my wife over the threshold. That's a thing, right?"

I bit my tongue, secretly delighted he thought of doing this and terrified I'd do something stupid like attempt to stick my tongue down his throat. His arms were so thick and strong, and I was dangerously close to his neck, which happened to smell especially amazing. The lumberjack pheromones were powerful. Someone should study this. I'd make a note to mention it to some of my biochem colleagues.

"Put me down," I said weakly, secretly reveling in the feel of my fake husband manhandling me with ease.

"Nope. Not a chance. Here, take a selfie of us."

I groaned and took the phone he still had clutched in the hand under my knees.

Effortlessly, he shifted me in his arms so our heads were close. I angled the phone and buried my face in his neck, using the opportunity to take a big old sniff of his manly scent.

He grinned, looking straight on at the camera, making sure the log cabin behind us was in the shots.

They were cute photos. The kind I'd think were real if I were mindlessly scrolling online. The couple in them looked silly and in love. Their expressions told a story that was in no way true.

But this moment? It was real. Remy carried me up onto the porch, unlocked the door with one hand, and then dramatically carried me across the threshold. Once inside, he set on my feet on the hardwood floor.

I crossed my arms over my thin T-shirt, angry that my traitorous nipples were trying to escape my cotton bra. I looked down, unable to make eye contact, lest I start humping his leg.

"You know, you're kind of cute when you are embarrassed," he said, tipping up my chin with two fingers.

Though my face heated, it was hard to look away from those dark eyes. He was smiling in that annoying way he had. His not-a-care-in-the-world smile. And I had the urge to smack it off his face.

But then I took a deep breath and reset my train of thought. Remy liked to tease me the way my older brother did. So why did this feel so different? Seductive. And certainly not brotherly.

I tried to center myself. This was platonic. We were friends making the best of difficult circumstances. Yes, my body was wildly attracted to him in this moment, but that was just biology. He was a big, strong, handsome man. And he had just carried me into our marital home, caveman style. Of course my hypothalamus was in overdrive, pumping hormones into my bloodstream. It was fine. He was just a good friend.

And right now, I was moving in with him.

I had spent my wedding night packing up what little I had in Dylan's apartment. He wasn't thrilled about me moving in with Remy, but if I didn't, there was no way we could sell this.

And my brother's apartment had gotten too small too quickly. There was no way I could keep sleeping on his couch. Remy claimed to have plenty of space. And that was an understatement. The cabin was bright and open and homey. I instantly fell in love.

"I moved in here a few months ago," he explained, rubbing the back of his neck. "After Crystal. Alice used to live here, but after she and the kids moved in with my brother, it was sitting empty. Henri usually rents it out in the summer, but he took pity on me." A strained look flashed across his face, but he masked it quickly.

I only knew bits and pieces about what had happened in the fall. And though I wanted to ask him more, understand why he was so down, find out what had really happened with his siblings, I was too scared. So I focused on admiring my new home.

Walking slowly through the main living space, I marveled at the panoramic view of the mountains outside the massive windows that took up the back wall. It was airy and bright and cozy. A large leather sectional took up most of the space, which had a wood stove in one corner and a large dining table in the other.

We made a few trips to the truck to unload my stuff, which didn't amount to much, and stacked it next to the couch. At one point, as we were finishing up, a moose ambled by, snagging my attention from where I was pulling a duffel bag from the bed of the truck.

"That's Clive," Remy said.

I had seen many moose in my life, and unless they were in front of my speeding car, I didn't much care, but this one was enormous and had a jagged scar across one of his hind legs.

Peering out from around the rear end of the truck, I beheld the creature. "That's a huge moose."

"Super old too." Remy nodded. "He's always around. Harmless."

For a split second, Clive made eye contact with me. I got the strangest feeling. Like this moose was sizing me up. He snorted, sending a spray of moose boogers into the air, then he continued his trek toward the tree line.

"We made eye contact," I said, still a bit unnerved.

"He does that. Sometimes I think he can see into my soul. But don't worry about it. When Alice moved in last year, she threw tampons at him, and he still seems to tolerate her."

"What?"

"Long story. I'll let her tell it. She's really funny. We can visit them."

I nodded and followed Remy to the house, carrying the last bag.

"It's on the remote side," he said, "but it's quiet, and Henri has equipment up at his house that I use for training. Plus, sometimes I get pity invites to their house for dinner." He waggles his brows. "Alice is an amazing cook, and I'm teaching Goldie how to climb trees."

Of course Remy was great with kids. He had such a fun energy. I bet children adored him. And by the way he talked about Goldie and Tucker, it was obvious he loved them. He would be a great dad someday. I'd be long gone by the time it happened, but I wanted that for him.

I went to the sink to wash my hands, then scanned the kitchen, searching for the cabinet that held the glasses.

"Here," Remy said, pulling two from the cabinet next to the sink and handing them to me.

When I'd filled them with water, he held his up in a toast. "To my new wife and roommate. Try not to fall in love with me, okay?" He smirked and took a long pull.

I laughed so hard I snorted. "I'm not worried about that happening," I said, then I hid behind my glass, taking a slow sip to cool myself down.

He tilted his head and scowled. "Why not? I'm very lovable." And in a flash, the frown he was wearing kicked up into a grin, and he winked.

While sixteen-year-old Hazel would have swooned on the spot, twenty-eight-year-old Hazel rolled her eyes. "Because I don't do that. Fall in love. It's not real and it doesn't last."

He reared back as if I'd slapped him. "Excuse me? Not true. My parents loved each other deeply."

"I know they did. And that's amazing. But I think we can both agree it's incredibly rare, can't we?"

He conceded with a slow nod. "You have a point there."

"From a young age, I vowed I wouldn't become my mom. I told myself I'd never let love blind me. Never let it destroy me. Or let some guy derail who I am and who I'm meant to become. So I date and I have sex and I've had a few relationships, but I don't expect much. And frankly, I haven't ever had my heart broken, so I feel like I'm doing pretty fucking good."

His brow furrowed. "How much sex?"

Jesus. Of course that was the part of that speech he zeroed in on.

I didn't respond. Instead, I took another sip of my water and glared at him. "None of your fucking business."

He shook his head. "You're right. It's not. But that whole philosophy sounds sad and lonely."

I slammed my glass down on the counter harder than I intended. "Says the man wallowing in heartache."

"Hey, don't judge me." For a second, I worried I'd offended him, but then his upper lip twitched.

"Sorry. That was harsh. I just mean that you had a horrible breakup. I'm looking at you right now, and all I can think is that I don't want to be in your shoes."

He scratched his chin. "You've got a point there." He put the glasses in the sink and propped a hip against the counter, crossing his arms over his chest. "We've established that there will be no falling in love in this marriage. Excellent. Now let me show you to your quarters, Mrs. Gagnon."

"Mrs. Markey-Gagnon," I corrected.

"Of course."

He cut across the kitchen and pushed through a door, revealing a small space with two decent-sized windows. A plush blue rug covered the floor, and on one wall stood an enormous steel desk.

"I got that for you." He nodded at the monstrous thing. "Alice let me take it. Said the school was going to donate it. It's kind of an antique."

Running my hands across the steel top, I took in its scarred surface. It looked like it was from the 1960s, with drawers on each side. My heart clenched. He'd gotten this for me?

"We can move it too. But it weighs a ton, so don't try it on your own. I had to bribe Henri to help me carry it in."

"It's perfect."

"It's not much, but I can get you anything else you need. Shelves, filing cabinets, whatever. This is your space."

He was watching me, his expression more bashful than I thought possible from a confident guy like him. And the hope in his eyes, like he really cared about what I thought of it, made my heart clench.

"That would be amazing." I wandered around the room, imagining the possibilities. White boards on the walls to keep track of my research, a small filing cabinet. I had never had my own private space before. Growing up, I'd shared a room with Dylan, and then in college and grad school, I'd lived with roommates. The past few years had been spent in a three-hundred-and-fifty square-foot studio I shared with an endless supply of critters that I would happily never see again.

This whole space felt like a fresh start. Where I could dig in and get my dissertation done. For the first time in months, a sense of relief washed over me. Like one massive item had been checked off my endless to do list.

The enormity of the last twenty-four hours hit me then. Marriage. Surgery. Moving in together. Tears welled up in my eyes, and a wave of gratitude hit me. "Thank you," I said, throwing my arms around his neck.

He went rigid at first, but then he wrapped his strong arms around me. "Nothing to thank me for," he whispered.

Tears crested, then spilled over my lashes as we stood, tangled together. I buried my face in his chest, breathing in the scent of him that I couldn't get enough of.

"No," I said into his shirt, the sound muffled. "You've already done so much for me. I just—"

And then the sobs began. I couldn't hold it in anymore. Years of tamping down my emotions, of being strong, independent, tough, flooded to the surface. And for one moment, I let myself be vulnerable.

Because I could. Remy was my friend. I could tease him and joke with him one minute and cry the next. I didn't have to worry about what he thought of me. And I wasn't trying to impress him. We were on the same team, and something about that realization made the tears flow faster.

I was feeling so many things at once. Fear and embarrassment, but also hope.

Because, after years of self-sufficiency, of barely scraping by, all my goals were within reach. I was so close to my PhD, and I could finally have the surgery I needed.

This man, this kind, beautiful person, was saving me. He was giving me health care and my own room to work, and the generosity of it all was just too much.

He would never understand what this meant to me. That

he'd stepped up like this when he didn't have to. It may have seemed insignificant to him, but for me, it was everything.

"Hey," he said, squeezing me tighter. "We're a team now. I help you and you help me."

"It's not the same." I hiccupped. "I owe you. And I hate being in debt."

He chuckled. "You certainly haven't changed, Hazel. But trust me, you have to pretend to be in love with me for the next year. You totally got the short end of the stick."

Resting my chin on his chest, I peeked up at him, tears still clouding my vision. But the stubble, the kind smile, the messy hair, I could see it all. And I had the sinking sensation that I may spend the next year doing more than pretending.

Chapter 11
Remy

I lay in my king-size bed and stared at the ceiling, studying the knots in the wood of each beam, unable to sleep. Never had been much of a sleeper, really.

My mom still complained, nearly thirty years later, about all her sleepless nights with me. How I would wake up at all hours, climb out of my crib, and wander around the house.

Growing up, it wasn't unusual for my dad to get up for work at four thirty and find me fully dressed and eating cereal while watching cartoons.

My brain and my body just couldn't be quiet.

Being up late, letting my mind wander, wasn't unusual.

But tonight was different.

My mind kept detouring to the spare room. Where Hazel was wedged in with her boxes of books, an enormous steel desk, and a tiny twin bed.

It felt weird, sharing my cabin with someone. Not bad weird, just different. I had lived with Crystal for three years. Had woken up next to her when I wasn't out working at

Gagnon camp. But somehow having Hazel on the other side of the wall was more intimate.

I had fallen in love with Crystal LaVoie the day she arrived in Lovewell in eighth grade. She was tall and blond and beautiful and popular. Her dad was a dentist who'd opened a practice in town, so she was rich too.

I spent years trying to get her attention while she dated every guy in town but me.

And then, in our early twenties, we started to hang out. For the first time, she was interested in me.

My siblings had always gotten all the attention. They were smart and hardworking and polite. Henri, the dependable oldest; Paz, the well-spoken, ambitious one; and Adele, tough as nails, smart as a whip and the apple of my father's eye.

Me? More often than not, I could be found climbing a tree or jumping into a creek.

My constant need to move made it hard to learn, despite my parents' best efforts. I couldn't sit still. I needed to be outside. My parents convinced me to try college, but that was a complete bust.

So I went to work. Dad and Henri put me out in the woods, and I learned the ins and outs of the logging business while I trained and competed on the side.

I had a job that let me move and kept me outside, a gorgeous girlfriend who'd said yes when I popped the question, financial security, and time with my family.

My life was moving forward.

And then everything fell apart.

I alienated the people I respected most in this world and

put others in danger. My father's legacy, my brother's life, all in jeopardy because of me.

For my whole life, I'd felt like the family fuck-up. But the last six months had really solidified that title.

But now, I had a second chance, a fresh start. I was married. And the woman on the other side of the wall depended on me. Needed me. Even if it was all fake, it still felt strangely satisfying.

I could provide for Hazel, help her get healthy and finish her degree. And yes, it wasn't a forever thing, but in the process of it all, I could finally get my shit together. Figure out what and who I was meant to be.

Content for the first time in what felt like forever, I rolled over in my massive bed, ready to settle in and force myself to get a few hours of sleep. With my eyes closed and my breaths steady, I let go of the thoughts that always ricocheted inside my brain, then froze at an unfamiliar sound. It was coming from inside the house, so it wasn't Clive, and it wasn't a bear rooting around nearby.

I got out of bed and headed toward the door, stopping to listen when the noise came again. Hazel. She was sick.

Running through the house, I flipped on the lights as I went, heading for the small bathroom. And that's where I found her, slumped on the tile, sweaty and pale.

I dropped to my knees beside her. "Are you okay?"

"Get out of here, Remy." She swatted at me. "I'm fine."

"You're not fine."

"I'm—" She gagged before turning toward the toilet and vomiting.

Worried, I pulled her hair away from her face and rubbed her back.

"Get out!" she yelled, still heaving.

"No," I gritted out. "I'm here and I'm not leaving."

I hopped to my feet and pulled a washcloth from the drawer. I wet it and went for her face with it, but she snatched it from my hand.

"Please leave," she pleaded, wiping her face with the cool cloth. "I've got to clean this up."

"No way."

I squatted and slipped one arm under her knees and the other around her back, just like when I'd carried her into the cabin. She was so tiny in my arms, the weight of her barely slowing me as I strode to the living room. Once my eyes adjusted to the light, I realized she was wearing only a T-shirt. Her bare legs were slung across my arm.

I laid her on the couch and grabbed a blanket, desperate to help. Witnessing how sick and helpless she was in that moment flipped some kind of protective switch in my brain.

"What do you need?"

She slumped back against the cushions. "Nothing. Just give me a minute."

I tugged the cool washcloth from her hand and draped it across her clammy forehead. "Okay. I'm going to clean up the bathroom, and then I'll be back. Don't get up. Holler if you need me."

After dealing with the bathroom, I returned to find Hazel curled up on the couch, sipping water from a glass.

"I told you not to get up," I scolded, my fists planted on my hips.

Into her glass, she murmured, "I'm not good at taking orders."

"You don't say. What can I get you? What do we do now?"

"We don't do anything. I'll make some peppermint tea and take my supplements and try to get back to sleep."

I huffed a sardonic laugh. Why couldn't she just let me take care of her? "I'll make tea."

"I got it." She stood, draping the blanket back over the couch. "It's passed. I'm fine."

I followed her into the kitchen, keeping my line of sight above her shoulders. Taking the kettle out of her hand, I gently nudged her aside. "You are clearly not fine."

"Are you always this domineering?" she asked, giving me some serious side-eye.

I stepped back and held my hands out in front of me, not wanting to upset her any more. She was clearly embarrassed. "Just trying to help." I took a seat on one of the stools at the island, taking a moment to fully process that my wife was standing in the kitchen wearing only a T-shirt.

It was gray and faded, and I couldn't comprehend the words written on it. I think they were English, but I couldn't tell when her bare legs were *right there.*

The shirt hit halfway down her thighs, and my brain was in overdrive, wondering whether she had panties on.

I dropped my chin and studied the countertop as she turned to put the kettle on the stove, depriving myself of seeing the hem inch up as she reached into the cabinet for a mug. I had to be strong. I couldn't be ogling my wife in the middle of the night like this.

And Dylan. I'd promised him. And I would keep my word. It didn't matter that my wife had a perfect ass that I wanted to spend time getting intimately acquainted with.

She turned around, and our eyes locked. Could she read my thoughts? Hazel was brilliant, but I doubted she had developed mind-reading abilities. I swallowed hard as her eyes dropped for one second to the waistband of my sweats before pulling back up. Huh. Maybe she wasn't immune to me either.

Trying to defuse the tension, I settled on a joke, though the second it left my lips, I mentally smacked myself because it made absolutely no sense. "I didn't realize you slept naked."

She huffed, pulling my attention back to her, and gave me an exasperated look. "I know it's late, dear husband, but this," she waved a hand up and down the length of her body, "is called a T-shirt."

Feeling dumb, I mumbled to myself. "It's barely anything."

She widened her stance and put her hands on her hips, which I secretly loved. "Ugh. You're one to talk. Coming out here in your low-slung gray sweats and no shirt."

I dropped my chin again and roughed the hair on the back of my head so she couldn't see my smirk.

"Jesus, Remy. Are you flexing right now? How many goddamn abs do you have?"

Damn, I loved when she was all sassy and fired up like this. It didn't happen often. Hazel was usually so serious, but I liked her joking at my expense.

She growled and went back to the stove, then returned with two steaming mugs of tea.

She set one in front of me and the other beside it, then climbed onto the stool next to me, tugging her T-shirt down her bare legs as she settled in.

We sat shoulder to shoulder for a moment, taking in the silence.

I blew across the surface of my tea. "Sorry I made things weird."

"You didn't. If you want, I'll wear pajamas."

That was decidedly not what I wanted. But I couldn't say that out loud.

"And I'll wear a shirt. I want you to be comfortable here. It's your home too." I brought my tea to my lips to test the temperature and took a small sip. "You know, most newlyweds are tearing each other's clothes off, but here we are, putting more on."

"Our union is as unique and special as we are," she said, raising her mug. "To more clothes."

"And a blissful marriage." I clinked my mug against hers lightly.

After we finished, I rinsed the mugs and headed to my room.

"Remy," she said softly.

I turned to where she stood in the doorway of her room, struck by how lucky I was that she needed me as much as I needed her.

I took a step closer.

"Thank you," she whispered. She looked up at me with wide, serious eyes.

All I could do was give in to the need to do what felt right. So I pulled her into a hug.

I rested my chin on top of her head and sighed. "All I want is to help you, okay? And that includes taking care of you. First thing tomorrow, you're calling to schedule that surgery. I already contacted HR. Henri assures me the paperwork will be processed quickly. We're going to get you healthy."

She pressed her cheek to my chest. "How can I repay you?"

"By being the most amazing wife ever and then divorcing my ass once I land my sponsorship deal."

She laughed into my chest hair, her warm breath against my skin sending tingles coursing through me.

"Deal."

"Good."

"Remy? Can you let go? It's getting weird having my face all up in your bare chest."

I heaved out a sigh. "Okay. good night."

Then she was gone, disappearing into her room and quietly closing the door behind her. And I returned to my giant, fluffy, empty bed and went back to staring at the ceiling all night.

Chapter 12
Remy

The last person I expected to find on my doorstep at seven on a Sunday morning was Paz. His BMW SUV parked next to my Chevy truck in the driveway only heightened the differences between us.

Paz had been born for something more than logging. He was the corporate type—smart, polite, clean cut. He had just survived another Northern Maine winter and still hadn't grown a beard.

He didn't want to be here, but after Dad died, he'd moved back and taken over the finance side of the business. Negotiated contracts, paid suppliers, and worked nonstop to get us out of the red. He and Henri were close, always in meetings behind closed doors and still treated me like the dumb younger brother who couldn't possibly understand.

The winter had been brutal. It was the busiest time of the year for Gagnon Lumber, and on top of that, we were cooperating with law enforcement. After Henri's accident, the logging companies reached a deal with the FBI to surveil parts of our logging roads for drug trafficking.

It had resulted in delay after delay, daily headaches, and far too many lost profits. All of which Paz had to manage. He was our corporate face, meeting with the governor, driving to Boston to sit down with the legal team, and constantly working to protect our bottom line.

And handling me. The liability. Because I'd lost the respect of my crews, thus ensuring I couldn't work alongside them. I'd caused tens of thousands of dollars in damage while simultaneously putting us days behind schedule. I was of no use to him. So he'd written me off, some days chewing me out endlessly and others completely ignoring my existence.

If he had his way, he'd be out of here tomorrow. Back to the city, where he could collect fancy watches and hit up cool restaurants. Where he could be someone else entirely.

The Paz of my childhood, the wise guy who sailed through school on his wits and then through the rest of life's challenges on his charm, was long gone. My older brother had always been the one to give me advice. He taught to ride a bike and bought me my first beer. Anymore, it was rare to find that brother of mine in the man he had become.

Outside the window, he marched up to the cabin, wearing his normal angry expression.

"Morning brother," I said quietly, opening the door.

Paz pushed past me without saying a word.

"What crawled up your ass?" I asked.

"You," he spat, his face twisted in what looked like disgust. "You need to stop being so fucking impulsive."

I wished I could say I was surprised by his outburst. But this was the way he spoke to me these days.

"You've been like this since you were a kid. Always shooting first and asking questions later. What the fuck were you thinking?"

He wore a light blue dress shirt with a few buttons undone at the collar and a pair of jeans that probably cost more than my monthly truck payment. Paz was not meant for this life. Yeah, he'd grown up alongside us, climbing trees and jumping in lakes, but he'd always wanted more than small-town life. Smart and ambitious, he sailed through school, and when he headed off to college, he never looked back.

He would come up for holidays and family events, but he was settled in Portland. Had a sick condo with ocean views and traveled all over the world.

Seeing him here, in this simple log cabin, wearing those expensive shoes, always felt strange. He didn't fit. It was obvious to everyone, but most of all him.

My parents had encouraged him to do what he needed to do, go where he needed to go. But when Dad died, he wasn't here. He'd missed out on years and years of working alongside him like the rest of us had been doing. And he was angry about that. About what had been lost. And he was taking it out on everyone and everything around him. And lately, I'd been the easiest target.

The realization that Dad's death had not been an accident only made things worse. Thing had been so tense since Adele's discovery that the four of us could barely communicate without finding ourselves in a shouting match. Everyone had theories and questions, and we were all blaming ourselves.

My sister had retreated. Adele blamed herself, and these days, if she wasn't working nonstop in the shop, she'd disappear. She was dating someone, that much we knew, but asking for details was a sure-fire way for one of us to get our head ripped off.

Paz had been back for two years, and he was still renting a small apartment, still kept a crazy schedule, still wore his Brooks Brothers shirts around town. He was biding his time until he could get out. Our business needed him. So out of loyalty to Dad's legacy and to Henri, he'd come back, stepping in as CFO and starting the long process of modernizing a fourth-generation family business.

I had always respected him. He worked hard and was good to our family, especially our mom. But we didn't have much in common. Not anymore. He had regarded me as the fuck-up little brother since birth, making it pointless for me to strive for anything more than the obligatory distant brotherly relationship we had.

"Lower your voice," I snapped. "What are you talking about?"

He pinched the bridge of his nose, already exhausted by my idiocy, I was sure. "Why the fuck would you go out and get married? I got paperwork from HR asking for my signature of approval for Hazel's health insurance yesterday. Along with a copy of your marriage license. You jaunted off to Bangor last Tuesday and got fucking married? What were you thinking? Never mind, I know that answer. You weren't."

His face was red, and his hands were shaking. Meaning

this outburst wasn't just about my surprise wedding. If it were, he wouldn't be here. Wouldn't have even bothered to mention it. In his eyes, it would be par for the course with me.

"You don't need to get married to legally bind yourself to someone. Especially someone who hasn't lived in this town for fifteen years. I don't get it."

"There is nothing for you to get. Hazel and I are happy, and that's enough."

He turned his back and stomped to the large windows that looked out at the mountains. "This is so Remy," he said to the view in front of him. "Always cutting corners. Never doing things the right way. Thinking with your dick instead of your brain."

That was too far. He knew nothing about Hazel and me.

I crossed my arms, breathing deep to temper the rage flaring up inside me. He was jumping to some pretty hurtful conclusions. "Like you should talk."

He spun around and glared at me from across the room.

"Who are you banging this weekend, huh? Miss Nipple Piercing? Or Miss Pink Skirt? What about Miss Redhead with Weird Ears? Give me your phone. Let's count the number of booty-call contacts you've racked up since you've been here."

In addition to being smart and ambitious, Paz had always been a playboy. Girls threw themselves at him as far back as middle school. He was tall and good-looking and had this air of indifference that, for some ridiculous reason, drove girls insane.

He'd always dated casually, but it wasn't until he came back to Lovewell that Henri and I got a peek of the contacts in his phone. Each one was saved using physical attributes and random details. No names. Turns out my big brother had a digital black book of hookups. He wasn't dating at all. No, he was fucking around with nameless, faceless women every chance he got. And while I was not one to judge consensual adult fun, the sheer number of contacts he had made the whole thing kind of gross.

"Shut the fuck up," he hissed, whipping around to face me finally.

"Because dehumanizing woman and objectifying them rather than using their actual names is super fucking healthy, dude." I took a step closer and dropped my arms. "Try therapy. It works."

"This isn't about me. This is about you"—he pointed a finger at me with far more violence than anyone should be capable of so early on a Sunday—"being a mess of a man who can't get his shit together."

"Wow," I scoffed, "your brotherly concern is heartwarming. Worry about yourself. I don't discard women like tissues."

"This isn't about me."

"Yeah, you said that. But maybe it should be." It was rare I stood up to my older siblings. I was a lover, not a fighter. And conflict was something I avoided if at all possible, especially with my family.

But this wasn't about standing up for myself. I was protecting Hazel too. We were in this together. I had convinced myself that people would understand and be happy for us. But standing here, staring my brother down, it hit me. They wouldn't. The bond we shared may have been unconventional, but it was ours. And I would do everything in my power to protect it.

"Henri and Adele aren't over here screaming at me. In fact, they've both congratulated me."

"Trust me, they're equally pissed. Henri's just too busy with work and his kids, and Adele is off fucking some professor."

I winced. Sure, Adele was a grown woman, but I avoided any mention of her dating life if at all possible. Details about my sister's sex life were hard to stomach. Especially because she had a type. Academic guys. Glasses and elbow patches. Treated her like shit.

She stayed far away from anyone who worked in logging. Hell, anyone who worked with their hands at all. She had taken shit from guys at work and in school over the years, so she overcompensated by seeking out men who were the complete opposite of those she'd spent her life proving herself to. Being a woman in our world wasn't easy. I didn't begrudge her happiness, but what she hadn't figured out yet was that these guys belittled her more than a good number of men who'd grown to respect her and her abilities over the years.

"So, of course, good old Pascal has to come and clean up the mess you made. Did you knock her up or something?"

A throat cleared a few feet away, and there was Hazel, standing in the doorway to her office, noise canceling headphones around her neck. Her glasses were crooked and there was a purple pen stuck in her ponytail.

Paz and I froze.

"Pascal." She said his name slowly, emphasizing every letter. I swore a shiver raced through him. "I can't believe you would even ask that. It's not 1950, for Christ's sake. And our relationship is none of your business."

The look on her face was pure venom. I'd known her all my life, and though she was serious and worked hard, I'd never seen such a stony expression from her.

If I hadn't been so terrified by the look on her face, I would have taken a moment to appreciate just how goddamn adorable my wife was.

Yoga pants, a tank top with a baby sloth on it, and her requisite dark glasses. That long dark hair piled on top of her head. She was tiny but formidable.

She walked to the center of the room slowly, every step deliberate. When she stopped in front of Paz, she propped her hands on her hips and tipped her chin up, scrutinizing him.

Paz, not one to be easily intimidated, especially by a five-foot nothing woman in a sloth tank top, narrowed his eyes. "Sorry, Pip," he said coolly. "I was just chatting with my brother."

"No." She crossed her arms and paused, giving him the kind of once-over that would make me pee my pants. "You don't get to come in here and call me Pip and verbally abuse my husband. I'm afraid I've got to ask you to leave."

"Jesus Christ." Paz ran a hand down his face.

"This is our home, and while thoughtful and respectful discussion is always welcome, shouting and insults are not," she continued.

Paz stood a little taller, fisting his hands at his sides. "This doesn't involve you."

She laughed. Straight up laughed in his face. I had never seen anyone do that before. Paz was Mr. Serious Business

Man. People usually looked at him in reverent awe or maybe a little fear. But Hazel's lack of veneration had his face turning red and his jaw clenching tighter than I'd seen it since the night I fucked things up at camp.

"It does involve her," I said, sidling up to Hazel and putting my arm around her tiny shoulders. "My wife is right. We don't welcome this kind of behavior in our home."

Hazel gave him a big, menacing smile. "I'll see you out. Come back when you can be civilized."

Paz looked between us, joined physically and spiritually, and sighed deeply. He trudged silently toward the door without looking back, and Hazel followed him, shutting it softly once his feet hit the porch.

We stood in silence for a few minutes, watching each other, until we heard his car drive off.

Then she opened her arms and walked toward me. The kindness of the gesture, the realization that she'd stood up for me to my brother, hit me in the solar plexus, and I welcomed her embrace. The feel of her tucked up against my body instantly eased the anger and the self-doubt swirling inside me and slowed my heart rate.

We stayed locked like that for a long moment, her head on my chest and me breathing in the scent of her shampoo. She was here for me, defending me and supporting me. I wasn't sure what to make of it. All I knew was that I needed to feel her in my arms for one more minute.

Our hug lasted longer than was strictly platonic, and finally, she broke away. She took two steps back and peered up at me.

"You didn't have to do that," I whispered.

She waved a hand at me dismissively. "Fuck yeah, I did.

What a dick. No one speaks to my husband like that." There went the hands on her hips again. Adorable.

I took her in from head to toe. The woman before me wasn't just Dylan's kid sister. Or my old friend, the nerdy genius. Not even the pretty girl I had married. She was formidable and fierce.

Crystal was pretty and she knew it. In fact, it was her primary personality trait. Her life revolved around being a blond, blue-eyed beauty. She religiously dyed her hair, and it took a minimum of two hours for her to prep to leave the house, even for a night out at the Moose.

I'd never begrudge anyone for doing what made them feel good about themselves, but in Crystal's case, the product was a woman who was so focused on how things looked that she never bothered to dig any deeper.

Which was probably why I didn't miss her nearly as much as I thought I would. I was hurt mostly. Embarrassed and humiliated. Confused and reeling from the rejection.

But I rarely felt genuine sadness over losing her. My life barely changed when she left. Like she had been a pretty accessory and not a partner.

Hazel could not be more different.

She had the kind of beauty that snuck up on a man and knocked him out cold. The longer we lived together, the more I appreciated it.

Her big chocolate brown eyes, her rosy pink lips. The round hips she tried to hide. Some days, looking at her felt like a punch in the gut.

She was so much more than cute.

She was fierce and smart and beautiful. And she was mine. For now.

"What crawled up his ass?"

I ran my hands through my hair. "I don't know. Paz has never been warm and fuzzy, but he's become a downright miserable asshole over the past year."

She considered this. "I think he's jealous."

"Of me? The family fuck-up?"

"First of all, you are not the family fuck-up. Stop telling yourself that."

"It's been this way forever. I'm the runt of the litter. Smaller and dumber. My siblings all got degrees; I dropped out after one semester. They all have clear career ambitions. I don't."

"Enough," she said, the heat back in her voice. "You are talented and driven and stupidly good-looking." She paused, and a blush creeped into her cheeks.

I let her words sink in. She didn't think I was a disaster. She liked what she saw.

"And. More importantly. You are kind and genuine and honest. Of course Paz is jealous, because you get up every single day trying to be a better human. And he's stuck in his own anger and misery."

I looked at her incredulously. Not just because of the way she described me. "I sincerely doubt Paz has been jealous of me for even one minute of his life. I'm the family disappointment. I'm not a leader like Henri. I couldn't handle the responsibility of keeping the community employed and prosperous. And I'm not Paz, he's the MBA financial genius. He's got lofty goals that are too big for Lovewell." I ran my hands through my hair, frustrated and maybe a little embarrassed. She couldn't understand the dynamics, but this was just how things were in our family.

"And I'm certainly not Adele."

"Definitely not." She cracked a smile. "She is much tougher."

I laughed. "They're all vital and useful and skilled. And I'm just Remy. I do what I'm told and go where I'm told and try not to fuck it up in the process."

"But do you even like it?"

Anymore, I didn't know. Maybe I never had. Our family was the business, and the business was our family. There was no distinction. It was my destiny, and I had never even considered doing anything else. "Not really," I admitted, dropping my chin to study the floor between us. Something about Hazel tore through my defenses and made me honest. "Cutting down trees is great. The world needs lumber. But it doesn't matter what I like. It's too late to change things now."

"Too late?" She scoffed. "You're not even thirty yet. Get over yourself."

I clutched my heart. "Wow, you don't pull punches."

She pushed her glasses up. "You know I don't have time for that. You have the rest of your life ahead of you. Do what makes you happy. Find fulfillment and passion and *live.*"

"Since Dad died, it's been all hands on deck."

"I hear that, and I think it's incredible that your family has rallied. But it's been almost two years. And at some point, it won't be that way anymore. When that time comes, you could pursue something new."

Her logic and reasoning were even more confusing than Paz's insults. "What else am I going to do? The only life I've ever known is out there in those woods." I nodded toward the tree line in the distance.

"You don't really believe that, do you?" She put a gentle

hand on my forearm, the touch sending a comforting warmth radiating through me. "You've done so much more. You have a huge opportunity in front of you. An opportunity to not only do something you love, but to be a role model for kids who are just like you were. Who'd rather climb trees than sit and read a book, kids who struggle to find themselves. Ever think about that?"

I shook my head. That warmth turned to dread. I'd never had an impact on the people around me, and I wouldn't know where to start.

"And what would it mean to Lovewell? If you went pro and competed nationally—maybe even internationally—that would only bring good things to this region. Not to mention lots of great exposure for Gagnon Lumber."

She tugged me toward the couch and pushed me onto the cushion. Then, dropping next to me, she squeezed my hand. "I believe in you. And it's time you started to believe in yourself."

Taking in her beautiful face, I nodded. She was right. She was always right. Life had given me an opportunity, and it was up to me to make something of it.

For a long moment, we soaked in the silence, sitting hand in hand. I felt calmer already.

She had my back, something I don't think I'd ever experienced before. And I'd have hers.

"We're a team," I whispered.

She smiled up at me. "Two underdogs. In it together."

Chapter 13
Remy

"I have something special for you."

At the sound of my mom's voice, I looked up from the railing I was repairing on her deck. I had become the de facto handyman in the family, mostly by necessity.

Paz had no interest in fixing stuff around the house, and Henri had no time. Adele would probably bring in a bull-dozer, rip the deck off the house, and reengineer a new one using suspension cables and scrap metal.

So here I was, the baby, doing odd jobs to keep things running at my parents' house.

I'd take it. After months of being stuck in an office, it felt good to be outside. To be productive.

As usual, my mom had insisted on making breakfast for me, and the scent of her world-famous banana bread floated on the air as she moved closer. She was likely baking several loaves so I could take some home, making up for lost time. Lately, we'd been doing that. I'd spent more time with my mom since Crystal left than I had in years. The two women had never really gotten along, although my mom had always been cordial. And my ex-fiancée had hated visiting, especially after Dad died. She claimed my family home was a "bummer."

So I'd stayed away. I had all but abandoned my mom when she was grieving. So I was trying to make up for it now.

Since taking a job at the elementary school as a receptionist, she was more alive and engaged than she'd been since we lost my dad. In addition to the job, she had gained two grandchildren this year, Tucker and Goldie, who she loved to spoil rotten.

And who wouldn't? It was impossible not to fall in love with those kids. I was thrilled for my oldest brother. But a part of me, a tiny part that lived deep in the sad corner of my brain, hurt each time I saw her interacting with them. I always thought I'd give my mom grandkids. But these days, that didn't feel like a possibility.

Because who would want to have kids with someone as reckless and irresponsible as me?

I shook off that thought and stood straighter. I had to look ahead, not behind, and in my current cranky state, I was more prone to wallowing. Hazel had bartended past midnight last night, and as always, I picked her up and drove her home. Since I'd agreed to be here early to work on the deck, I hadn't gotten much sleep. Not that I ever did.

Though I would have enjoyed hanging out with Hazel while she worked, I wandered aimlessly at home while I waited for her shift to end instead. I was avoiding the bar right now, keeping myself focused on training. *Fewer beers, more pushups* was my current mantra. And it was working.

My fitness and focus were both improving, and I had Hazel to thank.

She was loyal and fierce, and my trust in her grew more every day. The way she had lashed out at Paz still amazed me. And that day, I vowed to be the man she thought I could be. Because if someone like Hazel believed in me, then there was still hope.

Mom sat at the outdoor table and waved me over. "Take a seat. I made a fresh pot of that fancy coffee Pascal brings by."

I perked up. Though I was still annoyed with him, my brother had fine tastes, and it extended to fancy Guatemalan coffee that he imported by the case.

"As I said," my mom murmured, her eyes teary, once I'd settled in the seat beside her, "I want you to have this."

I took the small box she held out to me, dread settling in my stomach.

"Open it."

"Mom," I started, stroking the soft navy-blue velvet. "I'm not sure."

She pinned me with one of her looks. That *I mean business* mom stare that had me making my bed or taking off my shoes in seconds when I was a kid.

"Okay." I cracked the lid and peered inside. Draped across the velvet insert was a thick chain and a pendant. "Is this...?" I asked, fingering it, feeling its weight.

"A compass," she replied. "Your great grandpa Gagnon gave it to your great-grandmother on their wedding day. It's been in the family since. Your dad gave it to me when we got married."

"I don't remember you wearing it."

"It's big and heavy and old-fashioned. But I had a feeling Hazel might like it."

"Mom," I whispered, snapping the lid shut and holding the box out to her. "I can't."

"Hush. You can. Dad and I always planned to pass it down to one of you when you got engaged."

"But I proposed to Crystal almost two years ago."

She picked a nonexistent piece of lint off her cardigan and hummed. "It didn't feel right. I didn't want a precious heirloom around the neck of that stuck-up brat. She probably would have pawned it for eyelash extensions."

"Mom!" Damn. Loraine Gagnon was a kind woman who was active in the church and spent her free time knitting and tending to her roses. She didn't talk a lot of shit, but when she did, it was deadly.

She shrugged. "I've lived through some things. If I can't be honest with my baby boy, what's the point? For you, I tried. But she's just so rude and entitled. And her parents? They're from away. Never got how things worked here."

I had always wanted a partner, a person to depend on. My parents made it look easy. Loving each other through the hard times. Dad wasn't the world's most affectionate guy, but anyone with eyes could see how he looked at my mom. And she adored him right back.

When busybodies remarked about how many of us there were, my mom would waggle her eyebrows and say, "I really like my husband." It made us all gag, but it was guaranteed to shut down the people who stuck their noses where they didn't belong.

For a long time, I thought that was what I had with Crystal. And that if I gave her an expensive ring and threw her the wedding of her dreams, we'd settle into the kind of love my parents had. One filled with support and understanding and inside jokes.

But now I realized that she'd never wanted that with me. She was holding out for something better. Passing her time with me until she could access her trust fund.

I was a plaything. Nothing more.

Foolishly, I'd wanted to win the untouchable girl. Because that would give me validation. I strived for that bullshit rather than searching for someone I could connect with, someone I could have a real, loving, adult relationship with. And that was on me.

How ridiculous to base my value on the status of my significant other. To think that if someone like her wanted me, then I must be worthy.

This conversation was quickly going off the rails. I didn't want to even think about Crystal anymore, let alone have a conversation in which she came up. "Mom. I don't think—"

She patted my hand. "I mean it. Hazel is a lovely girl. Smart, hardworking. She deserves a happily ever after. Though I wish you hadn't kept your relationship with her quiet. That you'd let us throw you a big wedding. That girl deserves the world and more."

The guilt was burning a hole inside me. For the first time in so long, my mom looked happy, hopeful. She loved Hazel, everyone in town did, and she wanted the best for her.

And I hated knowing that I was nowhere near what my wife deserved.

"It's okay, you know. I'm sure your siblings are all up in arms over this. But when you know, you know. Your dad and

I had a whirlwind courtship. And we had thirty-six years together."

I squeezed her hand as a fat tear crested her lower lashes.

"Take it," she said, pushing the box at me. "It's not traditional, but I think it's perfect for you two."

I pulled the compass from its box and turned it over, squinting at the inscription on the back. "*Mon amour, nous naviguerons cette vie ensemble.*"

I read it slowly, the French my mom had insisted we all learn practically nonexistent anymore.

Mom raised a brow. She was always on us about honoring our heritage. "It roughly translates to 'my love, we will navigate this life together.'"

My breath hitched and my eyes strung at the realization that my mom wanted to give me something so precious. Something she had shared with my dad. The guilt once again gutted me.

Because this marriage wasn't even real. And it would be over before she knew it, devastating her and the rest of this town.

And inevitably, I'd be to blame. The fuck-up once again. But I'd happily shoulder that blame to protect Hazel.

"Make her happy, okay? That girl—Dylan too—was blessed with so little in this life. Give her everything. And I'm not talking about money. Give her your whole heart, all your love and attention. Listen to her and see her. Let her grow and follow her dreams."

My throat was tight, and my heart pounded in my ears, almost drowning out her words. "I promise, Mom."

And as the words left my mouth, I knew they weren't a lie. I would do just that for as long as she would let me.

Chapter 14
Remy

Since I'd moved into the cabin, I'd spent every day dreading going home to the quiet emptiness. Most nights, I went to Dylan's or to the Moose to avoid being alone with my thoughts.

But tonight, I couldn't get home fast enough. I had spent the day making spreadsheets for Paz that would allow us to track deliveries for the past few years by weight so he could create models for fuel costs.

My head had been spinning all day. Those damn tiny Excel spreadsheet boxes would haunt my nightmares, I was sure. There was nothing I hated more than tapping away on a keyboard all day in my windowless office. Paz barely spoke to me, and after our showdown last weekend, I didn't want to even look at him, so when the instructions hit my inbox, I hopped to it, knowing that if I didn't, he'd be in my office glowering at me again.

More often than not, I was desperate to get out of there, and that hadn't changed, but for once, I wanted to go home.

To my wife.

Strange didn't even begin to explain it. But it was still light out and the weather was pleasant, and for the first time in a while, I actually felt like working out. Each day, I had been pushing myself harder and harder to get back to the man I used to be. And thankfully, my body was on board today. My muscles craved movement and the strain of pushing them to their limits after a day at my desk. Even more than that, I wanted to check in with Hazel to see how her work was progressing and to ensure she was comfortable in the spare room.

The second I crossed the threshold, I froze. Hazel was in the kitchen wearing a pink frilly apron. The stovetop was crowded with pots and pans, and music was playing, but in my confusion, I didn't recognize the tune.

Should I walk back out and come in again? Was I hallucinating?

Maybe the spreadsheets had broken my mind?

I stepped in, tentatively at first.

"Hazel?"

She whipped around, her face flushed and sweaty, her gray T-shirt splattered with food.

"You okay?" I toed off my boots and hung my keys on the hook by the door.

She nodded. "Just making dinner."

Alarms clanged in my brain at that comment. Hazel did not cook. She could not cook. This was a known fact and had been since she was nine, when she put a package of pop tarts in the wrapper into the toaster at my parents' house and almost started a fire.

I did a quick scan of the room. No fires. Just a mess.

Literally everywhere. The island was littered with bowls and cutting boards and, inexplicably, a waffle iron. There was a massive head of lettuce perched on the edge of the countertop with a knife stuck in it. Just stuck in the head of lettuce, like it was the victim of some kind of grizzly vegetable-cide.

Mess I could handle. When she turned back to check on one of her concoctions on the stove, I discreetly shuffled to the coat closet and confirmed that the fire extinguisher was still there. Henri was obsessed with safety, so there were probably half a dozen more around the house, but it never hurt to check.

"Whatcha making?" I asked, tiptoeing through the kitchen toward my bedroom.

"Tacos. It's Tuesday, and it's our one-week anniversary. Alice gave me a ride to the grocery store since she was headed to town with the kids."

I nodded, biting back a cringe. My eyes burned as I sniffed, despite my better judgment, struggling to identify the scents that filled the cabin. I'd have to thoroughly air this place out. Maybe even hire professional cleaners.

It certainly didn't smell like tacos. More sour, with notes of... was that honey?

I sidled up next to her at the stove. "Can I help?"

She shook her head, bopping around to Taylor Swift. "I'm good. I just need more time."

"Okay. Thought I'd workout for a bit. Like thirty minutes?"

She waved a hand at me, shooing me out of the kitchen. "Sounds good." Then she whirled around and got back to work.

I jogged up the hill to Henri's to warm up, then hit the weights and did some mobility work. When I returned, Hazel had set the table, and, impressively, the kitchen was even messier than when I'd left.

She pushed a lock of hair out of her face and gave me a weak smile from where she stood next to the table. "I hope this isn't weird. But I was home and figured I should make dinner. That's a normal thing to do, right?"

I nodded, filling two glasses with water and dodging the dozens of pans and plates piled in the sink. "Yes. Thank you. We can't survive on pizza alone."

"Here." She pointed at the table, which had several bowls of unidentifiable food on it.

Once I was seated, she passed me a tray of tortillas that looked perfectly normal. One couldn't mess those up, right? So I plated a few.

"What kind of tacos are these?" I asked, eyeing a bowl full of a reddish-brown soup-like substance.

"Just regular beef." She shrugged, dropping a tortilla to her plate.

I stirred the mixture with the spoon she'd stuck in the bowl, and sure enough, tiny bits of ground beef floated to the surface.

"I'm not sure why the meat is so watery. I followed a recipe. I promise."

"It's great." After I'd held the spoon to the edge of the bowl to drain the liquid and scooped the beef onto my tortillas, I reached for the bowl of a brown pasty substance. Beans, maybe? Every item was a different color and texture, but none of it resembled food. Still, it was sweet that she'd tried to cook. One of us certainly had to figure it out, and she was way smarter than I was.

We looked at one another sheepishly before simultaneously biting into our tacos.

My mouth protested and my nostrils burned. My brain went haywire, registering the array of textures and tastes and even temperatures. One bit was piping hot, and the next was ice cold.

"This is really terrible, isn't it?" she asked, dropping the tortilla onto her plate and watching as the filling oozed out.

The earnest look on her face made me want to lie. To make her feel good about herself. It was a strange sensation, worrying so much about someone else's feelings.

"*Well...*" I started.

She pushed her glasses up, narrowing her eyes behind the lenses. "Do not lie to me, Remy Gagnon. You're terrible at it."

"Yeah, it's bad." I gave up and set my taco on my plate too. "I didn't know tacos could be so, so... soupy. And what happened to the beans?" I pointed at the stiff paste. "Were they involved in some kind of industrial accident?"

"Ha ha. Very funny."

"Not to mention there should be a chalk outline around that head of lettuce."

"Oh stop." She threw her napkin at me and cackled.

I gave her a wink. "But I applaud your efforts, wife. Even though it was inedible and probably a human rights violation, you tried."

"I did try."

"And we'll figure out the cooking together. It can't be that hard."

After we cleaned up the mess, we sat side by side at the kitchen island, munching on microwave popcorn.

"Wanna tell me what made you decide to cook tonight?" I asked.

She shrugged. "I need to learn so I can eat better. For my health."

"I get that. What causes the gallbladder inflammation?"

"Genetics and stress, but also diet."

"Ah," I said, pulling the popcorn bowl closer to me. "So we've got to get you off the junk food."

She scanned my face, shoulders hunched. "Food stamps don't buy a lot of vegetables. Growing up, I ate what I could get my hands on."

I blew out a breath. How hadn't I realized that? There were aspects of Dylan and Hazel's childhood that I simply couldn't understand. And there were things, like this, that had Dylan kept from me for years.

"Going home to your warm, comfortable house and a mom who put a hot meal on the table with all four food groups? That is the epitome of privilege, my friend. So watch it."

I held up my hands. "Sorry, I didn't realize. And I'm not judging. Just trying to understand."

"It's okay. So many people think that healthy, nutritious food is abundant and available everywhere. But it's not. Those who live in poverty don't get much choice. That's why we have poorer health outcomes. I've devoted my life to studying this shit. How public policy impacts the health of US citizens. How financial decisions made by jackass politicians impact the lives of real people."

"That's amazing," I breathed out. "You're amazing." And

I meant it.

She pressed her lips together and surveyed me, though she didn't respond.

"I get it," I went on. "But listen, I'm pathetic at cooking too. And I need to eat better for training. We can do it together. Figure it out."

She snorted. "Now you're concerned about training? I'm not sure a serving of broccoli will offset the entire pizza you ate last night."

I poked her in the shoulder, making her squeal. "Do you gotta be so literal all the time?"

She was right, though. I needed to get more serious about my training. And that included diet, hydration, and, most of all, sleep. With a little hard work, I could swing the first two, but the last was a pipe dream.

"I know I'm annoying. But at least that means you won't be tempted to fall in love with me."

I didn't respond. Because I wasn't sure that was true. Her straightforward nature was charming, and her lack of tolerance for my shit was refreshing.

"What's the point of my many degrees and years of education if I can't feed myself properly?"

I shrugged. "You said yourself you didn't have the opportunity or examples growing up, and you've been a little busy being a smarty-pants almost-PhD," I needled. "And second, don't you dare doubt yourself. There is nothing you can't accomplish."

She beamed at me, the expression making my heart clench. She was so damn pretty. "Except make tacos."

"Yes." I put my hands together and begged. "Please do not attempt this again."

Chapter 15
Hazel

"Stop fussing. I'm fine." I groaned.

Remy huffed and crossed his arms. I hated when he did that. It made his biceps bulge in his requisite T-shirt. I swear the man was allergic to long sleeves.

Then again, forearms that muscular needed to breathe.

"You had surgery." He pulled open the closet door and dug out yet another blanket.

"It's June."

"Correction, it's early June. Look out that window—there's still snow in the mountains. You're getting more blankets."

"God. I just got rid of Dylan. I could use a break from the fussing."

He had insisted on driving me home from surgery and lingering all damn day. Reading and rereading the discharge instructions and talking to Remy in hushed tones about my incisions. It was a relief to finally get rid of one hovering guy, but now I had to deal with another.

Remy had all but forced me to take over his bed. It was enormous and covered with a fluffy duvet and a dozen pillows. I had a hunch Alice had done some decorating before she moved out. It was way nicer than anything Henri or Remy would have chosen.

I reclined against the nest of pillows and sighed in relief. My surgery had been simple and straightforward. I was sore and exhausted, but with a prescription for antibiotics and another for pain killers—which I had no intention of actually taking—I was released. Remy had driven me home while I dozed in the car, and then he'd insisted on carrying me inside.

It would be adorable if it wasn't so damn annoying. I wasn't an invalid. That damn evil gallbladder was finally gone, and I could breathe. Recover from surgery and get serious about my research. A few days of taking it easy, and I'd be good as new.

After I gave in and let him drape another blanket over me, he thankfully left me alone for a bit, while I texted Lydia updates and responded to Dylan's endless check-ins.

I was just closing my eyes when the door creaked open. "We have a couple of hours until you next dose of Motrin. Hungry? I've got chicken soup."

Remy was standing in the doorway, holding a wooden tray with a steaming bowl and two slices of really excellent-looking bread.

"Depends." I yawned, then took a deep inhale of the comforting scent wafting around the room. "Did you make it?"

"Of course not." He chuckled. "Came from Bernice. But I heated it up. In a pot and everything."

Impressive. Probably better than I could do.

He set the tray across my lap and stepped back, watching me with his brows raised.

Suddenly starving, I snatched a slice of bread from the small plate. "This is excellent."

"The bakery."

"When did you have time to procure all this good stuff?"

He smiled. "I have my ways."

Of course he did.

"It's amazing," I murmured, dipping one edge of the bread in the soup. I ate in silence, savoring the feeling of being taken care of. I could count on one hand the number of times someone had done something like this for me, and that someone had always been my brother. It was strange, to be doted on by someone else, but not entirely unwelcome. As terrible as I felt, today had been a major turning point for me. I was going to get my health back, and I had Remy to thank.

But before I could thank my husband and medical savior, I had to deal with whatever was going on with him. He was so agitated he was pacing around the room. I appreciated that hospitals freaked him out. That wasn't surprising, given his family history. But we were home, and my recovery wouldn't take long.

"You don't need to pace," I teased. "I'm fine now."

He halted his movement and scrutinized me, working his jaw from side to side. "You are. And you're going to stay that way. I know you like to take care of everything and everyone else before you focus on yourself, but not anymore. I'm here now. And I'm going to take care of you."

I gave him an exaggerated eye roll and dropped my head back against the pillows.

"I'm serious, Hazel. No more junk food. We're going to work on bringing your stress level down, and first thing tomorrow, I'm going out to buy all those fancy vitamins the doctor recommended."

I sat up straight and crossed my arms over my chest. Who did he think he was, telling me what to do? "I already have an overprotective brother. I don't need another."

He pinned me with a glare that shut me up immediately. There was a fire raging in his normally kind eyes. "I am your husband." He growled. "Not your brother."

"Same difference."

He took a step toward the bed and loomed above me. "No, Hazel. Big difference. Huge."

I froze, my jaw slack in surprise. His bossiness was annoying, but his concern was doing things to me. Things— like ramping up my heart rate and sending tingles coursing through me—I couldn't understand in my post-surgical haze.

Biting my lip, I nodded, unable to tear my attention away from him and unsure whether I was enraged, turned on, or nauseated. Maybe a bit of all three?

"I care about you. You're one of my oldest friends. And I took vows. They mean something to me. Even if this marriage has an expiration date, protecting you is my job."

"I can protect myself." Though I meant it to be a proud, feminist declaration, it came out as more of a squeak.

"Agreed. But it doesn't change the fact that you're not alone anymore. You have me now."

"Thank you." I dipped my chin, giving in to the kindness he offered. "For worrying about me. I've never had anyone in my life besides Dylan."

"You have me now. I know I'm not the husband you would have picked, but I'm the one you've got."

His dark eyes softened at that admission. Vulnerability was not something I was familiar with, but in that moment, all I needed was to have him close.

"Do you want to sleep in here?" I asked. "The bed is huge, and we could watch a movie."

I didn't want to admit how terrified I was. How sick and weak and lonely I felt. I was a warrior. My independence was my superpower.

But right now. I was desperate for the comfort of my husband.

"You sure you're okay? I don't want to hurt you," Remy said, reclined against the mountain of fluffy pillows he had erected for us. He had changed into his gray sweats and a T-shirt (thank the Lord) and had commandeered the remote.

After a few episodes of *The Office*, we both brushed our teeth, then tentatively came back to bed. He pulled the blankets up around me, wrapping me tight, before settling in next to me.

He gently draped an arm around me, and I leaned my head on his shoulder, feeling warm and safe and comfortable.

Hours later, as Remy snored softly next to me in the massive bed, his words came back to me.

He was wrong. There were several alternate realities where I would happily marry Remy. Obviously, we could never be anything more than friends and short-term spouses, but he was selling himself way too short.

He was the best kind of person. Kind, generous, and loving. And it made sense, because his family was wonderful too. The Gagnons were doting, caring parents and active members of the community. They'd cared for Dylan and me so often. They'd done so much for us when we were children. Most of which I didn't realize until I was an adult. I couldn't remember a Thanksgiving or Christmas I didn't spend at Loraine's table.

Clothes, sneakers, and backpacks always magically appeared. There were books under their Christmas tree for me every single year.

My hand floated to the chain, as it often did, that held the compass around my neck. Another reminder of just how much I owed this place and this man.

I knew the statistics. How vulnerable Dylan and I had been. What could have happened. Most kids in foster care don't even graduate from high school, never mind make it to graduate school.

Shifting on the mattress, I inspected Remy. His dark hair falling across his forehead, his high cheekbones framed by his trimmed beard. He was beautiful. These were precisely the kind of thoughts I had to guard against. We could not let things get messy.

My feelings for Remy were tied up with my feelings for Lovewell. The familiarity and comfort of home.

The rightness of it all.

But I couldn't confuse my teenaged lust or my adult longing for home for true feelings.

The last thing I needed was to fall in love with my husband.

Chapter 16
Hazel

"I need to do this," I pleaded. "It's been two days. I feel disgusting."

Remy squinted at me and cocked his head. "Are you sure you're up for it?" He had been hovering over me since I was discharged. And I appreciated it. But at some point, I had to live my life.

"I've been up and moving. I promise, I can do it."

"Okay, but we've got to wrap up your incision. Will you let me help?"

While I waited for Remy to get a roll of plastic wrap from the kitchen, I picked out clean clothes and set them on the counter next to the sink. The bathroom was spacious, luxurious even, with a large tiled shower outfitted with a rain shower head.

Plastic wrap in hand, he stood near the door, staring at his feet while I undressed. I peeled off my T-shirt and shimmied out of my sweatpants, leaving me in a pair of panties and a worn sports bra.

Finally looking up, Remy took a step forward, his eyes laser focused on my face, his movements rigid. My hands shook slightly as I turned my back to him and lifted the bra over my head.

"Can you wrap it around my stomach?" I asked over my shoulder.

"Um. Sure." He stretched out the plastic and carefully lined it up under my rib cage, where the first of three incisions peppered my right side. I kept my hands covering my breasts as he slowly moved around me, wrapping the plastic around my torso several times before cutting the end and smoothing it down with his hands.

"There," he rasped, his focus on the floor again, "that should do it."

"Thanks," I said. "I can take it from here."

He nodded and turned. "Call if you need me."

I kept my back to him until I heard the door close and then let out a long sigh. My muscles ached from the way I'd kept every one of them locked when he was so close. Those hands. Big and strong, yet so tender and gentle.

I took pride in being a practical person. Never romantic or flighty. I wasn't the kind of girl who got swept up and spun out wild romantic fantasies. I'd had many relationships over the years, short and long, and never once had my brain danced around in a Disney style happily ever after montage.

But tonight, I was weak from surgery, and I was drunk on Remy. His kindness, his touch, his raw strength.

As I stepped into the warm water, scene after scene filled my head. A lifetime of romantic moments. The kind of sappy shit I would normally laugh at.

Clearly, I was delirious. Motrin just wasn't cutting it,

and I would not take narcotics on principle, so getting clean was my best solution.

As I stood under the spray, I was hit by a wave of pain, and soon nausea and dizziness overtook me.

I lowered myself to the tile floor, shaking as my body fought my mind. A shower, clean hair, and comfy clothes were all I wanted. Just to feel human again. But my body wasn't there yet. I was too tired, too sore.

And so I wept. Crying out my frustration and fear.

I'd lost track of time, but the water was still hot when I heard a knock on the door.

"Hazel? You okay?"

I said nothing, afraid I would sob if I opened my mouth. I curled up as the water pounded at my back.

"Hazel, I'm worried. Can I come in?"

"Yes," I finally croaked.

Keeping his eyes averted like the gentleman he was, Remy shuffled to the shower door. "Do you need help?"

"Yes," I sobbed. "Everything hurts, and all I want is to wash my hair." I could barely get the words out, my usual composure crumbling, washing down the drain along with my tears.

"Okay."

When he didn't continue, I picked my head up off my knees. Remy was taking off his T-shirt, then he unbuttoned his jeans. Through the steamy glass, I could make out the contours of his tan, muscular chest.

The door opened, and he stepped inside, thankfully still wearing a pair of black boxer briefs. "Let me help you," he said softly, carefully gripping me under my arms and pulling me to my feet.

I was too weak, too embarrassed to resist.

He swiped my shampoo from the ledge. "Tilt your head back," he said, pulling me gently away from the showerhead. "And tell me if I hurt you."

Gently, he massaged my scalp. I put one hand out to steady myself against the tile wall as the scent wafted around us and his hands moved down the crown of my head.

"What is this scent?" he asked, working those strong fingertips around the base of my skull.

"Rosemary." I murmured, closing my eyes as the suds slipped down my neck and shoulders.

"I like it. It's not girlie, but it's very you."

"My grandmother grew rosemary in a little pot on the kitchen windowsill of our trailer when I was a kid. I've always loved the way it smells. Earthy and sharp and like home."

He guided me under the spray, massaging the suds out as the water ran clean. I kept my eyes closed as he applied conditioner to the ends of my hair, letting the strands slip through his fingers. I couldn't look. The sight of water droplets dripping down Remy's muscled chest would probably cause me to lose consciousness. And the last thing I needed was a concussion.

He rinsed the conditioner from my hair, then reached around me to turn the water off. And that's when I felt it.

Solid steel brushing against my ass.

"Sorry," he choked out.

I covered my face with my hands. Was he hard? Because of me?

Thank God he'd kept his boxers on, or I definitely would have fainted. I studied the ornate pattern of the tile to avoid turning around and getting a look at the goods. This was not how I had imagined getting acquainted with Remy's penis. But now that it was out there, I could barely contain my curiosity.

By the time he led me out of the shower and wrapped me in a fuzzy robe, my nausea had dissipated. Such was the power of Remy's cock.

"Give me one minute," he said, settling me on the lid of the toilet in my robe.

He stepped out of the room, and when he came back a few minutes later, he was wearing gym shorts and holding another towel. Between the thick robe and all the steam, I was beginning to overheat, and my heart was racing. Okay, maybe it was my doting husband shirtless. That could have been a contributing factor.

I needed to get out of this bathroom and away from his hotness before I said or did something I would regret. But I stood too quickly and my knees buckled beneath me. Before I could fall, two strong arms caught me and held me up.

"Careful," he said, cradling me against his chest.

He carried me out of the steamy bathroom and set me on the couch before leaving the room quickly. When he returned, he had a glass of water, a sleeve of soda crackers, and a comb.

"Drink some water and eat something."

I took a sip of water and followed his movements as he rounded the couch. He was only out of sight for a moment before he ran my comb through my hair carefully. Section by section, he worked it through my long strands. Aside from my infrequent hair appointments over the last several years, I couldn't remember anyone ever combing my hair. Even as a kid, I did it myself.

"You can depend on me," he said softly, like he was reading my mind. He tugged gently on a tangle. "I'm not afraid of the scary stuff. I'll never hurt you, and I'll always be here when you need me. We've been friends since we were kids, and that will never change."

A tear rolled slowly down my cheek. He had no idea how much his words meant to me. I wasn't in any position to tell him, especially because my feelings were so jumbled right now, but I tilted my head back and gave him a teary smile as he continued to work.

I straightened again and closed my eyes, relishing the feeling of being pampered.

My entire life, I had felt so alone. Dylan, of course, had always gone above and beyond to protect and support me. But since leaving Lovewell at eighteen, I had been on my own. It was a point of pride, really. But at this moment, I liked being taken care of.

Remy had climbed into the shower and helped me. He could have rushed through the process and tucked me back into bed quickly, but he'd been patient, taking his time with me. Not only had he married me so I could be healthy, but he took his duty as caretaker far more seriously than anyone I knew.

"Do you want a ponytail?" he asked. "I can sort of do one."

I nodded, taking an elastic off my wrist and holding it above my head.

Instead of the suffocation I expected to accompany being cared for, a strange peace settled over me.

Remy was slowly scaling the walls I'd spent my life building. Thick concrete and rebar, forged from years of hardship and disappointment.

Normally, I would push back, launch some kind of emotional grenade to keep him away. It was what I always did when someone got too close.

But not this time. Not with Remy. And not just because I was exhausted and vulnerable. I wanted to let him in. Because, deep down, he was the only one I had ever wanted.

Chapter 17
Hazel

"Can I come out now?" I asked when Remy came in with a steaming mug of tea. He had insisted I stay in bed all day after last night's shower incident and had been waiting on me hand and foot. Dylan had come by with flowers and binged *Parks and Recreation* with me for a few hours. The laughs and his company had made for a fairly pleasant afternoon, but I was itching to see what was going on outside these four walls.

Dylan had distracted me with snacks and funny stories about his students, but I got the distinct sense that he and Remy were up to something. Remy set the mug on the nightstand and straightened. "For a few minutes if you want. But you need to rest up."

I swung my legs over the side of the mattress, wishing I was wearing something cute instead of an old T-shirt and faded track shorts. But hey, I'd just had an organ removed. I'd work on my appearance later.

He'd been cagey all day, ordering me to rest and making an unholy amount of noise on the other side of the closed bedroom door. He claimed he and Henri were working on a small home improvement project, but nail gun and other various power tool sounds belied that sentiment. My curiosity was piqued.

Though this project *had* kept him busy and out of sight, which thankfully meant we had not discussed what happened the previous night.

When we'd slept in the same bed and he'd held me close while I listened to his heartbeat and felt like everything was going to be okay.

This morning, as I floated back to consciousness, I'd assumed it had been a post-surgical dream. But no. He was there, with rumpled hair, squinting at the sunlight filling the room.

It hadn't been sexual at all. He'd worn kid gloves with me since my surgery. But the act had been so intimate. Especially because I was at my absolute worst.

But it also felt right. Having him close by after such an intense and scary day soothed every nerve. His presence comforted me and blanketed me in safety. Not that I'd ever admit that out loud.

We lived together and occupied this small cabin so seamlessly it felt as though we'd been doing it for far longer than six weeks. So much had changed since the day we'd said our vows in Bangor.

He helped me to my feet, ducking low and studying me, like he was making sure I felt okay. "I did something. It's sort of a surprise. For you."

I raised a brow, but he ignored the expression, instead turning and guiding me toward my room. At the closed door, he stopped and gently covered my eyes with his one hand.

"Get ready," he whispered into my ear, sending shivers down my spine. The door creaked open, and I could hear the flick of the light switch. Then a soft *surprise* as he pulled his hand away from my face.

"Oh my God." I gasped.

I took a careful step forward, trying to understand what I was seeing. My tiny room slash office, which was stuffed to the gills with paperwork and boxes of books and research, had been transformed.

The entire back wall was covered with bookcases. Gorgeous, gleaming solid wood.

I ran my fingers along the shelves, taking in each knot. "I can't believe it. You made these? For me?"

His smile split his face in half. It wasn't his signature easygoing Remy smile, the one he pasted on when he was expected to play the role of laid-back joker. No, this was his real, secret smile. The one he rarely showed the world. "Yup. I had some help. It was Henri's idea to trim everything with crown molding to make it fancy, but it looks good, don't you think?"

"That's an understatement. This is unbelievable, Rem. I've always wanted floor-to-ceiling bookcases like this."

"I figured. You cart massive boxes of books with you everywhere you go. They need a place to live. And this is your home. If you're going to live here and write a kick-ass dissertation in this room, then you need the proper setup."

He shuffled his feet and studied the floor below him,

looking like a proud but bashful little boy. "If you don't like them, I'll rip 'em out tomorrow."

"No!" I protested a little too loudly. "I love them. No one has ever done anything like this for me. Remy, I'm serious. You've done so much. I truly can't thank you enough." Tears pooled in my eyes. I hated this feeling. Of being in debt, of being needy. It wasn't who I was. Though it was obvious how happy this reveal made him, and that knowledge eased my discomfort. Remy didn't have a clue what a huge gesture this was. To him, it was a practicality, but to me, it was so much more.

"I just wanted to give you something you would love and use. And you just had surgery, so I wanted to do something special."

"How did you manage all this in one day?" I turned in a slow circle, mentally cataloging where everything would go and internally squealing. My own little library. Literally my childhood dream come true.

"I measured and drew up the plans weeks ago. Then Henri and I have been building them in the shop at work. We loaded up the pieces this morning and installed them. Did the trim work and everything."

Hence all the noise.

"This is too much." I sniffed, fighting back tears.

He waved me off. "Nah. We're a team. Husband and wife. For a little while, at least. And what my wife wants, my wife gets."

Then he bit his lip, as if he could read my mind about what his wife wanted. I tried to fight the blush I could already feel creeping up my cheeks, because what I really wanted right now was to throw my arms around my husband's neck and kiss the shit out of him.

And then get naked and do lots of filthy things with him. I had spent my teenage years dreaming about Remy and, being the excellent observer that I was, I had drawn a few conclusions.

First, he was excellent with his hands. Second, he was attentive and eager—both excellent qualities in a lover—and third, he had excellent stamina, you know, from all the wood chopping and tree climbing. This very scientific analysis had led me to the conclusion that he would be unbelievable in bed, and probably make me scream so loud it would wake up Clive, along with all his forest friends.

It took a long minute after I'd relived my brief fantasy about making out with the world's kindest and most thoughtful husband to realize that we were standing awkwardly and silently in the middle of my room.

He gave me a lopsided smile. "You want to spend all night arranging your books, huh?"

I laughed. Shit, he knew me well.

"I definitely do."

"Okay. But no heavy lifting. Tell me where you want them, and I'll set them up."

I clapped, almost giddy with the prospect of finally unpacking my books.

Remy unpacked the boxes, insisting I sit in the desk chair he'd brought home from the office a few weeks ago and give orders. I tried to follow directions and take it easy, I swear, but I ended up on the floor, going through each one before he shelved it. My books were my most treasured possessions.

We had so little growing up, so what I did possess had always been special. I'd toted them from shitty dorms to shitty apartments over the last ten years, and I would never, ever part with them.

"Where did you get all these?" he asked, carefully arranging the spines of my *Lord of the Rings* trilogy.

"Remember when the library would have summer book sales?"

He nodded.

"Every year, I'd save every penny I could get my hands on and then go wild, picking up my favorites for twenty-five cents apiece."

"Some came from your parents at Christmas. And some of these," I held up a collection of Emily Dickinson poetry, "I found used in bookshops all over the place. Every time I visit a new city, I find a used bookstore to see what treasures I can unearth." I flipped through the pages of the book, smiling at the inscription on the inside cover. "And I really love it when someone has left notes or an inscription inside. It makes me feel like I'm stepping into another life."

He took the book from my hand and placed it on the shelf we had designated for poetry. "You know, my wife, you're kind of adorable."

I studied a biography of Eleanor Roosevelt to avoid eye contact. Because comments like that made it feel impossible to stay platonically married to this guy. He was taking care of me after surgery, had built a bookshelf for me with his bare hands, and now he was calling me adorable. Thank God I'd just had surgery, or I'd be throwing my panties at him.

Before I could respond with something witty, a book I

hadn't read in years caught my eye. "Hand that to me," I said, carefully taking the book from him.

The green canvas cover was frayed, and the spine was broken, but I held it close. "My grandmother gave me this. It was right before she died, so maybe third grade? We read it together, and I've read it hundreds of times since. I have the whole series here, too, but this one is one of my most special possessions."

I held it to my chest, taking a moment to remember Grandma May, who had done right by us when my mother could not. We lost her too early, but she had given me so much.

Remy settled on the floor next to me, studying the cover when I set it in my lap. "I've never read *Anne of Green Gables*," he said. "But Adele loved the series."

"Anne was one of my childhood heroes. She's an orphan, kind of like me, and smart and curious and small. It's always been my dream to go to Prince Edward Island, where her story takes place."

"You should go. It's not all that far."

"I've never been to Canada."

He laughed. "You haven't? Canada's only a couple hundred miles that way." He pointed out the window. "You could drive there. I've crossed the border more times than I can count hauling logs. It's not a big deal." Once again, Remy made things sound so easy, so accessible.

But I had things to do, research to finish.

"How about this?" he said, brushing his fingers down the cover of the book I was still holding tight to. "When you finish your dissertation and officially become a doctor, I'll take you there. I'll even read the book first. We can take a celebratory road trip together."

I grinned. A road trip to Avonlea with my brother's dreamy best friend. Teenage Hazel had officially died and gone to heaven.

"That sounds nice," I said softly, unable to articulate all the gratitude I was feeling toward him.

Chapter 18
Remy

"I love her for you," Alice whispered in my ear while giving me a warm embrace. "This is a good thing."

I smiled weakly and handed her the daisies I'd picked up for her.

My brother didn't socialize unless brute force was applied, so this dinner was no doubt Alice's doing. But Hazel had been stuck in the house recovering, so the break would be good for her.

Henri was the one sibling whose attitude toward me I could predict. He was steady and focused and had picked me up when I was at my worst.

"Uncle Remy, Uncle Remy!" Goldie came running down the hall, dragging a massive stuffed sloth behind her, and jumped into my arms. "How could you get married without me as your flower girl?" she pouted.

"Sorry, GoldBug." I spun in a circle, knowing just how to improve her mood. "Trust me, Grandma is super mad about it too."

She pushed my hair out of my eyes and gave me a big smacking kiss on the forehead. "Did you bring me anything?"

I set her on her feet and ruffled her hair. "Ask Aunt Hazel."

She turned to Hazel, who was standing beside me, and gave her a lopsided grin.

"I may have brought these," Hazel said, holding out a box of fresh molasses cookies from the bakery.

Goldie ripped it out of her hands and took off running through the house to find her brother.

"How are you feeling?" Henri asked, taking Hazel's coat.

"Better. This guy"—she grabbed my arm and squeezed—"has barely let me get out of bed, even though my doctor told me I'd feel like my old self after a day or two. But I feel great, really. Excited to be on the mend and getting back to work."

"Hazel," Alice murmured, giving my wife a gentle hug, "come keep me company while I put the finishing touches on dinner."

When the women had disappeared, Henri raised an eyebrow and gave me a nod. For such a small gesture, it had significant meaning. I was taking care of my person, just like he took care of his people. And that acknowledgment made me feel better than any words from him ever could.

"Dig in," Alice said once we were seated around the table. She picked up Goldie's plate and scooped a spoonful of carrots onto it. "So, Hazel, tell us about your work."

"It's boring," she protested with a shrug, sipping her water.

"Not at all. We're all so impressed, right kids?" Alice

looked at them with that mom look she'd been perfecting over the last several months. When they grumbled in half-hearted agreement, she gushed, "Aunt Hazel is going to be a doctor."

"Not a medical doctor," my wife corrected. "I wanted to be one for a long time, but a few semesters of the pre-med program at Brown convinced me that I could not manage the physician life. Treating individual people is a very noble calling. But I found myself really interested in the big picture problems. Studying systemic problems causing disease and sickness and suffering and searching for solutions."

"So you want to help a lot of people; not just one person at a time?" Tucker asked. The kid was sharp as a tack.

She smiled at him. "Exactly. Helping people who are hurt or sick is wonderful, but I'd rather do a quantitative analysis of drinking water quality and contamination and public infrastructure to support efforts to combat water cont-amination, you know?" She dipped her chin, turning pink, clearly embarrassed that she had nerded out at the dinner table.

"That's fantastic," Henri said. "Is that what you're researching here?"

She pushed up her glasses, her face lighting up in a way I didn't think I could ever get tired of. The expression she donned when she talked about her research made me wonder what it would feel like to spend my days devoted to something I truly loved. A greater purpose rather than just getting by.

"No. My initial proposal was focused exclusively on a few rural Maine counties. I planned to do an analysis of public health programs, sociological factors, and health data. But I've hit a few roadblocks with the state government. I've been submitting public records requests every day, but the delays in response have been a challenge."

"Oh no," Alice said, pursing her lips in a frown. "I'm so sorry."

"It's okay. If anything, it's giving me an opportunity to learn more from the local level. Right now, I'm interested in how communities can combat opioid abuse and trafficking. What kinds of outreach, programs, and education will actually make a difference in people's lives."

A hush settled over the table. Goldie was happily pushing mashed potatoes around her plate, but Tucker was slumped in his chair. I didn't know the details, but I knew their mom was an addict, and I knew Tucker had seen more than a child his age should. And like Dylan, he'd spent his short life protecting his sister.

"Hazel is really smart," I said softly, "and she's gonna help a lot of people."

"Some people don't want to be helped," Tucker muttered, his chin to his chest and his eyes locked on his uneaten food.

We continued to eat in silence, the adults around the table wearing frowns and probably feeling just as heartbroken as I was in that moment.

But Hazel, being the incredible, thoughtful woman she was, cleared her throat and broke the tension. "Since we're family, I should probably tell you more about why I'm back in Lovewell. I grew up here, like you two, and like Henri and your Uncle Remy. My mom was an addict. She died several years ago, but I hadn't seen her since I was twelve or thirteen. Addiction took her away from my brother and me, and ultimately, it took her life."

Tucker's haunted eyes shot up and locked on Hazel.

"A long time ago, I promised myself that not only would I avoid the same fate, but I would help. I would use the gifts that I have to make at least a small impact on this problem." Her eyes welled with tears, but she didn't look away from my nephew.

I took her hand and pulled it into my lap. I knew all of this. Hell, I'd had a front-row seat for it, but hearing her tell Tucker and Goldie gutted me.

"Can I help too?" Tucker asked.

She gave him a watery smile. "Of course you can."

"I'm good at fixing things, and I know a lot about technology."

Hazel nodded, one side of her mouth kicking up into a half grin. "Then you're just the man I'm looking for. I can't for the life of me sync my printer. And I have so many documents to scan."

He sat a little straighter in his seat. "I can fix that for you."

"If it's okay with your parents, how about you come down to the cabin after school tomorrow? You can help me get everything networked."

Tucker beamed and picked up his fork, going back to the dinner he'd abandoned and jumping into a story about troubleshooting the copy machine in the school's office. From there, his mood lightened exponentially.

After dinner, Alice put the kids to bed, and Henri and I

tackled the dishes. "I just wish we had found something," he said.

I shook my head. "They didn't exactly do much. After all the meetings and negotiation."

Hazel dried a large platter with a kitchen towel. "I don't want to pry, but it's not a mystery how illegal opioids are coming into Maine."

"Nope. From Canada. Usually on rural roads and through the backcountry. Logging roads, like the ones we own, are usually easy for traffickers."

"Exactly. And that's part of what my research is revealing." She turned and propped a hip on the cabinet so she was facing us. "A disconnect between what we know about the problem and what's being done to fix it."

"You sound like our dad," Henri said. "He was always asking these questions, fighting for more supervision and police support. Over the course of the last few decades, he watched how opioids hurt our communities, and he wanted to do something about it."

"He was a good man," she murmured, taking a clean dinner plate from me and wiping it dry.

"He was." Henri cleared his throat. "And that's why we need to do more, to figure this out. To get to the bottom of what happened to him."

"I'm not a cop, but I know my way around research. I'll keep you posted on what I'm learning."

"Actually," Henri said, his voice low and strained. "If it helps, I've got a bunch of documents I'll pull for you. Maps, random musings, notebooks. All our dad's old stuff. Haven't been able to make much sense of it all, but you're welcome to take a look."

Her face lit up. "Really?"

"They're a disorganized mess, but you're welcome to everything."

"I want to help," Hazel insisted. "And I'll do whatever I can."

Chapter 19
Remy

I rubbed my eyes. A five-a.m. run had felt like a good idea this morning. I was hitting my stride with my training, but ramping up training while still maintaining a full-time work schedule was getting tricky.

Paz and Henri were keeping me busy in the office, especially now that I had gotten better at excel spreadsheets thanks to Hazel's coaching. I was feeling useful for once, and I truly was grateful to still have a job after all that had happened. But it was draining me a little more every day.

My mind was consumed by training and competition and strategy. I woke up energized and determined to stick to my plan and push myself a little further. Nationals was something I had dreamed about since I was a boy, but for so long, it was nothing more than that. A dream. I had been competing in timber sports since middle school. But I had never taken anything seriously. In high school, I'd partied too much and trained too little. Even through my twenties, I'd been too consumed by work and keeping Crystal happy to focus the way I should have.

But things were different now. I was different. And I owed so much of that to Hazel.

I guzzled coffee and signaled Bernice for a refill when Dylan slid into the booth. We hadn't seen much of each other recently. Outwardly, I blamed my training schedule, but it had far more to do with wanting to spend all my extra time with Hazel than I would ever admit. And that fact made me feel like a shit friend.

"How is she?" Dylan said, stirring his coffee once Bernice had stepped away from the table. That woman's ears were legendary. And like many of the people in this town, she was fiercely protective of Hazel.

"Working hard," I said and left it at that because I had absolutely no poker face, and if anyone could see through my bullshit, it was my best friend. Could he tell I was developing an unhealthy attraction to my wife?

Guilt coursed through my veins as I looked at my best friend. I had given him my word that I wouldn't cross the line with Hazel.

And technically, I hadn't. But deep down, I knew that was a lie. There had been so many moments of true intimacy between us. And even more moments of lust wrapped in delicious tension.

And, shamefully, I wasn't trying to avoid it either. In fact, I loved walking around shirtless, knowing Hazel couldn't keep her eyes from roving all over my body when I did. And how many times had I rolled over in bed and savored the sight of her creamy thighs or round breasts under those massive T-shirts she always slept in?

So I was hating myself while we chatted about the end of the school year and his plans for the summer.

Dylan had always been the serious one, even back in grade school. He had to be. I could be the class clown and the spoiled baby of the family, but he had been forced to provide for himself and Hazel at a young age.

And unlike so many others in challenging circumstances, he kept himself on the straight and narrow, getting good grades, working hard, and charming everyone he met.

It was no surprise that after putting himself through community college, he transferred to UMaine on a full academic scholarship and graduated with a degree in education.

When he finished, he came straight back to Lovewell and threw himself into teaching, coaching, and mentoring kids. And developing an unhealthy rivalry with Lydia over who would win the annual teacher of the year award. It came so naturally to him, giving back and embracing the community.

As did being an overprotective brother. Unsurprisingly, he had steered the conversation back to Hazel. "I can't believe how quickly she's recovered. She's already back to texting me nonstop about her research."

I laughed. "That's Pip. Never stops. At her follow-up, the doctor was impressed with how well she's doing. And she's up and about more and more."

"She said you've been really great." He hung his head. "Thanks, man. I appreciate it so much. What you've done for her."

"It's nothing." The swell of guilt rose in my stomach like bile. He clearly didn't know we were sleeping in the same bed every night, our bodies a few centimeters closer every morning.

His brow was furrowed and his eyes were stony. "No, it's not. It's huge. You very well may have saved her life."

I paused, meeting his stare. I wasn't sure how to respond. Because I couldn't tell him that I would do it a thousand times over. That Hazel was important to me. That my eyes had been opened, and I was finally seeing her for the gorgeous, fierce, accomplished woman she was. So instead, I kept my mouth shut and answered with a simple nod.

"As much as I was opposed to this 'marriage'"—he used air quotes, the gesture making my stomach clench—"it's been the best thing for her. Getting good health care? It's something she's literally never had. She needed this surgery. I've been worried for months."

"It's the least I could do," I muttered.

"And the way you've taken care of her? Giving her an office and building her bookshelves? And your mom popping in to check on her and bringing meals? We don't deserve you guys."

"Dyl. Yes, you do. You and Hazel are my oldest, closest friends. There is nothing I wouldn't do for either of you. Same for the rest of my family. You're Gagnons too."

Though Dylan wasn't the emotional type, his eyes were glassy. "I owe you, man."

I swallowed a sip of my scalding hot coffee to mask my emotions. It was so unlike him to be so open, but he had devoted his life to taking care of Hazel. I was proud that I could help them both and swore to myself I'd keep my feelings in check. A little snuggling and visually appreciating my smoking hot wife would have to be enough. This couldn't go any further.

With that, my guilt over the fantasies of her I'd been having compounded, so I cleared my throat and changed the subject again, this time really putting effort into steering our conversation away from his sister. We spent the rest of our breakfast chatting about the upcoming competition season, the STEM summer camp he was working to get up and running for budding engineers like Tucker, and looking at possible dates for our annual rafting trip.

Through it all, though, my conscience ate at me. Our friendship was changing, and this new distance I'd put between us—one he wasn't even aware of—was uncomfortable. Like a favorite pair of jeans that just didn't fit after Thanksgiving dinner.

And I wasn't sure I could go back to how things used to be. Not after this time with Hazel.

Dylan was one of the best people I knew. And he had taken care of me. When I had alienated my family, threatened our business, and hit rock bottom, he'd picked me up, dusted me off, and propped me up while I got my shit together.

He had let me sleep on his couch and had listened to every one of my rants about Crystal. He'd been the kind of friend that anyone would be lucky to have.

And how was I thanking him?

By thinking about his sister naked while I jerked off in the shower every morning.

I was a piece of shit.

And Dylan was perceptive enough to know it. If he hadn't figured it all out yet, it was only a matter of time.

Chapter 20
Hazel

"You look nervous. Smile." I resisted the urge to elbow this guy in the gut. Tim was ageless and pushy, and he was dressed like he was going to an art exhibit in Miami instead of a lumberjack competition in Vermont.

"I'm fine." I shifted on the bench seat. I was in the VIP section of the small stadium near Stowe. The entire Gagnon family was squished around us, every one of them amped up and ready to watch Remy compete. This was the regional qualifier, which determined who could go to the National Championship in Wisconsin in August.

Because Remy had won the Maine state championship last year, he was automatically eligible to compete. That was a blessing because while he had done a few local competitions and exhibitions in the last few weeks, he still wasn't at his best, and his frustration was weighing on him.

Today was a big day. He had been uncharacteristically quiet on our drive over last night, so I'd filled the silence by chatting about my research and random town gossip I had picked up from Bernice. And by the time we got to our hotel, it was late. Just like at home, we took turns washing up and then climbed into opposite sides of the king-size bed. At some point, we'd have to have a conversation about this bed sharing situation, because since my first night home after surgery, we'd kept up with it, but I didn't want to burden him while he was working so hard to keep his head on straight.

This place was really something else. I'd been to a few of these growing up, usually makeshift stages set up in high school football fields or parking lots.

But the Northeast Regional Timbersports Championship? Professional lighting, a judging panel, and even fancy bathroom trailers.

It had the energy of a state fair, with food trucks and beer tents and all kinds of kids' games.

It was perfect. The atmosphere was just chaotic enough that I didn't have to talk much, which my inner introvert appreciated, or do anything more than watch what was happening, which satisfied the natural observer in me.

There were dozens of trailers filled with tools and so many teams.

Lots of beards, lots of plaid, and lots of talk about trees.

Remy and I had existed in our own little cocoon for the past couple of months. Between our quickie wedding and my surgery, we hadn't really had to test drive our relationship around anyone beyond our families.

So I was more than nervous about messing this up for Remy. He'd already fulfilled his end of the bargain; I was two weeks post-op and feeling better than I had in years.

Now it was my turn to help him succeed. But I didn't understand this world or its expectations.

So I asked. Because in my experience, people loved to tell others what to do.

Shifting on the bleachers, I faced Tim and tried to muster a smile. "This is my first competition. Is there anything I can do to help Remy?"

Tim turned and gave me a curious once-over. "You know, very few of my athlete's wives have ever asked me that."

I pushed up my glasses and shrugged. "What can I say? I like research and procedure and rules."

"Great." He rubbed his hands together. "Right now, we cheer and hope he places in the top five. That will qualify him for nationals and be a great way to introduce him to a few of the sponsors who are here today.

"After that, you and I will head to the athlete area. I'll introduce you both to a variety of people. Just smile, shake hands, and talk about how hardworking and dedicated your husband is. Easy enough, right?"

It sounded fine. And literally the least I could do for Remy. I gave Tim a smile. I wasn't much for small talk, but if it helped Remy, I'd give it my all.

"He's a good kid and a hell of an athlete. He just needs discipline and focus. But you seem like a good influence. He's training and even posting updates to social media after I bug him enough. Looks like his head is finally back in the game."

Ducking my chin, I did my best to hide the blush blooming across my cheeks. It was a strange thing to get coy about, especially given my feminist leanings, but I secretly loved that this marriage was helping him in a small way.

Because he deserved that. A partner who could build him up and help him reach his goals. And although this was temporary, I took pride in encouraging him.

So I was here, dressed the part and ready to support him in a denim skirt, a cute pair of boots Lydia had loaned me, and a blue flannel shirt that I'd ordered from Racine's website so that my outfit coordinated with what he wore when he competed. Lydia insisted I tie it at the waist, and though I'd scoffed and argued that it was cheesy, I secretly liked it.

The massive chainsaws scared the shit out of me, but the events were all fast paced and exciting. Goldie, Tucker, and I perused the food trucks, and I cheered along with the entire Gagnon family when Remy came in first in the block chop, his best event.

The speed climb was the final event of the day. After the announcer gave a brief overview of what to expect—a ninety-foot climb up a cedar pole, where each contestant would ring a bell before returning to the ground using only spiked shoes and a steel core climbing rope—I buried my head in Alice's shoulder, too terrified to watch.

No matter how many times I reminded myself that he was an expert tree climber and would be wearing safety wires, it never got easier. Watching him practice on the trees at home, which were far shorter, always made my stomach clench and my heart rate race, and not in a good way. And this? It was so much worse.

"It's okay," Alice said, draping an arm around me and patting my back. "He's been doing this since he learned to walk. Plus, he's going to kick Cedric LeBlanc's butt."

The name sounded familiar, but I couldn't place it. He

wasn't from Lovewell, but maybe Remy had mentioned him when talking about tournaments. There were so many guys in Maine who competed that it was hard to keep all the teams and families straight.

Remy was waiting for his safety gear check, standing near a generic-looking, fair-haired lumberjack.

My husband, on the other hand, looked like he had just stepped out of a Racine catalog, even after finishing his fifth event of the day, several of which included using chainsaws.

But something was off.

While the previous set of competitors were being unhooked from their harnesses, at a time when Remy would normally be shouting encouragements—because my husband was that kind of guy; he was the best of the best, but he cheered everyone on as he went—his posture, though normally relaxed, was tense. His broad shoulders were bunched at his ears, and his attention was fixed on his boots.

After his last event, he had been blowing kisses to his mom and taking photos with every kid who approached him, but sometime in the last thirty minutes, his mood had tanked.

Tucker leaned across his mom. "Aunt Hazel, is Uncle Remy okay?"

I studied him, watching his pale, drawn face, my stomach plummeting. Surveying Remy's surroundings in search of what could have such an effect on him, I found the culprit. Crystal. Looking like Malibu Barbie after a bender, she was flicking her hair extensions and cooing at the other guy. He looked like a generic corporate guy. A little out of place at a lumberjack competition, but this was Maine, so I supposed it wasn't all that strange. Heck, Paz, Mr. Brooks Brothers, had supposedly competed on a team with Remy and Henri in some of the smaller events in the past.

Ahh. This had to be the *him*. The one she cheated with. A lawyer or something, from what I'd heard. Remy had predicted that it would be difficult to see them together. And by the looks of his body language, he was right.

She was obnoxious, pawing all over him and taking selfies. She'd probably be posting them to Instagram with grammatically incorrect captions later. I clenched my fists, wishing that I could punch her.

But Crystal didn't matter right now. First, I needed to help my husband. Though at the moment, my logic was inaccessible. Instead, I acted on pure instinct.

I turned to Lydia. "Distract my brother."

She nodded and I stomped to the competition area and hopped over the plastic fence that separated the spectators from the competitors—without landing on my face, I might add.

"Gagnon!" I yelled.

He looked up and scanned the crowd, stopping when we made eye contact. My heart was racing, and I probably looked like a crazy person trying to crash a tree climb, but I didn't care. All I saw was the spark in his eye when he caught sight of me.

I waved him over, and when he was an arm's length from me, I grasped the front of his blue Racine shirt and tugged so he was flush up against my chest.

"Look at me," I said softly. When he complied, I went on. "You are going to kick ass right now. You are stronger and smarter and so much better-looking than that douche canoe over there."

He laughed, a small but genuine smile creeping up his face.

"I mean it. I'm proud of you."

That smile grew, and he closed his eyes for half a second like he was letting the truth sink in. "Thanks."

But it wasn't enough. He needed to forget about all the draining drama standing a few feet away and focus on what was really important.

So I did it.

I took a risk.

Grabbing the collar of his shirt, I pulled him down and kissed him. His body relaxed into me instantly, and he kissed me back, taking it deeper and wrapping one hand around my waist. It was sloppy and rushed, but it did the trick. He pulled away, his eyes wide and his jaw unhinged.

Then he gave me one of his devastating Remy grins. "You been waiting a while to do that, Pip?" he whispered.

"Only since eighth grade," I said, blushing. We could talk about it later. "Now go make your wife proud."

Chapter 21
Remy

I was flying. Finishing in second place and qualifying for the National Championship after seven grueling events had something to do with it. It had been my goal for years, after all. And finally, I was getting there.

But mostly, I was soaring because I had my wife tucked under my arm as I laughed along with my family, all the while stealing glances at her lips.

Because she had kissed me.

And Dylan had congratulated me and given me a one-armed hug before driving back home with Lydia, so he clearly hadn't seen his sister plant one on me, or else I would have received a punch in the face for my troubles.

So it was officially one of the best days of my life. Family and friends all here to celebrate my success and a kiss from the woman who occupied every thought inside my head.

It wasn't a long kiss or a particularly passionate one. But Hazel had put her plump, rosy lips on mine, in public, and my blood was singing in my veins. The world was a beautiful, amazing place.

She had seen me like no one ever had. She'd seen me struggling and she'd pulled me out of it. The depth of our connection was unnerving and terrifying. But I craved more.

The needy part of me wanted to pull her aside and demand she tell me what that kiss was about. And maybe kiss her again, properly this time, just to make sure she got a full demonstration of my skills.

Maybe she had kissed me to get me out of my own head so I could compete. That was the most likely scenario. Hazel had already demonstrated how she could read me better than anyone I'd ever met. She knew what I needed before I did.

And although I never would have believed it, in that moment, all I'd needed was a good luck kiss from my wife.

Placing first in the speed climb certainly helped me qualify. And I'd set a personal record to boot.

My mother was snapping photos of everything, and Henri and Adele were debating about how to improve my chainsaw technique before nationals.

Me? I couldn't stop smiling.

Hazel and I hadn't test driven our relationship in public much. Since her surgery, we had grown closer, comfortable with each other, but we'd spent most of our time together in the cabin, away from the speculation and observation of the people of Lovewell.

We'd made a nightly ritual of climbing into my big bed—both wearing pajamas, of course—and watching an episode of *The Office*. She had suggested we try it since I was currently stuck in office hell, and she had never had a lot of time to watch TV before now.

So after I trained and she finished her work, we would settle into the mountain of pillows left over from when Alice inhabited the cabin and laugh until we cried at the antics of Michael and Dwight and the rest of Dunder Mifflin.

She hadn't yet gone back to her room. Instead, she slept next to me. Even if it was all the way on the other side of the massive mattress. We respected the unofficial boundary drawn down the middle, but it was nice.

Every night, once she was asleep, I'd drift off, content with the knowledge that I was keeping her healthy and happy. I wanted more. What red-blooded man wouldn't with a woman like Hazel? But I was content for now. Somewhere out there, my dad was watching me grow into the man he had always wanted me to be, and I knew he would be proud.

After the awards ceremony, Tim led us up to a private area of the stadium to meet with the event organizers and sponsors and get necessary information for nationals. My brain was already racing. The competition was in six weeks, and I still had so much to do.

But as Tim steered us through the crowd, those thoughts took a back seat. This was our first big public outing as a couple. We should have had a conversation ahead of time. It would have been wise to make a plan. But right now, we were winging it, and so far, it was working.

Winging it, fortunately, involved me putting my hands all over her and her tucking herself under my arm and sticking her hand in the back pocket of my jeans, which, hello, was neither unwelcome nor uncomfortable.

I couldn't stop smiling at her. I didn't know when she'd

had the time to learn, but she knew far more about timber-sports than I expected, asking thoughtful questions to the various bigwigs Tim introduced us to.

"Remy, I want you to meet Josh Hanlon. He's a marketing executive from Racine."

I stood straight and smiled, offering him my hand.

"Great job today," he said. "That springboard chop? Man, you can move."

"Thank you, sir," I replied. The older man had a friendly face and a midwestern accent that immediately set me at ease.

"This is my wife, Hazel," I said, making the introduction.

"Pleasure." He held his hand out to her as well.

"He's a great tree climber," she said proudly once she'd tucked herself back under my arm. "He's got to be. We have an errant moose at home. Clive's harmless, but sometimes you've got to get up a tree to avoid those antlers."

Josh and Tim broke into laughter, and I beamed. Of course she'd be ready with a cute Maine anecdote to make me look good.

"And you know"—she gestured to her flannel shirt, which was tied up around her waist, making her look somehow sexy and adorable at the same time—"I bought this online. I'm loving the new women's cuts you've added."

That was all it took for her to win Josh over. From there, he dove into how seriously they took the integrity of the fitting process, making sure each garment was built to last.

Hiding behind Hazel's shy nerd exterior was a curious and brilliant mind. Put her in a room full of interesting people, and her natural curiosity blossomed.

"You two are a hoot," Josh said, slapping me on the back.

"You're signed up for our wife carrying competition, right? We're excited to debut it at this year's event."

Hazel peeked up at me with her brow all scrunched up and a suspicious look in her eyes.

"Oh. You've got to try it. You two are beyond perfect. It's easy. Remy here will pick you up and carry you through an obstacle course in the woods. It's a lighthearted, silly event. It's our charity event this year. Nationals are a full weekend of competition, so we sprinkle in fun stuff for the fans."

"Sounds challenging," she said, giving me a side-eye.

"And to make it interesting, the winning team will be featured in the fall Racine catalog. You know we only use real working folks as models. We take pride in it. Steelworkers, farmers, even have had a few artists and a scuba diver. So we thought, why not award a contract to the winning couple?"

Hazel pressed her lips together, the wheels in her head turning, I was sure. I'd love to commit, but I couldn't ask that of her. She had done enough. Just being here today was above and beyond the call of duty. I was ready to politely bow out of the conversation with a noncommittal response when I spotted a familiar face only a few feet away.

I sucked in a breath, my body going rigid as I prayed she didn't see me.

Hazel looked up at me and then followed my line of sight to where Crystal was standing with Cedric LeBlanc, looking smug and overdressed for a lumberjack competition in a very short, very tight pink dress.

And then she was approaching and wedging herself into our space, her long blond hair flying in her wake. "Mr. Hanlon, did you say a contract with Racine?"

I took a step back, desperate to put distance between us as she dragged a sheepish-looking Cedric behind her. He had placed fifth overall, just good enough to make the cut, and so I'd have the pleasure of seeing them again at nationals.

"I've always wanted to be a model," she said, tossing her hair again. *Good lord, how had I ever thought that was attractive?* "My fiancé and I would love to participate. He's super strong." She turned and gave Cedric an exaggerated wink that made me want to vomit before holding out her left hand to display a diamond the size of a golf ball on her ring finger.

"Oh, how fun!" Hazel gushed in a theatrical bubbly voice. "We'll definitely be competing. Remy and I are happy to support Racine *and* their charity work." Her eyes were blazing. If I didn't know better, I'd swear she was possessed.

If Crystal had been a smarter woman, she would have gotten the hell away before my wife put a hex on her or some other demon shit, but she was instead batting her lashes at Josh. After a comically long time, Hazel's comment finally soaked in through her trashy extensions, and Crystal's head snapped around at high speed. "It's for married or engaged couples," she said, looking down her nose at Hazel.

But the attitude didn't faze my wife one bit. Nope, she just pulled me closer, her short nails digging into my ribs, and smiled. "Oh gosh, didn't you hear the happy news? Remy and I are married." Her voice had a fake, singsong quality that was petrifying. My wife never failed to astound me.

Crystal narrowed her eyes and arched one painted-on brow. "What are you talking about? Remy married *you?*"

At that, I couldn't help but break out in a huge grin, leaning down to kiss the top of Hazel's head. "Hazel and I tied the knot a couple of months ago. I've loved her since we were kids. It took a lot of work, but I finally wore Dylan down. You know how overprotective he is."

"Great," Josh said, interrupting the showdown between my ex-fiancée and my wife. "We at Racine are so excited about this. And I love a little healthy competition. Chainsaws and axes are great and all, but this will be a fun addition to the weekend."

Hazel beamed at him. "It's a lovely idea. And Team Gagnon will be there, ready to compete."

My heart soared. *Team Gagnon.* I loved the sound of that.

And I really loved touching her. The way she shifted against me, always keeping our bodies connected. The smell of her hair, the sound of her laugh. It was exhilarating.

After we excused ourselves, leaving Crystal and Cedric far behind, she motioned for me to lean down. I dipped closer, growing giddy by the proximity.

"We will destroy them," she whispered in my ear.

***

"I want to say something, but I'm worried it'll upset you," Hazel said, munching on a slice of dried mango as she drove. Since Stowe, Vermont, was a little more than four hours from Lovewell, we were taking turns behind the wheel.

"Go for it," I said, leaning back in my seat. Right then, I didn't think anything could upset me. I was tired, sure, but energized and still in awe that I'd qualified. And now the real work began.

"I need you to make me a promise."

"Okay."

"After... you know." She gripped the steering wheel hard with both hands, her attention fixed on the road ahead. "After we get divorced or whatever. Promise me you'll find someone worthy of you. Please don't let yourself get sucked into a relationship with someone who doesn't value you."

I laughed, though it was hollow, because I didn't want to talk about what came after this. What came after Hazel was gone. And I definitely didn't want to talk about Crystal.

"I mean it," she said, finally peeking over at me. "Don't sell yourself short. You are a beautiful person, inside and out. And she is..."

"Bratty," I offered.

She shrugged. "I was going to say a sociopathic demon with a perverse princess complex, but bratty works too."

I swiped the bag of mango from her lap and grabbed a piece. "You think I'm beautiful? I've never been called that before."

Shaking her head, she rolled her eyes to the ceiling. "Oh please. You saw those execs drooling over you today. You know you're hot."

My breath hitched at her comment, and all I could do was stare straight ahead while I processed her words. Hazel thought I was hot? For weeks, I'd caught her looking at me when she thought I wouldn't notice. And I'd noticed the way her pulse sped up when I was close. But here she was, saying it out loud. I considered pinching myself to make sure I hadn't dozed off in the car and fallen into a post-competition fantasy land.

"You've got that whole country boy charm, plus the chocolate puppy dog eyes, the dimples, the arms..."

"What do you mean?"

"I mean"—she blew out a breath and turned her head, piercing me with a glare so powerful it was obvious even lit only by the light of the moon above us—"you should cut the sleeves off your shirt. You'd probably gain another hundred thousand Insta followers if you did."

I almost choked on my mango. "Mrs. Gagnon." I gasped. "Are you implying that I should be displaying the guns in public?" I held up one arm and flexed.

"Oh, Mr. Gagnon, I certainly am. What kind of timber wife would I be if I didn't want to show off those axe-throwing, log-chopping muscles?"

My smile almost cracked my face in half.

"Don't read too much into this," she said, eyes locked on the road again. "It's just a suggestion." She patted my shoulder. "Now rest up while I drive home. Because tomorrow, we start training."

Chapter 22
Remy

I wanted this. I wanted to be the best at something. No longer the idiot little brother, the bad student, the guy who used his charm instead of his skill to get through life.

Paz's words echoed in my brain. *Half-assed. Shortcuts.* I wasn't that guy anymore. Life had handed me an opportunity, the chance to do something with my talent, and I was going to see it through. I was going to nationals. And I'd give it everything I had.

Because I was good at this.

Chopping and climbing and throwing. They'd all come naturally to me my whole life. For years, I had competed, but never seriously, never pushing myself fully. But I wanted it. The next level.

And it wasn't until Hazel called me out that I realized why I had held back. I was afraid to fail. I was self-sabotaging, just like I did with every other fucking thing in my life.

I wasn't living to my potential. But my time with Hazel was showing me what true determination looked like.

I'd leave for work, and she'd be hunched over her desk, making spreadsheets. When I got home, she'd be on the phone, trying to track down information, or she'd be typing furiously, glasses on, pencil stuck in her hair, and head-phones in place.

That tiny room had been transformed. White boards lined the walls. The old desk was covered in computer moni-tors and Post-it notes. Her bookshelves were artfully arranged and almost filled to capacity.

And Hazel's research consumed her. She was so damn dedicated.

I wanted that. To feel the fire in my belly and push for more.

And so here I was. It was five a.m., and I was running through the woods. The days were getting warmer, but the mornings were frigid and wet. I had layered up, but I was still freezing my balls off. I ran the trails on Henri's land, looping around the forest and coming back up the main road.

My lungs burned and my quads ached, but I felt... at peace.

The trails, the woods. And Hazel. That was all I needed. Though I wasn't sure how to—or if I should—admit it out loud, but my feelings for my wife were growing. It was all so new and confusing. She had always been funny and inter-esting and sassy. I'd admired her since we were kids. But I'd never really noticed her, maybe out of respect for Dylan, or maybe because I was so infatuated with Crystal for so long. But things were different now. The connection between us was evolving, and I was completely out of my depth.

As I rounded the final copse of trees, the cabin came into view, and standing on the front porch, wrapped in my tan Carhartt jacket, was Hazel.

I sped up, showing off a bit. Hey, I was a human. And this was my wife, standing in the chilly air in my jacket.

Subtly yet distinctly, my belly flipped. My wife. My partner. Mine.

I had never felt this way with Crystal. Not in the beginning, and not after years together. Not even after I proposed. She'd never felt like mine. Never felt like a partner. She was a pretty, shiny object I'd spent years working to obtain. Then, once I'd succeeded, I'd fought a constant battle to keep her.

Hazel was like the missing piece to a puzzle I'd spent my life trying to solve.

On the porch, she stood, holding a steaming mug of coffee. "I made this for you," she said as I jogged up the steps. "Figured you could use the warmup."

"You didn't have to wait outside," I panted, ushering her into the cabin.

"I had a feeling you'd be back soon, so I went out to check. It's supposed to be in the seventies today. Great training weather."

I was sweating, and my heart was racing, but a tranquil sensation spread inside my chest at the idea that she'd gone out of her way to care for me.

She wagged a finger at me. "Don't go getting ideas. I'm not one of those women who'll wait on you hand and foot."

I laughed. "No?" I tapped my chin. "I thought for sure we were falling into one of those routines where I came home from work, all sweaty and manly, and you'd be in the kitchen, cooking dinner while wearing nothing but an apron."

She punched my shoulder playfully. "Maybe your next wife. I'm going to get changed. Eat something. We need to start training."

For most people, athletic training involved sneakers and sweat. But Hazel? She started our first training session with a PowerPoint.

"Okay," she said, pushing up her glasses. "I've spent the last week researching. This," she said, handing me a neatly stapled stack of papers, "is our training plan. We've got less than six weeks, and you still have work and your normal training. So I did a deep dive on the data, and hopefully my shortcuts can get us there in time."

I casually flipped through the training schedule while she showed me different carrying positions on her laptop.

"Competitive wife carrying is all about teamwork, communication, and flexibility. We have to move as a unit and anticipate one another's movements. And we both contribute to your balance and stability through the course."

I reviewed the exercises she had outlined. In typical Hazel fashion, it was a lot.

"We don't have to actually do this," I said.

Her face was stony. "Dear husband," she seethed, although there was a hint of humor lurking there too. "I'm taking this extremely seriously, and you should too. This competition is another great opportunity for you, and we're not letting it slip away."

Protesting, I started, "But—"

She held up her hand. "No buts. I've never been sporty. It wasn't an option because sports costs money and require transportation to and from practice and games. Someone who will buy the right shoes or whatever and cut up the orange slices for halftime. I never had that luxury. So I honed my competitive streak at school."

"And I think we can both agree that worked out really well for you," I said, sitting forward and planting my elbows on my knees.

"Yeah, maybe it did. But when I do something. I do it. The Gagnons are going to crush this. We may not win, but we'll be the most hardworking team out there."

"So you're a Gagnon now?" I bit my lip to keep from smiling.

"Hazel Markey is getting a PhD. Hazel Gagnon is going to be one half of a wife carrying championship team and crush Crystal and that sentient saltine she's engaged to."

And with that, I lost the fight to keep from smiling. In fact, I flat out through my head back and guffawed. Damn, I loved when she was like this, fiery and feisty and on my team.

"So get focused," she demanded, eyeing me until I got my laughter under control. "We won't know the course until we get there. But the standard wife carrying course involves running uphill and downhill on uneven terrain, two land obstacles, and one water obstacle. There are usually logs to jump over and lots of mud."

"So I'll be giving you a piggyback ride through it all?" I asked, scanning the different positions she was explaining.

She scoffed. "A piggyback ride? You sweet, simple man. This is so much more than a piggyback."

On her laptop, she toggled to a photo of a man carrying an upside-down woman on his back. It wasn't just an upside down piggyback either. The woman's crotch rested on the back of his neck, and her legs draped over his shoulders. She wrapped her arms around his waist, her face inches above his ass. If I didn't know better, I'd think this was some weird, rejected karma sutra position.

"I've studied competitive wife carrying extensively, and we're going to do the Estonian carry."

I shook my head, trying to keep all my sexual thoughts under control. "Sorry. One more time?"

"There are many ways to carry your wife on your back. However, the most effective is the Estonian carry. Especially if your wife has short legs that won't impede your peripheral vision."

"Okay," I drawled, dubious. How on earth could I jump over logs like this? Hazel was small, but she was still an adult human being. And this was... intimate. We would be getting up close and personal with one another's parts. And while I was very open to that possibility, in the woods, sweating and fully clothed, was not my ideal scenario.

"So if I'm upside down and hanging on to your back with my legs wrapped around you, the bulk of my weight will be distributed to your shoulders, which frees up your legs. You can use all your lower body strength to push us up hills and control yourself running back down."

My thoughts were still spiraling, but I cleared my throat and sat back again when she pushed up her glasses and dug back into her theories.

"It also allows us to be more aerodynamic. The most important thing for me to remember with this position is to not squeeze too hard with my legs, because I could cut off your air supply. You could pass out, so we don't want that to happen. To avoid that, we need practice, but I'm feeling good about this."

My brain swam with all this new information. "I appreciate all of this," I said slowly, "but I have to train for the competition events too. The charity event looks fun, and I'd love to kick Cedric's and Crystal's asses, but I should focus on what's going to help me get the sponsorships I need. I don't have a ton of time, and I may never get this chance again."

"Flip to page four." She nodded at the packet still in my hands. "I don't want to take up too much of your time. So we'll focus on teamwork and balance together, and everything else you need, you can build from your current training. There are so many crossover skills.

"If we want to win, you need to be strong, powerful, and agile. What do you need to be a great lumberjack?"

I nodded. Of course she had already thought of everything. "All of those things," I grumbled.

She pumped her fist. "Exactly! So you keep running and lifting and swinging your axe and leave the strategy to me." She jumped up and bounded for the front door, where her shoes were waiting on the mat.

"Because if there's one thing I do understand, it's physics."

Chapter 23
Hazel

As his fingertips grazed over my butt for the eleventh time in as many minutes, I reached a very scientific conclusion. Analyzing the data was a lot different from letting one's husband of convenience put his hands everywhere.

And they were big, callused hands with strong fingers. And as we practiced, they were *all* over my body.

After a few tries, we sort of got it. Getting into the position was the hardest part. I stood, legs spread, and Remy crouched and tipped forward, putting his head between them and then throwing me onto his back. When I'd fantasized about his head between my legs, this was *not* what I was thinking about.

It was bumpy and a bit terrifying. My legs were literally wrapped around his neck and shoulders, and I was eye level —upside down, of course—with his very round, very firm, very muscular ass. Sure, I'd noticed it before. But up close? *Damn*, this thing could crack walnuts. It was the kind of detail I didn't need to know about my husband, especially as I was clinging to him like an upside-down spider monkey.

If I was the kind of woman who could convincingly lie to herself, I'd say it didn't matter. That I wasn't attracted to strong, round, muscular man butts. But alas, I was truthful to a fault, and I had to concentrate really hard on not accidentally taking a bite out of it.

Instead, I focused on getting the hold correctly. It was far from comfortable, but once we got it, I could see the advantage. He had use of his arms, and our weight was well distributed for balance. Way better than a piggyback or a fireman's carry.

But my crotch was rubbing up against the back of his head. So not totally ideal.

Once we nailed the hold. It was time to try running up and downhill.

I tossed a stainless-steel water bottle to Remy and peeled off my T-shirt, leaving me in my shorts and a sports bra.

His eyes widened when I dropped my tee on the porch steps, but I did my best to ignore it. We needed to stay in the zone.

"Take off your shirt," I ordered.

With his hands on his hips, he cocked his head to the side. "Why?"

"Because we need to feel each other. We need to learn how to move as one. When you shift or move, I have to move with you. Otherwise, we lose balance and fall."

He raised one brow and stared at me. It was warming up outside, yet my nipples hardened under his gaze. I liked the way his attention on my body felt, even though tiny bubbles of insecurity popped up in my brain.

"This is the best way to train.," I explained, blowing out a breath and taking control of the situation. "It's important that we be perfectly in sync in the way that we move as you run uphill, downhill, and around the obstacles. I was watching videos of the World Championships from last year..."

I was getting breathless just looking at him looking at me. *Focus, Hazel. Focus.* "And granted, I don't speak Finnish, but Google translate did a pretty good job. One of the keys they emphasized is really being able to feel each other. So we're going to train skin to skin."

He bit his lip and nodded, scanning me from head to toe. "So that's why you're wearing just a sports bra." He spoke slowly and deliberately.

I tried to remain scientific despite the urge to clench my thighs. "Yes. The less between us, the more we can feel one another's bodies and muscles. It'll help me learn how you move and vice versa."

He stood up and shrugged. "Okay, boss." Then he slowly peeled off his damp T-shirt.

And the clouds parted and angels sang and I almost passed out, practically suffocating on the testosterone emanating from every pore.

I had seen Remy shirtless plenty of times when we were kids, and he had always been athletic. But now he was all man. Recently, I had become very familiar with his body, since he seemed allergic to wearing shirts in our cabin. Chest hair, rippling muscles, and a farmer's tan that revved my engine more than I ever thought it could.

Beard, pecs, abs, and a happy trail leading right to the elastic waistband of his gym shorts. And he was already sweating from carrying me around. No, not sweating. That was too pedestrian for someone who looked like he had been carved from rare Italian marble. No, Remy glistened. And once I'd given him a far too thorough perusal, I regretted my whole "train shirtless" scheme. No amount of competitive advantage was worth whatever was happening to my body and brain.

My thoughts were suddenly hazy and my body was buzzing and my brain's ability to send signals to my eyes to stop staring was temporarily malfunctioning.

"Hazel?" Remy asked, his hands on his hips. "What do we do next?"

Finally, I forced my attention to his face, but with one look at his dark eyes, I almost swallowed my tongue. Next time I got fake married, I'd definitely choose someone I hadn't been lusting after since puberty.

"Right," I croaked. "Let's try running a bit."

He nodded and strode toward me. He crouched low, and before I could process it, I was on his back. And now, instead of obsessing over his ass, I was obsessing over the feel of his back muscles against my skin. I closed my eyes and tried to focus on how his body felt moving as he took off at a jog.

"You okay?" he hollered over his shoulder, picking up his pace.

My hands were wrapped around his stomach, so I gave him a thumbs up.

"Okay. I'm going to head downhill."

I should have warned him. All the videos claimed downhill was the hardest. But I was in a trance, soaking in the way his body moved and how his skin felt against my bare abdomen. I didn't realize we were going down until my shoulder hit the ground.

I got my other arm free, and Remy caught one of my knees, pulling me onto him so my face didn't hit the dirt.

"Hazel. Jesus, are you okay?"

I sat up in a daze, then dropped to the grass beside him, slowly dusting the dirt off my chest. "I think so."

"This is crazy," he said, gritting his teeth. "You just had surgery. We're not doing this."

I leveled him with a glare. "I had surgery weeks ago, and I've been cleared for all activity. Including vigorous exercise. Which, I may add, the doctor encouraged me to do more of. For my health."

"You can go to the gym with Lydia or do yoga or something. You do not need me dropping you on the hard ground in the forest."

I heaved myself to my feet and crossed my arms with a huff. It was one little fall. "I'm healthy now, remember? I eat my veggies and work out. And if this activity is enriching my health, then you really should keep your opinions to yourself."

He stood and loomed over me so our chests were almost flush. I glared right back, my chin up and my jaw set. He was not giving up on this. We were going to figure it out, and we were going to nationals.

He reached down, his hand brushing against my neck, and my breath hitched. Then he pulled a pine needle from my ponytail and held it between us. "You're a mess," he said, his soft tone in direct opposition to the way his chest was heaving.

"Back to work," I said, desperate to end whatever this

was. Focus and data and planning. That was what I should be thinking about. *Not* my shirtless husband standing much too close to me.

He slung me onto his back and turned back toward the hill he'd barreled down. This time, he moved more slowly, more deliberately, and I worked to calm my breathing while I focused on the feel of his body.

"I'm going to turn left and work my way through a trail or two," He explained as we headed up toward Henri and Alice's cabin.

My chest got tight, and my head swam a little, and not just because I was hanging upside down. This was way more challenging than I had anticipated when formulating my training plan. And I was starting to feel self-conscious.

I had a healthy relationship with my body. From childhood, I'd known I'd have to use my brains to get by in life, so I didn't stress about the way I looked. In high school, I wasn't obsessing about my hair or my nails or whether my thighs touched. They had always touched, and that was fine with me.

I was naturally petite, like my mom and my grandma before me. Sure, I guess my thighs could be smaller, but time spent worrying about the circumference of my thighs was time spent not studying.

And so I'd tossed my concerns over my looks to the side, leaving them for future Hazel to worry about. Someday, future Hazel would be gainfully employed, and she'd get facials and highlights and go to Pilates class with friends. Future Hazel would prioritize self-care. But present-day Hazel had way too much going on.

But right now, with all my blood rushing to my head and

feeling every inch of Remy's muscular torso, I was starting to regret the choice to shelve those concerns. I was thinking about all the workouts and spray tans and manicures I'd missed in my twenty-eight years and wondering whether that was the kind of woman he was attracted to.

I was a data geek. And the data, in the form of his demon spawn ex-fiancée, indicated that he was. All the more reason to stop crushing on my husband. Because all the elaborate, sexy fantasies I'd been concocting in my head would never come to fruition.

I'd never cared much about what guys thought of my body. My entire life had been devoted to being taken seriously and being seen as a smart and powerful woman. And being as short as I was meant I had to work hard for those things. So did my high-pitched voice.

I'd never had much trouble with dating. Maybe because I'd never stressed about whether I was single or in a relationship. I'd had a few boyfriends, nothing serious. And a decent friends-with-benefits deal that lasted through grad school.

But this? There was a deep, primal need inside me for Remy to appreciate my body. For him to want me.

I knew he valued my brain. He'd made that clear since we were kids and especially since we'd gotten married. Every time I looked at the bookcases he'd built, I smiled. He supported my work and encouraged me to get healthy so I could finish my doctorate.

But, despite my better judgment, I wanted him to lust for me the way I lusted for him. To feel the frustration I felt. Because he made me feel valued and smart and celebrated, but he also challenged me. It was that deeper level of connection that made me want more from him. Need more from him.

And when I kissed him last weekend, I had foolishly thought that it could be the start of something. He had seemed so surprised and delighted when it happened. But by the time we'd left the tournament, he'd cooled.

The uncertainty and frustration were killing me, and that was dangerous. Especially because I was currently half-naked and upside down, clinging to him like a baby sloth.

"You okay?" He dropped low and put me back on my feet.

He was panting and soaked with sweat.

All the blood rush from my head, making me wobble. I couldn't focus on a single point in front of me, and I suddenly felt cool and clammy.

"Hazel," Remy said, holding my shoulders.

"Can I sit?" I asked, rubbing my temples. "I think I was upside down for too long."

He led me to a grassy spot under a large tree where I sank to the ground and leaned against the trunk.

"Sorry. Head rush."

He dropped to the grass next to me, his shoulder brushing mine, and looked out at the forest.

"Thank you," he said softly.

I hummed and put my head on his sweaty shoulder.

"You're a pretty kick-ass wife."

"You're a pretty kick-ass husband."

For a long moment, we were quiet, catching our breath in the shade of the trees around us. I had missed this in the city. The peace and quiet, the rustling of leaves and the buzzing of insects.

"Can I ask you about the kiss?" he murmured, folding a maple leaf between his fingers.

I nodded, hugging my knees to my chest and dropping my chin to them.

Without looking at me, he asked, "Why'd you do it?"

"Because," I cleared my throat, "I wanted to. You were doubting yourself, and I wanted to remind you that I was in your corner and had your back."

"Were you telling the truth? About wanting to kiss me since eighth grade?"

I dropped my forehead to my knees, wishing I could hide. But there was no use lying now. "Yes," I squeaked.

He nudged me. "Come on, I need more info than that. Did it live up to your eighth-grade fantasies?"

I nodded, still curled up in a ball and mortified. Was he teasing me? God, this was way worse that having his ass in my face.

"Hazel. Look at me." His voice was deep and his tone serious.

So I obeyed. I slowly picked up my head and turned to face him. We were so close I could see the gold flecks in his dark eyes and feel the heat radiating off his body. Scanned my face, his attention landing on my mouth, and I froze.

"I've been obsessing over that kiss for the last week." He pressed his lips together. "Was it a pity kiss? Were you just helping me, or were you signaling that you want more? I wish I was the kind of guy who could be cool about this, but you're my wife, and we sleep in the same bed, and I just really want to kiss you again. Properly this time. Because I need it. I need you."

My pulse thrummed and my heart soared. I couldn't

speak. Instead, I was trying to control the chemical reaction exploding inside my body. Everything was on high alert, and I didn't dare move for fear of breaking the spell that had come over me.

His eyelids were heavy, and his chest heaved with exertion. "I need you," he rasped.

And before I could process it, he was cupping my cheek and leaning in. And then his mouth was on mine, giving me the kind of slow, languid kiss I'd never shared with anyone and hadn't known I needed until that moment.

His lips were soft yet firm, his fingertips rough as he brushed my neck and slid them down the column of my throat. His gentleness barely concealed the hunger deep inside him. His touch was commanding but comforting.

Our mouths met in the most perfect way, exploring one another thoroughly. He pulled back, only to take a breath and dive in again, hungrier and more urgent. I reciprocated, letting myself sink further into the abyss that was his mouth.

I was flying.

Then he was pulling me onto his lap, grasping my hips and dragging me closer, his tongue moving frantically with mine. The feel of his strong hands on my hips made me shudder. The combination of physical power and emotional vulnerability had my entire body aching for release.

Clawing at his bare chest, I threw my head back when he kissed my neck. I sank into the moment, relished the way he nibbled my flesh and the feel of his erection against me. This was what I had been missing. This urgency. This want. This need.

I moaned at the sparks that lit me up inside as those strong hands roamed over me, grabbing and grasping. I caught his mouth again, letting the feel of his tongue and the taste of him consume me.

It was too much, too good, too soon. But I couldn't stop myself from grinding down on his lap, savoring the groan that escaped him as he tugged at the top of my sports bra, freeing my breasts.

The feel of his tongue on my skin was making me dizzy with lust and ramping up the ache in my core that had been slowly growing for months. Since the day we'd said our vows and shared that chaste kiss at city hall. I didn't know where this was going or what we were even doing, but I needed more.

Sliding my hands down his ribs, I brought them between us, feeling the ridges of his abs, the soft hair below his navel that led—

Before I could follow that trail, we were interrupted by a loud vibrating sound.

"What the hell?" Remy rasped as I whipped my head around.

"Fuck," he cursed, pulling me close protectively. About ten yards away, at the edge of the clearing, was a massive bull moose.

His braying was a loud almost honking, almost mooing sound. One I had never heard at such close proximity. It was deep and flat, making the hairs on the back of my neck stand up.

I squinted. I had left my glasses back at the cabin so they wouldn't fall off while I was hanging upside down. "Is that Clive?"

Remy growled. "Fucking Clive. Go away Clive!" he shouted.

The moose turned slightly, displaying the large scar on his hind leg. Yep. It was definitely Clive.

I sank into Remy's chest.

"He's usually not aggressive." He scanned the clearing, his chin brushing against the top of my head. "I don't see any ladies for him to impress. Give it a minute, and we'll get up and head back."

I nodded, a little scared but mostly embarrassed.

"It's like he's looking right at us," I said. "And judging us."

"He's probably trying to protect your virtue. Cock-blocking asshole moose."

I couldn't help but laugh. Of all the things to derail the hottest make-out session of my life, it was a moose.

After a few minutes, Clive got bored and wandered off, giving us an opportunity to dust ourselves off.

I tucked my boobs back into my sports bra and searched for something, anything, other than Remy to focus on. "I gotta get to work in a bit," I said, not sure how to address what had just happened.

In my periphery, he nodded. "You shower. I'm going to head up to Henri's to lift weights. I'll give you a ride to work when I'm done?" His eyes were bright and hopeful, and his lopsided grin was so sweet. I couldn't help but think about the way he'd kissed me. His body was big and strong, but he'd held me so gently and kissed me so desperately. Almost like he had also been wanting to do it since eighth grade.

Chapter 24
Hazel

"Sooo..." Lydia dragged out the O sound while stirring her vodka tonic. She tipped forward, elbows on the bar, and whispered, "Have you consummated the marriage yet?"

I threw a bar towel at her. That was the last thing I needed to be thinking about. The very last.

"Shut your mouth." I scanned the area around the bar. It was early, so the place wasn't full yet, but there were several people in the booths eating dinner and a few playing pool.

"You *did*." She pumped her fist. "Excellent. I won't tell Dylan, of course. But I need details." She took a long pull of her drink and blinked at me expectantly. "Spill, lady. The other teachers will be here soon, so you better talk fast."

"You look amazing, and not in a *just had life-saving surgery* way. It's more of a *getting busy with your hot husband* glow."

"Shut up," I snapped again, heading over to greet a pair of regulars on the other end of the bar. I'd relived the hot and heavy make-out session in the woods at least a dozen times so far tonight. Remy had driven me to work silently, and instead of coming back to pick me up later, he'd hunkered down with a glass of water and was now playing pool with Dylan in the back corner.

The trip was the same as it had been since our arrangement began, except for the part where he had been biting my nipples while I ground against his erection a few hours earlier.

I could not tell Lydia. Or could I? Who was I kidding? She would get it out of me by the end of the night.

I looked down the bar at my oldest friend. As usual, she looked beautiful in an effortless way. Her wavy red hair was tousled but not messy, and her nineties style mom jeans were slouchy but managed to make her waist look tiny and her ass look amazing. She tapped her freshly manicured nails on the wooden bar, eyeing me while she waited for me to finish up, no doubt so she could resume her interrogation.

Every time I looked up, Remy caught my eye. Even as the Moose got more and more crowded, I could feel his dark gaze on my skin. It was unnerving and told me he was thinking about what happened earlier just as much as I was.

When I stood across from Lydia again, I topped off her glass of chardonnay and discreetly looked around to make sure we wouldn't be overheard. Lovewell was a small town, and if one wasn't careful, things did not stay private for long.

I leaned forward so our faces were almost touching. "Nothing," I said. "Nothing will happen. We're friends, and that's it."

"Stop lying to yourself. You are smitten and so is he." Lydia pulled back and grinned.

Silently, I wiped down the counter and set out a new stack of drink napkins, not trusting myself to even respond. I wasn't known for my poker face.

"You sleep in the same bed."

"Opposite sides," I hissed.

"Not for long. Any day now, you'll be jumping his bones." She narrowed her eyes. "If you haven't already..."

Choking on a cough, I shook my head vigorously.

"Why not?" she asked, tapping her chin. "Does he have dozens of creepy teddy bears set up on his bed? Or—ooh," she crowed, clearly on a roll, "is his body covered with hideous scars?" She shook her head. "Nah, scratch that. Scars are hot. Let's be honest, you'd still hit it."

Slumping my shoulders, I dragged a hand down my face. "Please stop talking."

"I'm just saying. You bought the cow, may as well enjoy the milk while you can."

"Could you be any more disgusting?"

She smiled and steepled her fingers like a Disney villain. "Challenge accepted, my friend. What does he wear to bed? Boxers? Briefs." She paused. "Ooh. Ooh. Gray sweats? He strikes me as a guy who goes commando. But I haven't taken a good look at what he's packing." Planting her hands on the bar top, she stood on the rungs of her stool and peered around the bar. "Where is he?" she asked, dropping back onto her seat. "I'll check out what he's working with."

"Don't you dare." I growled. "If you look at my husband's junk, I will kick your ass."

Lydia slammed a palm down on the bar. "There it is. The Hazel fire. You try so hard to be little miss meek and mild, but I've known you forever. Get jealous, get man. He's your man now."

I had been played.

Pinning her with a glare, I leaned over the bar. "I hate you right now."

"Nope. You love me. Because I don't sugarcoat things. And now you're gonna take a deep breath and tell me what's really going on."

"Fine." I huffed. "We've kissed. It was hot and intense, and I don't know what's happening except I can't stop thinking about it."

"Fuck yeah." She did an exaggerated fist pump, drawing all kinds of stares.

"Subject change," I said, hoping no one had overheard any of that. Unlikely, given Lydia's penchant for the dramatic. "Let's talk about you."

"Ha. Sure thing. I got stood up last night. Then another guy messaged me asking for photos of my toes."

"Did you send them?"

She twirled her wine glass slowly and lifted her chin. "Well, he's employed, has hair, and my preliminary background check indicates that he's actually single and not some creepy married guy trying to get some on the side, so I most certainly did."

I gasped.

"Like you're one to judge. I'm kink friendly to a point. And given how limited my options are these days. I'd be stupid to disqualify a suitor over a little foot action."

I laughed so hard I broke out into a coughing fit.

"Careful, I know I'm hilarious. But you just had surgery. Don't rip your stitches."

"It was weeks ago."

"Still. They removed an organ."

"I'm fine."

"Sure thing. You're totally fine. You're not desperate to fuck your hot lumberjack husband, and you're not in denial at all, yup. Sounds about right!" She raised her wineglass and gulped half of it, as if toasting my delusion.

Jim brought another tray of clean glassware out, giving Lydia a nod and me a look of pure disgust.

"Good to see you, Jim," Lydia said.

He ignored her. "Still can't believe this one got married," he said, shaking his head.

"I've told you a dozen times. It's none of your damn business."

He ignored my response, instead turning to Lydia. "I really thought she was smart enough to know better than to get hitched to a Gagnon."

Lydia snorted into her wine.

"Ignore him," I said, stacking the glassware under the bar.

"I've thought about it," he said, scratching his beard. "You're fired."

I rolled my eyes. "You fire me at least once a week. Who else is gonna close for you tonight?"

"Nah. This time I mean it. When I hired you, it was only because you promised you would get out of here. You swore to me you'd move on to bigger and better things."

"And I'm doing just that. When I'm not behind this bar, I'm busting my ass doing research."

"But now you're stuck with a Gagnon boy. And not even

one of the good ones with the good jobs and educations. Nope, you got the youngest."

Lydia laughed. "Now Jim, that's not fair."

"Life ain't fair, missy. We all had such high hopes for Hazel."

"Deliver these to the bikers down at the end of the bar," I said, pushing three drafts at him and shooing him with my hands. "You're not firing me. And quit distracting me. I'm not here to make friends."

He laughed. "Good. I hate friends."

"Me too. They slow me down."

He collected the beers and headed toward the other end of the bar, but halfway there, he turned and pinned me with a look over his shoulder. "Maybe you aren't as dumb as I thought."

The weather had been mild, and people were in a generous mood that night, if my tip jar was any indication. I was rushing around making drinks, wiping down the bar, and mentally planning a trip to Bangor so I could buy more supportive shoes before next weekend when Jim caught my arm.

"Can you deliver a food order to booth three?" he asked, pouring a draft and nodding to the order waiting in the kitchen window.

I nodded, slinging my towel over my shoulder and heading that way.

Plates balanced, I weaved between tables, headed for the table of men speaking in hushed voices. As I approached, they fell silent and stared at me. Mitch Hebert held court in the middle of the corner booth, flanked by his younger brother, Paul, and a few cronies I didn't recognize.

The Heberts were sort of like the Kennedys of Lovewell. An old timber family and by far the richest, with the most land. They even owned their own mill a few towns over—the opening of which was one of the reasons the mill here in town closed in the nineties, costing us hundreds of jobs and devastating most of the town.

Mitch Hebert walked around town with his nose in the air, like he was better than the rest of us. His hair was dyed black and slicked back, his fingers covered with gaudy rings, and he wore the kind of smirk that suggested he was really, really pleased with himself.

He had five sons. They'd gone to school with us, every one of them the epitome of a spoiled rich kid. Always traveling to hockey tournaments or getting new trucks for their sixteenth birthdays. Their charmed lives couldn't have been more different from how Dylan and I had grown up.

And so I'd always harbored a low-level disgust for the family. They'd never done anything to me personally, but the Gagnons hated them. There was bad blood between the families going back at least a few decades, and both sides stayed far away from one another.

Mitch ran his business with Paul. A shorter, dumber version of his brother, who drove around town in a Mercedes G wagon and was known to have too many drinks and then sexually harass half the female population of Lovewell. I'd had to cut him off several times in the last few weeks, and he was a shit tipper to boot.

They made my skin crawl. So it was no surprise when Mitch whistled at me like a goddamn dog to get another round. Bastard. He was lucky I was too classy to seriously contemplate spitting in their beers.

How unfair that people like him got to roam this earth with their money and status and comfort while hardworking, loving people like Mr. Gagnon or my sweet grandma were taken too soon.

These days, the younger Hebert boys kept a low profile. A couple of them had moved away. One was a plumber, and I think another joined the military. Remy had mentioned working with the oldest, Gus, out in the woods a few times, though he hadn't elaborated.

I was grateful. The fewer assholes in this town, the better. Rural communities like ours had enough problems. We didn't need entitled shitheads running around, making life harder for the rest of us. But the Heberts were everywhere. Always throwing money around, putting their names on things, and reminding the rest of the hard-working citizens that they were better than us.

I forced a smile as I returned with the round of beers.

"One more, Hazel, dear," a voice called from behind me, then Chief Souza slid into the booth to my right, giving me a wink. Our chief of police was a graying man who had been in his position for longer than I'd been alive. As an adult and a public health professional, he was ineffective at best, but I could never dislike him. He had shown great kindness to Dylan and me, as well as my mom, several times throughout my childhood.

"Of course, Chief," I said. He was a regular, so I didn't bother asking what he'd like. Allagash White—he only drank local beer—and a glass of soda water with lime.

"How's the research going?" he asked kindly, then turned to his companions. "Not sure if you know, but Hazel here is a brilliant student on her way to a doctorate. She's an opioid expert, and my office has been helping her connect with some of the bigwigs in the state for her research."

I forced a smile. Helping was an overstatement. He'd given me a few phone numbers, and then he'd shrugged when I asked for drug arrest data, saying he'd get to it. So I wasn't holding my breath.

Mitch Hebert scrutinized me, his gaze turning even colder.

I stood a little straighter and held my chin high, staring right back at him to let him know I wasn't intimidated. "I'll grab those drinks, Chief," I said, turning and getting as far away from that table as I could.

Once I rounded the bar, I caught Remy's attention. He was playing pool with Dylan and not so subtly keeping an eye on me. He raised a concerned brow, and I responded with a subtle nod and went back to pouring drinks. He was always checking on me. We didn't talk about it much, but he had quit drinking, and I worried hanging around in a bar would be difficult for him, but he showed up time after time, sipping on water and watching me.

I inadvertently touched my lips, still reeling from our afternoon together. Every time I looked up, he was watching. His gaze unnerving and such a turn-on.

I had the rest of my shift ahead of me, but when I peeked over at him for what must have been the hundredth time and caught his hungry expression, I knew one thing—Remy had plans for me, and it was going to be a long night.

Chapter 25
Remy

I wasn't the jealous type. Never had been. Even with Crystal. And with the way she flaunted things, maybe I should have been. Her skimpy outfits, her constant social media posts, her need for attention—I never thought twice about any of it.

I let her be herself, and then she cheated on me. Humiliated me and ruined my life. Wasted six good years.

Though six years was an exaggeration since I'd done her bidding for the first two before she even agreed to go out with me. And I'd wasted so many years before that, desperate for a chance with her.

In hindsight, it was obvious that by the time she'd gotten around to me, she had exhausted her options. She was just as stuck as I was. And I was a way to pass the time. A diversion. Something to do while she waited for her trust fund to kick in. All the while, her parents indulged her, never saying no and contributing to the creation of the monster she became.

The loss of that time was what hurt the most. Time I

could have spent furthering my education or career. Opportunities lost because I was trying to be someone I wasn't. Focusing so much energy on trying to please someone who didn't really want me.

She had been so dismissive of my training and groused every time she traveled to competitions with me. On the rare occasion she actually went. Or complaining that I was no fun because I had to get up early to work out.

But things were different with Hazel. Maybe because we had grown up together and shared a familiar level of comfort. She had always been around, usually reading a book while Dylan and I built forts and ran around, making trouble.

I had always been protective of her, like any boy would be with a little sister.

Except she wasn't my little sister. That was for sure. It would be easy to say I'd never thought of her in that way. Because at some point during my teen years, Hazel the annoying little sister in her brother's old clothes turned into something else completely.

It was the summer before my senior year, and a group of us were at South Birch Lake, messing around on the beach and drinking beer someone's older brother had bought us.

Hazel had come with Dylan, like she always did, and when she took off her T-shirt and exposed that purple bikini, every neck snapped. There was not a guy on the lake that day that didn't notice.

She had always been a scrawny kid who wore clothes a few sizes too big. But in that bikini, she was a goddess. All curves and creamy skin.

After that moment, I had trouble keeping her in the *sister* category in my mind.

Regardless, she never dated. She was too busy with school to bother, I was sure, and Dylan would have lost his mind anyhow.

So I'd safely tucked away that desire and let Crystal consume my thoughts instead, keeping Hazel locked firmly in the *off-limits* category.

But now, everything had changed.

Hazel was my wife. *Wife.* I could not stop saying it in my head. Or out loud, for that matter, every chance I got.

And we had kissed. It would have been a hell of a lot more than kissing if we hadn't been interrupted by Clive the cock-blocking moose. Every time I looked at Dylan, I cringed. A friendly game of pool had become a minefield, the guilt overwhelming me every time he cracked a joke or smiled. He had come out tonight to keep me company. It was a lot easier to pass the time drinking water and eating salad when I had company.

He had always been a good friend. But these past few months, he had been there for me more than my actual siblings had. And here I was, hiding something major from him.

But this connection with Hazel was overwhelming. Our marriage had brought us closer and forced us to lean on one another. The competition last week had been a game changer. She showed up for me in a big way, more than any person, save my parents, had ever done.

When I was with her, I didn't feel alone. I didn't feel like an impostor or the idiot little brother who brought no real value to any aspect of life.

Tonight, I came to the Moose determined to be close to her while she worked. Dylan had kindly distracted me for a bit, but now it was late, and I sat alone at the bar, pretending to look at my phone. I wasn't proud of it, but the guys I'd been playing pool with were long gone. Henri was with his family, and I wasn't speaking to Paz. And no one knew where the hell Adele was spending her time these days. So it was just me. Drinking water and trying to control the sudden jealous urges I was experiencing.

Because Hazel in that tiny tank top and red lipstick? Tending bar surrounded by grizzled mountain men who looked at her like the most delicious snack at the candy store? She brought back feelings I'd stuff down years ago. Desires I'd spent my adult life channeling into other things.

The Timber Trio was playing tonight, which always brought in a big crowd, and people were dancing and playing pool and having a good time. But me? I was officially losing it.

Brooding at the bar, gripping my water glass, chugging it like it was something stronger, shooting dirty looks at every fucker who even made eye contact with her. I never intended to be the jealous husband, never in my life expected I'd become one. Not at all. But anymore, it didn't feel optional.

Thankfully, Hazel was too busy running around and pouring beers and working in her usual focused, strategic manner to notice. She always had the right glass within reach, always had a bar towel in the back pocket of her jeans. Everything about her exuded competence. And it was such a fucking turn-on.

Finally, well after midnight, the place was clearing out. The band had packed up and the kitchen had closed, and I helped Jim stack the chairs and mop while Hazel handled the bar tasks.

"Can you two lock up?" Jim asked. "I trust this one"—he nodded at Hazel—"but I'm not sure I like you."

I rolled my eyes. "You were my little league coach, Jim."

"That I was. You were trouble even then. And now here you are, married to the smartest girl ever to come from Lovewell. You best not screw this one up, son."

With a nod, I dropped my chin and busied myself with the mop bucket. If only he knew just how hard I was trying not to do just that. My marriage to Hazel, as fake as it was, had been the best thing to ever happen to me. I was healthy, happy, and finally getting my shit together.

It may not be traditional or look like other marriages, but it was working for us.

Which was why I had to learn to keep my hands to myself.

After what happened in the woods earlier that afternoon, I knew we could never go back. But I wasn't sure we could go forward either.

Hazel and I stocked the bar in silence until Jim's truck rumbled out of the parking lot. Then she spun to face me, planted a fist on one hip, and pinned me with a glare.

"While I appreciate the help cleaning up, maybe next weekend you don't come babysit me at work? You scared away all my tips tonight."

The swing of her ponytail, the arch of her brow, all those things that were so... Hazel lit me up inside and sent blood thrumming through my veins.

I took a step closer to her. "I'm not sorry," I rasped. "Didn't like the way those guys looked at you."

She scowled. "Excuse me? You are out of line."

"You. Are. My. Wife." I took another step closer.

"Not really."

"In the eyes of the law, you are mine. And I hate that every asshole in the county came here tonight to look at your tits and your lips and your hair."

She slammed that one fist on the bar top. "What has gotten into you? Why on earth are you thinking about my tits all of a sudden? They aren't even that impressive."

"Jesus." I roughed my hands through my hair to keep from grabbing her and shaking some sense into her. "Not impressive? I dream about those tits every night. I would do anything to touch them again. Lick them and bite them and watch you squirm."

"Remy." Her tone was sharp, but her chest was heaving.

"You'd love it, too, wouldn't you? You like a little bit of a rough touch, I bet."

"Stop it," she commanded. Her voice quivering.

"I want to stop," I growled, stalking closer. "But I can't." I pushed forward, backing her up against the bar, caging her between my arms. Because of our height difference, I had to dip low, close enough to hear her pulse pounding, to whisper in her ear.

"I can't control myself around you. You are mine. And I want every asshole in this bar to know it."

"I'm wearing your wedding ring. Isn't that enough?"

We were so close now, almost chest to chest, that the heat radiating off her body soaked through my shirt, warming my skin. I gripped the bar so hard to keep my hands off her I thought I might leave dents in the oak.

"No. It's not good enough for me. I want all of you, Hazel. And it's eating me up inside. I want to touch you and possess you and have all of you."

There. I had said it. The words I had been holding in for weeks.

They lingered between us as she stared up at me, her brown eyes wide behind her glasses. There was a fifty-fifty chance she'd kiss me or knee me in the balls.

The silence was punctuated only by the sounds of our heavy breathing.

"Why not?" she finally asked, her voice no more than a whisper. "What's stopping you?"

I growled, desperate to contain the animalistic urges taking over every cell in my body. Because another taste, one more kiss, and I'd be done for. The self-control I was holding on to by a thread would snap. Then it'd be gone forever.

"I'm not good for you," I growled. "And I promised Dylan. So I've got to keep my distance. Be your husband in name only. Doesn't make it any easier to watch other guys flirt with you, though."

Faster than I'd ever seen her move, she snatched at the fabric of my T-shirt at my chest.

"But what about me? What about what I want?" she asked softly.

I shook my head, but before I could respond, she was pulling me toward her, catching my mouth in a hungry kiss.

Without my permission, my hands found her hips and tugged her closer as I explored her mouth.

She tasted sweet, and her perfect mouth drove me wild.

I needed more. I wanted more. Fuck, my brain could barely function.

Then my damn hands were taking control again, dragging the neckline of her tank down and exposing the top of her bra. And I couldn't hold back. I kissed my way down her neck, down her chest, to the swell of them, loving the weight of them in my hands.

"I was right," I said, gently biting her nipples through the lace of her bra, then tugging that last layer of fabric down. "You like when I'm rough with you." Again, I brought my teeth to one bud, grazing her skin as she writhed under my touch.

She moaned, arching her back, the sound so tempting I knew that if I didn't stop this, I'd be fucking her on the bar in no time. And although that sounded perfectly wonderful, I wouldn't do that to her.

"We should stop," I said, brushing my lips back up her neck as she palmed my rock-hard cock over my jeans.

She shook her head in protest, but I pulled away.

"This isn't right."

The second the words left my lips, the look of lust in her eyes was replaced by anger.

"I'm sick of your caveman shit. You want to fuck me? Do it. Show me what it means to be yours."

Grabbing her shoulders, I loomed over her, glaring. But I couldn't stop myself from taking in her exposed tits and messy hair. Fuck, she was gorgeous.

I pushed her back against the bar, caressing her hips and then lower, until my fingertips brushed the hem of her denim skirt.

Against my better judgment, I dropped my mouth to hers again and inched the fabric up her legs.

"This is what you want?" I asked, stroking her inner thighs, reveling in the way they quivered. "You want to be mine?"

She gasped as I ran my fingers over the damp cotton at

her center, then dipped inside it, finding the perfect spot.

"Oh, you're already soaked. That's my sexy wife."

I thrust two fingers inside her, watching her eyes roll back in her head at the intrusion. She was wet and tight and warm and so fucking exquisite. My cock protested in my jeans, desperate to join the party, but I had to stay focused.

"You are my wife," I said, curling my fingers inside her and rubbing her clit with my thumb.

She cried out, the reaction spurring me on. I was acting like a ridiculous caveman, just like she said I was, but I couldn't stop myself. The line I had crossed in my head so many times had been completely obliterated.

"You belong to me. I don't care if it's only temporary. I don't care what our reasons are."

I pumped my fingers, dipping my head to take one pink nipple in my mouth, loving the taste of her skin and the feel of her clenched around me. With my thumb, I drew circles on her clit as she pushed back against me, riding my hand timidly at first.

"That's it," I growled. "Ride it. Come all over my fingers."

"Please," she moaned, her face and chest flushed and her eyes glassy. Her body trembling, on the brink.

"Say it," I demanded. "Who do you belong to?"

"My husband," she cried, coming undone, throwing her head back, her breasts bouncing and her chest heaving. She spasmed and bucked, moaning loudly. It was the most beautiful thing I had ever seen.

"Who takes care of you?"

"You do," she gasped. Panting and writhing.

"Good girl."

Chapter 26
Hazel

The ride home was silent and filled with tension. It was for the best. I was still recovering from the orgasms to end all orgasms. It had been a while for me. I wasn't about to break out my favorite vibe while I was sleeping on my brother's couch or sharing a bed with my formerly platonic husband.

And living with my hot lumberjack husband hadn't helped the situation. He was allergic to shirts and shaving and spent most of his time working out. No wonder I'd combusted after a little exceptional hand action and a few dirty words.

And he was *dirty*. Remy was a laid-back guy. Not a jealous, possessive alpha male. Or so I'd thought. Now I wasn't so sure.

All I knew was that I was addicted to this side of him. And although we'd waded into dangerous territory tonight, I couldn't help but want even more of him.

He rounded the hood of the truck and opened the door

for me, but before I could step out, he slung me over his shoulder.

"Come on, wife," he said, gravel in his voice. "I'm not done with you yet."

He carried me carefully into the cabin, then toed off his shoes and locked the door behind us.

He carried me through the dark living area and kitchen and into the bedroom, where he eased me onto the mattress and untied my shoes. He threw them onto the floor one at a time and then got to work unbuttoning my skirt and sliding it down over my hips.

"I want you so badly," he rasped, his chest heaving as he took in the sight of my soaked panties.

I situated myself on my knees in front of him, placing my hands on either side of his rib cage.

"Not as much as I want you," I said, pulling the hem of his T-shirt up.

He helped me pull it over his head, then tossed it aside while I ran my hands over his chest. I was familiar with this chest. We had seen a lot of each other during training and while sleeping beside one another over the past few weeks. But now I could touch him and explore every inch of his skin, and I didn't want to stop.

He tilted my chin up and brought his lips to mine, the kiss deep and passionate but also gentle.

"I've wanted this for so long," he said, pulling back and studying me.

I laughed, unbuttoning his jeans. "Not as long as I have."

He shucked his pants off with a chuckle. "Really? Sweet, nerdy, high school Hazel wanted to get in my pants?"

I tossed my tank top to the floor and made quick work of my bra.

We were facing one another, wearing only underwear, my entire body flushing with heat as I drank him in. The beating of my heart punctuated the silence.

This was Remy. My friend, my husband, and the person I trusted most in the world.

And in that moment, I was liberated. Set free from my insecurities and worries. Existing in this moment with this man.

"Do you want to know a secret?" I asked, emboldened by his hungry gaze.

He nodded, biting his lip and fisting his hands at his sides like he was holding himself back from touching me.

"The first time I, you know." I looked away. Maybe I didn't have the courage to tell this story after all.

"I don't know, Hazel," he said, running his fingertips down my arms, making the fire inside me burn even brighter.

"The first time I touched myself, I thought about you."

He froze, his attention locked on me and his dark eyes molten. "That is the hottest thing I've ever heard. My naughty wife." He angled in and kissed me again, rougher this time, one of his hands grasping my neck while the other palmed an aching breast.

"I think about you all the time," he confessed, kissing down my neck as his fingers explored the waistband of my panties. "I jerked off in the shower thinking about you this afternoon."

I pulled back. "Really?"

He shook his head. "And so many times before that too.

After our training session and the hottest make-out session of my life, you couldn't expect me to not take care of things."

I closed my eyes and let myself sink into the sensation of his lips on my skin.

"Tell me more," I said.

"I think about fucking you. About what you'll feel like wrapped around my cock. About the sounds you'll make when I make you come."

I gasped, clenching my thighs together. How could I be this close already? Dirty words and excursions to second base apparently did it for me these days.

"Then do it," I said, tugging down his boxer briefs to reveal a very hard and very impressive erection. I gripped it, reveling in the size of him and how turned on he was.

He moaned and tossed me onto the bed, yanking down my panties the second my back hit the mattress.

"I'll never deny my wife what she needs."

And then he was looming over me, biting his lip and lining himself up with my center.

"I have an IUD," I blurted out, aching for him but attempting to be somewhat responsible.

"We should have discussed this first," he growled. "I was tested after Crystal cheated on me. And I haven't been with anyone since."

"Same. I was tested recently. And all good."

"Are you okay with this?" He nudged my clit with his crown, his attention fixated on our connection.

"Yes," I breathed as he slid his length against me. "Yes. I want it. I want you. Nothing between us."

"Have you ever...?"

"Never," I said. "I've never done this with anyone."

"That's right," he said, biting one of my nipples and lining himself up. "Only your husband gets you bare."

He sank deep, stretching and filling me in ways I had never experienced. It was too much, yet I wanted more. So much more.

"Please," I begged, my body aching with need.

He caged me between his arms and dropped his chin, his focus locked on my face. "Spread your legs wider for me. Oh yes, that's perfect."

I bucked my hips, clenching every muscle, watching him squeeze his eyes shut. "Harder, please," I begged.

"Okay, okay," he gritted out. "What my wife wants, my wife gets."

He circled my wrists with those long, talented fingers, then pinned my arms above my head, picking up his pace, thrusting deep and hard and reminding me of just how powerful my husband was.

I wiggled beneath him, my body on high alert already. Dazed and buzzing and so close. Reduced to a puddle of need, begging for more. He kissed his way down my chest, and when he took my nipple between his teeth and clamped down hard, my world exploded. I cried out, screaming as I fell apart, every cell in my body combusting with pleasure. And with a growl, he surged inside me, then collapsed on top of me.

He was still inside me as he rolled over, bringing me with him and stroking my face. "I hope I didn't hurt you."

Dazed and smiling, I opened my eyes. "Not at all."

"Good." He kissed me softly. "Because next time, I'll last a lot longer. No wife of mine is finished after only one orgasm."

Chapter 27
Remy

I rolled over, pulling Hazel close. If she wasn't a snuggler now, I'd convert her. The bed we had been sleeping in for weeks was suddenly too big.

I needed her close, tucked up against me where she belonged.

"Remy," she whispered as I nuzzled her, peppering her neck with kisses.

"We should talk."

"Mm-hmm." I kissed her shoulder blade, roaming her naked body with greedy hands.

She turned to face me, her eyes swimming with worry.

"We fucked up," she said softly.

My heart seized. Because until she uttered those words, I was on cloud nine, thinking we had just turned a major corner after admitting our desire for one another and finally getting what we had both wanted for so long.

Because that spark of desire I first felt during that chaste kiss at city hall had caught fire, slowly building and burning into a wild inferno of lust and possession.

Before me, she was nibbling her lip, her eyes darting back and forth between mine. Knowing her, she was ready to overanalyze this to death, but I refused to go there with her. If I had any say in the matter, we'd keep doing what we were meant to be doing.

I shifted, pulling her beneath me and caging her between my forearms, then dipping down to give her a kiss that would help her see sense.

In response, she arched up into me as my cock hardened against her thigh and let a tiny moan escape. I kissed her again, more fiercely this time, and was rewarded when she grabbed my face and bit my bottom lip.

"We need to talk," she said between kisses.

"So talk," I grunted, kissing down her neck and collarbone.

"We should put clothes on."

I shook my head, nipping at her breasts. "Unnecessary."

"Remy Gagnon, I'm serious. How can we properly discuss what happened and its ramifications if we're half naked and your boner is rubbing up against my leg?"

I smiled up at her. Of course having my mouth on her nipples wouldn't affect her vocabulary.

"Ramifications? You mean all the orgasms? Should we talk about how many times I made you come and how many more times I plan to do it tonight?"

"Nice try. I mean how we totally changed our arrangement and blurred lines and made everything much more confusing."

With my lips hovering above her hard pink nipple, I peered up at her. "Okay. Since you clearly need to hear this, I'm going to say it once and then get back to work."

I sat up, pushing the covers back to expose both of our naked bodies, and she clambered up to her knees after me so we were eye to eye.

"We're married. The entire world thinks we're fucking, so why not? I can't keep my hands off you anymore, Hazel." I slid one finger from the base of her throat, down her breastbone, to her navel, my eyes transfixed on the goose bumps that erupted on her skin as I did. "You are so smart and sexy, and you push all my buttons. If you don't want me like that," I pulled my hand away and eyed her, searching for any sign that she felt that way, "I will back off. But given what happened between us in the woods, and then again last night, I'm not sure I buy that."

"I want you too. I've always wanted you." She looked away and picked at an invisible speck on the sheet beside her knee.

"Then it's settled. We keep going. I make you come whenever you want. And if you want to stop, tell me, and I'll respect your decision."

She studied me from under her lashes. "You make it sound so easy."

"Because it is. We agreed to stay married for a year, and so far, I'd say our marriage is going great. As long as we work as a team and communicate, we can let this evolve into whatever it needs to be. And when it's over. It's over. I'll respect your wishes." I winked, hoping to sell the lie. My feelings had been developing for a while now. If I was being honest with myself, I probably started falling for her on our wedding day. When I took her hand and promised her everything would be okay.

But last night had changed our dynamic in so many ways. We hadn't just crossed the line. We had crushed it and then set fire to the rubble. There was no going back. I had felt her come on my fingers; I'd been inside her body; and I'd felt our hearts racing together, syncing, as I held her close.

"Because I'm not staying." The words sent panic flaring inside me, turning that inferno of desire into a scorching pain.

"Of course you're not. I know I can't keep you forever."

She smiled, but her eyes swam with tears as she squeezed my hand.

"But I'd like to have you while I can." I brought that hand to her cheek, hoping she could sense my genuine need for her.

She pulled out of my hold and scrambled out of bed. Grabbing her robe from the back of the door, she whipped around and then wrapped it around her naked body, putting a physical and metaphorical barrier between us.

"I don't want to tell Dylan."

I froze, taken aback. The guilt had been eating me alive for weeks. Now that this was officially something, I assumed we'd tell him. Wanted to tell him. We'd deal with his inevitable freak-out and then move on.

"My sex life is none of his business," she continued, pulling her robe just a little tighter around her. "I'm a grown-ass woman. I date who I want. When I want. I don't need him getting all patriarchal on me."

"Of course not. But I feel like he should know if this isn't platonic anymore."

She shook her head. "The last thing I want to deal with right now is his overprotective bullshit."

I stared at her, not sure how to respond. On the one hand, it was none of his business, but on the other, he was my best friend. And I promised him I wouldn't cross the line.

"It's just..." She turned to the window, taking in the spectacular view of the mountains. "I've spent my entire life planning for the future. Sometimes living only for the future when the present was particularly shitty. And for once, I want to enjoy the now."

I stood and rounded the bed until I was standing behind her. Cupping her shoulders, I squeezed her, hoping to reassure her, then wrapped her in my arms, ignoring the way my erection pressed into her delicious ass.

"I've got this amazing husband, a gorgeous log cabin with my own damn library, and I'm back in my hometown for the first time in ten years. Life is good. I don't want to fuck it up by adding expectations and disappointment."

I tipped my head and kissed that special spot where her neck met her shoulder. "Then let's enjoy the now and not worry about the future just yet."

She turned, still wrapped in my embrace, and traced her fingertips over my chest. "Do you really mean that? We can keep things between us? And just enjoy the temporary?"

"Yes," I said, placing two fingers under her chin and lifting until she was forced to look at me. "We have fun together. You finish your dissertation, I train, and we do not talk about the future."

Finding her waist, I tugged on the belt of her robe and kissed my way down her neck.

"And now that we've got the business out of the way," I said, gently pinching one nipple and making her squeal, "I need to get back to work."

She moaned as the robe hit the floor.

"It's my husbandly duty to provide you with at least three orgasms a day." I backed her up until her calves hit the bed and pushed against her shoulders, grinning as she let herself fall onto the mattress. Dropping to my knees, I took the opportunity to push her legs wide open.

"Is that right?" she said, arching her back off the bed. "I'm so impressed by your dedication to the job."

I shrugged, biting her inner thigh. "What can I say? Being married to an overachiever is rubbing off on me."

***

After our morning sexathon, I took off to train for a bit, feeling better than I had in years. Sex with Hazel was better than any protein shake. I ran faster and lifted heavier, and I would be swinging my axe with purpose now. I was a man possessed. After my session in the gym, I wandered out to the area behind Henri's house we used for training.

Next to the shed filled with axes and chainsaws and climbing spikes was a massive pile of fresh logs waiting for me. Donning gloves and picking the heaviest maul, I got to work.

About a dozen logs in, my oldest brother came out of the woods, his dogs, Heathcliff and Rochester, beelining for me.

The two of them worked together to almost take me down, jumping all over me and covering me with slobbering kisses.

"Training or blowing off steam?" Henri asked, tipping his chin toward the maul I'd left stuck in a thick log.

"Training," I replied, wiping the sweat from my brow. "Can't disgrace the family name at nationals."

Lumbering over, he grunted. "Then I suppose I'll join you," he said, picking up another maul from the pile of equipment I'd created just outside the shed. "Alice has been feeding me so well, I could use the workout."

I elbowed him. "Domestic life making you soft?"

He shrugged. "If being happy and exhausted all the time is soft, then yeah, I guess it is."

All I could do was grin. My eldest brother, the family grump, the quiet, serious one who never missed a day of work and never missed an opportunity to take on even more responsibility, had been transformed into a doting family man, and he was loving every minute of it.

"How's Hazel?" he asked between splits, already huffing and puffing.

I split another log, just to show off, and smiled. "She's good."

"Paz was against this quickie marriage, but I think she's good for you."

I relished the compliment. Henri was not the effusive type.

"And I think you're good for her too. But what's gonna happen when she finishes her degree? I don't see you as the big-city, university type."

That stung a bit, but I shook it off and went back to work. I certainly wasn't going to bring up the elephant in the room

—my future at Gagnon Lumber. So I tiptoed around it, settling for the easy truth. "Not sure yet. But I don't care where we go as long as I'm with Hazel."

It was early afternoon before I finished, and when I stepped into the cabin, I found my wife seated on a stool at the kitchen island, typing away, wearing teeny, tiny shorts and one of my T-shirts, which hung off one shoulder, revealing her lack of bra. Christ, I'd just put my body through a grueling workout, but suddenly, I was filled with restless energy.

I bent down and gave her a sweaty kiss.

"I made us lunch," she said, waving to two plates on the counter without looking up from her computer. I flinched but recovered quickly. I still hadn't quite recovered from taco night.

Not quickly enough to go unnoticed by my wife, though. "Just PB and J," she said, getting up to fill water glasses.

"Thanks, babe." Famished, I dropped onto the stool next to her makeshift workstation and took a big bite of the sandwich. From the outside, it looked like any old PB and J. But good Lord, it was somehow grainy *and* a little slimy. I chugged half my water, working to get the bite down and gave her a smile. "Thanks for thinking of me."

She beamed. "No problem." She made her way back to her seat and took a bite of her own sandwich, her smile quickly turning into a grimace. "Fuck," she said, dropping the rest of it onto the plate. "Why does that taste..."

"Oily?" I offered.

She wiped her mouth with a napkin. "And cold and wet and hard and soft at the same time."

"It's okay." I lifted a shoulder, trying to make her feel better while wondering how on earth anyone could screw up the world's most simple sandwich.

"I even used the fancy bread. You know, the multigrain stuff we got at that health food store in Bangor?"

"It was in the freezer. Did you defrost it before you put the sandwiches together?"

She shook her head. "Why? Bread thaws."

I pointed to the crystallization in the middle. "Not fast enough."

She sighed. "And the peanut butter is all oily and nasty. But that one's on you. I wanted Jif, but you insisted on the fancy natural stuff."

"Did you stir it first?"

She raised an eyebrow at me.

"The natural stuff, when you open it, you gotta mix up the oil that collects on the top with the actual peanut butter below it. It separates."

She threw her head back and guffawed. "Yeah, I didn't do that. I just thought it was oily because it's healthy."

I couldn't help but laugh along with her, dumping both sandwiches in the trash and pulling smoothie ingredients from the freezer.

Soon, we were both howling, the sheer insanity of the last twenty-four hours catching up with us.

"I made you a frozen peanut oil sandwich," she said, slapping her thigh. "Wife of the year over here!"

Leaning across the kitchen island, I planted a smacking

kiss on her lips. "I didn't marry you for your cooking abilities."

She covered her face and snorted. "I hope you didn't marry me for my laundry prowess either."

I froze. Had Hazel attempted laundry? I'd been throwing a load in most mornings before she got up to keep her away from the state-of-the-art machines Henri had in the cabin. Looked like my hunch that she'd be just as awful with laundry as she was in the kitchen was right.

"It's fine," I said, preemptively steeling myself for the news she was about to deliver.

"I threw a big load in. Towels, clothes, the works. And I used hot water because I figured it would kill all the germs."

"And..."

"I have no idea what I'm doing, okay? I always dropped my laundry off in the city. It was a pay by the pound kind of thing. The Polish family that lived in the triple decker next door owned the place. I tutored their daughter in math, and they did all my laundry and dry cleaning for free."

"So..."

"So you know those mesh running shorts you're always working out in?"

I nodded, one eye twitching.

"They kind of shrunk." She popped up from her stool and shuffled to the laundry closet. Cringing at me, she opened the door and snagged a pair of black shorts off the top of a pile of haphazardly folded clothes.

They were tiny. Truly tiny. Like the size of a pair of underwear. Like if I hadn't known better, I would have thought they belonged to her.

"On the bright side," she said, holding them out in front

of her and giving me a wink, "they'll really show off those gams!"

I darted over to her and slung her over my shoulder, giving her ass a slap. "Such a bad wife," I growled, though it was mixed with laughter. "I better punish you for being so bad."

She giggled and pinched my ass. "I think I'm going to like my punishment."

I spanked her again, a bit harder this time. "Oh, babe, you are going to love it."

Chapter 28
Hazel

Lydia eyed me suspiciously over our coffee and veggie omelets at the diner. "You're glowing, and I know hydra facials aren't your thing, so it's clearly orgasms. Spill."

My face flamed as I whipped my head from one side to the other, terrified someone had overheard her. The gossip mill in this town was insane.

"What's the problem? You're married. No one with eyes would think you weren't hitting that fine lumbersnack."

"Can you please stop?" I hissed over my mug. "Things are really complicated right now."

Lydia almost snorted out her coffee. "Oh please. Complicated?" She wiped at her chin with a napkin. "Nope. I can see it clear as day on your face. You're in love with him. And taking a ride on his big lumbercock confirmed what I already knew."

I buried my face in my hands. Clearly, I wasn't hiding

anything from her. "It was more than one ride," I said, still not making eye contact.

"Good man." She pumped her fist. "I knew he'd step up. And I'm proud of you. Getting those marital benefits. Joint tax returns aren't the only plus, you know. The twenty-four seven access to excellent cock is part of the deal too."

Looking at my oldest friend right then, I had to fight the overwhelming sensation to shake her. This was so not the time or the place for this conversation. "Stop talking about my husband's cock," I whispered.

She took another sip of coffee and shrugged. "You started it when you walked in here bowlegged and glowing. And now." She leaned in closer, an evil glint in her eyes. "I need details. Length, girth, stamina, tongue dexterity, flexibility, and creativity."

I glared at her while she tilted her head innocently and twirled a lock of her fiery red hair.

Bernice sauntered up with the coffeepot, then, no doubt eavesdropping. Lydia had the good sense to keep her trap shut, and I gave Bernice my most friendly smile while I inquired after her grandkids.

Once she was safely in the kitchen and out of earshot, I huffed at my friend. "First of all, I'm not telling you any of that, and second, I need your help. I'm in over my head here. We had an agreement, and now there's no way any of this will end well."

"You're both sexy humans, and given that you have been lusting after him since middle school, let's face it, this was bound to happen. Do you think it's out of your system? A mediocre bang, and now you can go back to being friends?"

"Nope." I hung my head in shame. "It was amazing."

Like I knew it would be. Remy was intense and masculine, yet tender. He had incredible strength and grace. And his dedication to challenges meant that he, of course, figured me out immediately and discovered things even I didn't know I enjoyed, effectively ruining me for other men.

"Does Dylan know?"

"Of course not! And we're not telling him. We're just having fun. I don't need Dylan's approval to have fun."

"Of course you don't. But Remy is his best friend. And you're..."

"Save it," I said, holding up a hand. "I'm having fun and living in the moment right now. And it's pretty great. The last thing I need is an overprotective brother making everything even more complicated."

"I understand," she said, bringing her coffee cup to her lips. "But for the record, I disagree. Back to the good stuff. How did it happen? Who made the first move?"

"I did." My face burned as a blush overtook my body. "I literally started it. Straddling him in a forest and sticking my tongue down his throat." And I would have done so much more had we not been interrupted by a moose with a grudge. It wasn't my finest moment. I was usually less... desperate. But he was sweaty and shirtless and had been carrying me around like a caveman for an hour. We had been skin to skin, working together as a team, and my hormones had gotten the better of me.

And once I kissed him? Forget it. There was no way we could share a kiss like that and then not explore what was growing between us. It was inevitable. We were inevitable.

My face went hot again just thinking about our first night together. I picked at my omelet and debated whether to give Lydia, who was studying me with curiosity, any of the details.

"So, there's one thing," I said, angling closer. "He is very possessive. It's hard to describe. The way he made me feel, it was thrilling."

Her mouth fell open and her eyes widened, but for once in her life, she was silent.

"I've never had anyone want me like that." His jealousy and frustration, while objectively annoying and cavemanish, made me feel cherished and desired. It was strange to say out loud, but I liked him like that. Desperate and possessive and obsessed.

"I'm gonna need more, Hazel." Lydia held her hand palm up and curled her fingers in a *gimme* motion.

"No one's ever wanted me in that way. All of me, the good parts and the bad. And the fire in his eyes, the intensity of his touch, wasn't what I expected at all. It was animalistic. Like he didn't just want me. He needed me. Like it was painful to not touch me. To not be inside me."

Lydia scooped up her napkin and fanned herself, still wide-eyed.

"Not in day-to-day life," I clarified. "He's so sweet and supportive and he lets me do my thing. But once we get physical, he changes. He's all bossy and intense, telling me I belong to him."

With that, she balled up her napkin and chucked it at me. "You lucky bitch. Fuck. He's a damn book boyfriend come to life."

"I don't even know what that means."

"Do you have Kindle Unlimited? I'll text you some recs."

I shook my head. It was like the words she was speaking

were in a foreign language. "Focus, Lyd. Is it wrong? You know... that I like it so much?"

She pinched the bridge of her nose, giving me a long, disappointed look. "Hazel, sweetheart. You have hit the fucking man jackpot. Listen to me. Do *not* question this. Do *not* overanalyze this. You are going to fuck your husband and enjoy the shit out of it for as long as you can, because men like Remy Gagnon do not exist in real life."

She stood and dug a few dollars out of her pocket and tossed them on the table.

"And now," she straightened her skirt, "I've got to get to school so I can shape young minds. But you, my friend, are going to finish breakfast and thank every god and deity for your good fortune. And then you are going to beg them to have mercy on your best friend, who can't find a decent man within a one hundred–mile radius. Are we clear?"

I stood and gave her a hug. "We're clear."

After finishing my breakfast and chatting with half the town about the weather, the state of my research, and Remy's training regimen for nationals, I headed to the Gagnon Lumber headquarters. I'd been inside the building a handful of times in my life, but today I had work to do.

After diving into the files Henri had shared with me, I had found some helpful bits and gotten sidetracked by the history of the Golden Road, which was the main logging road that stretched from Northern Maine to Canada. It had been built through a private partnership of logging families to open up the northernmost forests and provide timber and jobs for the region, replacing a network of roads and trails and streams that had been used for hundreds of years prior.

Henri had invited me to chat with employees and check records, and I wasn't going to pass it up. I was veering off track, satisfying my fascination with the logging roads and drug trafficking, but I couldn't stop myself. The records I'd scoured hinted to so much more, and I intended to figure out all the secrets hidden along the Golden Road.

My work analyzing the data from state programs to treat and prevent opioid abuse was chugging along, especially since Henri had connected me with a clerk at the state police, who had helped me with an official records request. But the secrets of the lumber business, and the ugly underbelly of these lonely roads, kept pulling me in.

Remy was in a meeting with his brothers, so I chatted with several members of the administrative team and the late Mr. Gagnon's secretary, who helped me scan a slew of documents we had unearthed from an old filing cabinet.

I pored over old logging maps, obsession tightening its grip on me. There were several antique ones framed around the office, and others I found in various old files. They revealed a network of old roads and trails and camps that followed the rivers through the vast wilderness. A way of life completely abandoned once technology changed the industry.

Needing a break from the documents I'd been compiling, I wandered out to the machine shop. It was bigger than the office building, with a massive parking lot filled with parts, scrap, and dozens of intimidating-looking machines.

I found Adele inside the shop under the hood of something massive. Music that I could only identify as heavy metal was blaring, and when my shadow fell over her, she popped her head up quickly, then ducked back down and continued working, ignoring me for several long minutes while I stood near a worktable and waited.

"Hazel," she said coolly. Adele was intimidating. Both in stature and attitude. She had been cultivating an air of *don't fuck with me* since grade school. She wore dark blue coveralls tied at the waist and a black tank top, which showed off her impressive shoulder muscles. She was tall, probably almost six feet, and her long dirty blond hair was pulled back in a ponytail.

Her cheekbones were high and her eyes were big and round and her mouth was set in a hard line.

"Here to talk about my brother?" she asked, taking a sip from a stainless-steel water bottle and wiping her hands on a rag. "I agree. You can do better."

I respected her attempt at diversion. Henri had asked her to answer some of my questions about the truck and machinery and how things worked, but he'd warned me that she may not be receptive.

"I'd rather not talk about my marriage," I said primly, clasping my hands in front of me and instantly regretting it.

She stood to her full height and sauntered closer, glaring at me. "Fun. And I'd rather not relive the trauma of my father's death and my brother's accident, but here we are."

I closed my eyes, searching for the right words. Usually, I was skilled at interviewing subjects, but unsurprisingly, my experience was failing me with Adele. I had known her since we were kids, and in all that time, she'd been known to take exactly zero shit. Growing up, I had stayed far away. She had always been one of the boys—

playing sports, climbing trees, and beating everyone along the way.

And She was smart. Everyone knew that. Most of all, her. And while Remy had cautioned me, there were just too many questions. I couldn't stop the curiosity that simmered inside me.

"Why are you even here?" she asked, opening up her laptop and typing. "Shouldn't you be making excel spreadsheets or something?"

Her tone said it all. She did real work, and I was nothing more than a desk jockey. Not an uncommon attitude up here, where so many worked with their hands, so I was ready for her.

"I'm conducting research about the opioid crisis. Specifically its impact in rural communities here in Maine. How the drugs get in, how social factors make certain populations more susceptible, and how local and state governments and NGOs can help."

She didn't bother looking up from her computer, so I went on, though I wasn't sure she was even listening.

"What is actually efficacious and what is a waste of time and resources. But the big question is always how are they getting here? So I wanted to ask you a few questions about the trucks and the roads."

"You're not a cop," she interrupted.

"I am not."

"So why do you care?"

I took her sneer and raised her a smug smile. "Hmm." I crossed my arms and stepped closer. "Maybe because I've devoted my professional life to this? Or maybe because I lost my mom to addiction. Dylan and I lost her long before she lost her life. This is personal for me."

At that admission, she looked up, and her face softened faintly. It wasn't often I talked about my mom, but she needed to understand that I wouldn't let her shitty attitude stop me from getting the information I came here for.

"So no, I'm not a cop, and I'm not a mechanic, or a lumberjack, I have one skill set. I understand data. I collect and synthesize huge volumes of information. So you do your job and let me do mine."

She straightened, scanning me from head to toe, squinting as if she were debating with herself. "I really don't want to talk."

"Do you have something to hide?" I asked gently.

She scowled. "Of course not."

"Good," I said, pulling my notebook out of my bag. "Then answer my questions."

She tapped her chin and cocked a wicked brow. "Fine. But first, tell me why you married my brother."

She thought she could get under my skin, rattle me. But she was seriously underestimating me. "Easy," I said, giving her a toothy grin. "Because I'm madly in love with him. Now can I do my job, please?"

She laughed. "Come on, Hazel."

And that was it. I could take her insulting me or my research or *anything* else. But I had reached my limit.

I slammed my notebook down on the table next to her laptop and pointed a finger at her face. "You know something? I am so sick and fucking tired of all of you piling on Remy. I get that he's the youngest, but you're all grown-ass adults." I was several inches shorter than her, but I pulled myself up to my full height and sucked in a breath. "Why do you treat him like a poorly behaved puppy? All he wants is your love and approval and to be treated as an equal. Instead, you condescend to him and insult him and undermine him every chance you get."

She took a step back, clearly shocked by my outburst. But she deserved it, and I wouldn't back down. All these years, I'd envied the Gagnons, the happy, loving family with the two parents and the big, noisy house. But the more I got to know them and their sibling dysfunction, the more I appreciated Dylan and our sad little trailer. Because we did not treat each other like this.

Her eyes narrowed. "Oh, you want to defend him? Great. Where were you last year? Huh? When he crashed a truck and caused tens of thousands of dollars in damages and lost productivity? All money we don't have, by the way. When Henri had to drop everything and run up to camp to deal with his drunk, depressed ass? Henri, Paz, and I are working without pay, around the clock, to save this business and my father's legacy. And all Remy has done for the last six months is climb trees and pout."

"Stop it," I shouted, still glaring at her. "He's apologized. He's tried to make amends. But you and Paz won't forgive him. Grow the fuck up and get past your childish shit. If you're angry with him, use goddamn words and work it out or get the fuck over it."

Finally, I blew out a steadying breath, though I was still shaking with anger and more than a little fear. Most people did not scream in Adele Gagnon's face and live to tell about it.

She ran her hands through her hair. "Shit," she said, dropping her gaze to her feet.

"Yeah, shit," I agreed.

She looked at me, narrowing her eyes. And then she took a deep breath. "I approve."

"Huh. Too bad, because I don't want your approval." Who did this woman think she was?

"Good. I assumed you wouldn't. But I'm giving it anyway. I'm glad my brother has someone who is willing to fight for him. But I'm allowed to be angry about his choices, and I'll work through it when I'm ready."

I was floored. Was I having a genuine moment of connection with my sister-in-law?

"I'll answer your questions now," she said, grabbing some tools I couldn't name.

I picked up my notebook and pen, and, brushing a strand of hair away from my face, I gave her a professional smile. "Excellent."

Adele explained the types of trucks they used, the road conditions, and a long list of challenges that came with navigating hundreds of thousands of pounds of lumber. She showed me photos and drew diagrams, walking me through the transportation process.

She even made me a cup of tea while we talked. She was clearly passionate about what she did and loved talking about it. It was strange, bonding over heavy machinery, but I was enjoying it.

I was flipping through photos on her phone of the disc brakes that had been tampered with while she attempted to explain them to me when a call came through.

When *Stretch* flashed across the top of the screen, she

ripped the device out of my hand and stabbed at the Decline icon before shoving it back into her pocket.

"Do you need to get that?" I asked, secretly desperate to know who the hell Stretch was.

"Fuck off," she replied. Abruptly ending our bonding session.

Chapter 29
Remy

I pulled into the driveway, my limbs heavy and my chest tight. During our morning meeting, instead of answering my questions or listening to my ideas, Paz had yelled at me, humiliating me in front of the administrative staff, and then he'd stomped out of the office.

Normally, this kind of thing would stick with me for days or even weeks. Letting people down, especially my family, gutted me. But it was a lot easier to let his insults roll off my back with Hazel's encouraging words floating around in my head.

Given how distracted I had been recently, I made sure to hit the gym in town before coming home, because if not, it was likely the only workout I'd get would be the naked one I'd been looking forward to all day.

In the past two weeks, my life had transformed. I woke up every day grateful and ready to deal with whatever shit the world was slinging. Work, training, all of it was easier because of Hazel.

And having a front-row seat to her curiosity, her ambition, and her determination every day inspired me. There was a whole world beyond Gagnon Lumber. Beyond these woods and the tradition carved out by my family.

It had taken me almost thirty years, but I'd finally realized that I was capable of more. I was setting goals and working hard to achieve them. And more and more, I was coming to the conclusion that working in the family business was not my dream.

I hopped out of the truck, grabbed my gym bag from the back, and jogged for the door, ready to see my girl. Inside, nothing was burning, so I paused for a moment to send up a silent thanks that Hazel had not attempted to cook dinner again.

The cabin was dark except for the glow of a dozen or so candles. I toed off my boots, catching the soft strains of music floating through the air.

"Hazel?" I called, assuming she was finishing up her research for the day.

Then she appeared, sauntering out of our bedroom wearing nothing but my blue flannel Racine shirt and a tiny pair of panties. The shirt was unbuttoned, exposing her creamy skin and making my mouth water.

I dropped my gym bag to the hardwood as every ounce of blood in my body rushed south.

"Holy shit." I groaned as she prowled toward me.

"Hard day?" she asked, tipping her head.

"I-I can't remember," I stammered. "I think my brain is malfunctioning. I just dreamed that I walked into my house and found my sexy wife naked and waiting for me."

She pulled her bottom lip between her teeth and

watched me from under her lashes. "I've been lonely."

I stalked over to her, picked her up so she could wrap her legs around my waist, and kissed her.

"Your man is home," I said, then dove in again, reveling in the taste of her mouth and the feel of her body wrapped around me.

She clutched my face, kissing me back with abandon. We clawed at each other, wild after being separated all day. She was intoxicating, making all my insecurities melt away and my inner animal take over.

I placed her on the kitchen island so I could pull my shirt over my head and shuck my jeans.

"I need you," she panted, chest heaving, the flannel shirt slipping down her shoulder as she dropped back on her forearms, arching her back as I laved and nipped at her nipples.

"Already?" I slid her panties down her legs and spread them wide, stepping between them.

She bit her lip, nodding.

"Too bad. Because I need to eat this delicious pussy first."

I pushed her back onto her elbows, drinking in the sight of her naked body laid out for me, my shirt slipping off one of her shoulders. Spreading her thighs with my hands, I took one long, leisurely lick up her seam, tasting her wetness and loving the feel of her squirming beneath me.

With my tongue, I circled her clit, savoring her moans as I picked up the pace and buried my face in her heat. Hands in my hair, she raked her nails over my scalp and gripped the strands, driving me wild. I responded by pushing two fingers inside her and sucking her clit into my mouth, feeling her clench around me.

"Yes. Remy. More." She moaned, tugging my hair harder. Obediently, I curled my fingers inside her, preparing to make her detonate. I worked my hands and tongue harder, faster, and steadier, feeling her body tighten as she barreled for the finish line.

She went wild, riding my face and pulling my hair so fucking deliciously I could barely contain myself. I wanted nothing more than to thrust inside her, but I had a job to do first, one I took very seriously. And seconds later, my efforts were rewarded with my favorite sight in the world. Hazel coming undone. She threw her head back and screamed my name at the ceiling as she came, clenching and spasming and shaking. Heart pounding, I reveled in the power of making her scream. Of giving her this pleasure. Determined husband that I was, I kept up my work, licking and sucking until she pushed me away and slumped onto the countertop.

"Holy shit," she breathed, her chest heaving.

Slanting over her, I kissed her hard, then offered her my fingers. She licked them clean and sucked each one into her mouth, making me harden painfully.

She snaked a hand down and circled my aching cock, and I wasted no time lining myself up and slamming into her, grabbing her hips to keep myself steady.

Pulling one of her perfect pink nipples into my mouth, I bit down, just like she liked. Her responding gasp amped up my need even more.

"This is what you wanted, isn't it?" I murmured, my thrusts steady. "Putting on my shirt like that."

"Yes. I thought about you all day. I wanted you to come home and fuck me."

I kissed her. It was sloppy and hungry and so fucking

right. The feel of her clenched around me was already making my vision blur, but I didn't care. I just wanted to get lost in Hazel.

Straightening, I watched where we were joined. "Look at that," I said, "look at how I stretch you. Look at how well you take every single inch of me."

"It feels so good," she gasped. "I'm close." Sitting up, she gripped my shoulders, her body going impossibly tight around me.

I slammed into her again for good measure, then swept my hand up her chest, pausing at her collarbone before palming her throat. She was so tiny, my hand covered her neck.

"Is this okay?" I asked.

"Yes." She moaned, throwing her head back and meeting me thrust for thrust. I could feel it, the clench. She needed me as badly as I needed her. I was so close, but I wasn't done yet.

"Look at me," I growled, my hand still loosely gripping her neck. "Look at your husband while you take my cock."

The second her eyes met mine, she clamped down on me, spiraling into oblivion and dragging me along with her.

As we came back down, I rested my head on her shoulder, struggling to calm my racing heart. Fucking Hazel was better than hill sprints.

"Remy," she said, scratching my scalp. "I..."

"I know," I murmured, picking her up and carrying her to the couch. I dropped to the cushion, holding her in my lap, and threw a blanket around us.

She curled against me, sweaty and panting. I felt like a king. Nothing would top this feeling.

"How was your day?"

"It was kind of shitty. But then I came home and my smoking-hot, practically naked wife greeted me. So it pretty quickly turned into one of the best days of my life."

She giggled. "It was pretty good for me too. You know," she nudged me, "you're pretty bossy."

I shifted her until she was facing me, taking a moment to appreciate just how beautiful she looked with messy hair and an orgasmic glow. "Listen." I kissed her collarbone. "I'm happy to take a back seat most of the time. Sit back and let you shine. I'm lucky just to exist in the same timeline as you, never mind marry you."

Another kiss, this one a little lower, smiling against her skin when her nipples hardened against my chest. "But you need to know one thing." I straightened. "When your clothes are off, I'm the boss."

Smiling, she nodded, clearly enjoying this side of me. "I'm the boss of this sweet pussy," I said, dropping down again and taking one nipple into my mouth.

"Yes you are." She whimpered.

"And these delicious tits."

"Mm-hmm." She moaned.

"Are you okay with that? Being mine?" If I was the kind of guy who overanalyzed things, I probably would have determined that my possessiveness was a result of being cheated on. But that obvious answer didn't tell the fully story. I wanted Hazel. I needed Hazel. More than I had ever needed anyone in my life.

She threw her arms around my neck and kissed me. "Yes," she breathed against my lips. "I'm all yours. Only yours."

Chapter 30
Remy

Sunday dinner at the Gagnon house was never a quiet, tranquil affair. Nope, it wouldn't be a Gagnon gathering unless there was a full tackle football game going, endless hugs, a handful of arguments, and the requisite shame session from our mother for not eating enough.

It was a warm, breezy summer afternoon. Mom was busy in the kitchen with Alice, chatting about school, where she worked with Alice, who was the principal.

Mom still wouldn't accept pay, a major point of contention with both Alice and Henri. But what they failed to understand was that before she'd taken the position, she had barely been able to get out of bed most days.

Going to school every day, where she stayed busy and built relationships with the kids and teachers and the parents, had brought her back to life. She was looking more and more like the woman who'd raised us. Chatty and always in motion. Baking banana bread, volunteering, working, bossing us around and butting into our lives.

Under the table, I squeezed Hazel's hand. She had survived hundreds of these dinners over the years, always smiling politely when my mom tried to force feed her or interrogate her about her life. She was comfortable here. She'd been a Gagnon since long before we tied the knot.

"Remy, sweetheart," Mom said, standing beside the table, holding a platter. "You didn't like the meatloaf?"

"Mom, I love your meatloaf."

She gave me a forced smile. "But you barely ate any."

"I had two helpings," I said, leaning back in my chair and patting my stomach. "I'm training. I can't gorge on your cooking until after nationals."

She put another piece on Paz's plate. "Hmm. I guess I can forgive you, then." She rounded the table and squeezed my cheek. "My baby boy. A professional athlete. So exciting."

Paz snorted and Adele coughed a "mama's boy" under her breath. Then all three of my siblings burst into laughter.

Turning in Adele's direction, my mom pinned her with a look.

"We know he's your favorite, Mom."

Mom's face paled. "Adele Celine Gagnon, how dare you insinuate that I have a favorite child? I love you all equally. You all have special places in my heart."

"Sorry, Mom." My sister hung her head, not because she was genuinely sorry or scared by the mom look she'd been on the receiving end of. More likely, she was just eager for a topic change.

"You bet you are. And eat the brussels sprouts. They're homegrown. Green food won't kill you."

Tucker and Goldie erupted into hysterical laughter. No one spoke like that to Adele and lived, except my mom.

Adele rolled her eyes like a teenager and speared one brussels sprout, inspecting it for several seconds before taking a bite and frowning. The kids laughed even harder.

"Why don't you kids show Auntie Adele how it's done?" Alice said, grinning at her kids, who had also avoided eating their vegetables.

They grumbled simultaneously, then Tucker shoved one into his mouth dramatically. Henri followed suit, followed by Hazel.

Pretty soon, the entire family was racing to eat the Brussels sprouts, grabbing the bowl and asking for more. My mother sat at the head of the table, laughing and grinning from ear to ear.

"That's better," she said. "Now, who's ready for pie and ice cream?"

After dinner, we cleared the table and cleaned while my mom, Hazel, and Alice sipped iced tea in the sunroom. The sun was starting to set, and I was anxious to take my wife home and enjoy this glorious summer night. Things had changed so much between us, and our connection was even stronger than I could have ever imagined.

I caught her eye as I slung a dish towel over my shoulder, and she bit her lip. I had to turn away before I got hard in my mom's kitchen.

Beside me, Henri nodded and his jaw ticked, the action silently telling us to follow him to the porch. We gathered, the mood turning somber, even with Goldie and Tucker and the dogs running and shouting happily nearby.

"Any updates?" I asked, looking at Henri's serious face.

He shook his head. "The occupational safety inspector declined to take another look, even after Adele showed him the slack adjuster."

"Fuck."

"And the police haven't done much either."

"I think we should hire a private investigator." Paz scratched at his chin.

"This isn't a movie, Paz, this is real life."

"The safety board, the state police, none of them have come up with anything new. Adele can literally prove Dad's death wasn't an accident, but we're still missing so many pieces."

Paz propped himself against the doorframe, crossing his arms. "We need to hire a private investigator," he said again. "We can't just fuck around forever."

Maybe he was right. I knew nothing about investigators, how to find one, or how much they cost, but in theory, it was probably a good move. "This is bigger than just Dad," I added, looking at Henri.

The signs of tampering Adele had found on the brakes of Dad's truck matched what she'd found on Henri's. Last fall, he lost control and jumped out of the cab, injuring himself seriously but surviving. My dad had not been so lucky.

"We don't know who we can trust. We need someone discreet and who knows how to follow money and leads. Someone who won't draw suspicion," Paz continued. "We can sit around and hope no one else gets killed. We can ignore the fact that our business and our heritage are at risk due to narcotics trafficking. Or we can take shit into our own hands."

As much as Paz and I had been butting heads lately, I agreed with his approach.

Adele dropped to the porch swing, her head in her hands. No one had taken this harder than her. She blamed herself and, against Henri's wishes, had inspected what was left of the truck Dad had been driving for possible clues. She was the one who discovered it hadn't been an accident. And she was struggling to process all the implications.

Over the past few months, she had become a ghost. She was never around and did her best to avoid all of us at work. She was dating someone, but we'd never met the guy. She hadn't even told us his name.

"We need closure," she said softly.

We turned to her in unison. Normally, Adele barked orders, lecturing us on why she was right and we were wrong and throwing a few punches if necessary.

"But how do we find someone? How do we keep this a secret?" Henri asked, removing his hat and running his hands through his hair. "I don't even know how this all works."

"I'll take care of it," Paz said. "We just need to gather all the information we have and hope it can all be sorted out."

"Hazel can help," I added. "She's been studying Dad's notes and the old maps."

Paz scowled at the suggestion, but I ignored him. "You should see her office." I popped my head inside, where it looked like my mother and Alice were interrogating her about our wedding. "Can I steal my beautiful wife for a moment?" I asked, giving them my patented Remy smile.

Hazel jumped up, a look of relief crossing her face.

"Was she trying to convince you to get pregnant?" I whispered when she approached. "No. She was trying to convince me to have another wedding. A big one with a church and party and all that shit."

"Ignore her," I said, letting my hand graze her ass. "We've got more important things to discuss."

I caught her up on our discussion, and she took a seat next to Adele on the porch swing.

"Were you able to look at those files I gave you?" Henri asked in a tone far more polite than usual.

She nodded. "I've been combing through them. My plan was to create pivot tables of narcotics arrests in this county to assess the efficacy of diversion and needle exchange programs. But—"

"But?" Paz interrupted.

"But I've been distracted. I don't want to get your hopes up, but I get the sense your dad was doing something off the books. He was reviewing all the old stuff too, leaving notes and memories and a bunch of breadcrumbs."

"Leading to what?"

"Not sure yet. But my suspicion is that he knew more about the drug trafficking than he may have let on."

Paz stood, his fists clenched. "Don't fucking insinuate he had something to do with it."

I pushed myself in front of him, ready to go toe to toe for the tone he was taking with my wife.

"Relax, Remy," Hazel said. "I've got this."

I retreated, looking to her for reassurance. No matter how angry Paz got, Hazel remained serene and focused. It was unnerving and really fucking sexy.

She pinned Paz with a withering look, making Adele snort behind her. "I'm doing no such thing. If you had listened instead of jumping to insane, paranoid conclusions, I was going to tell you that I think he had suspicions, but he was trying to keep things on the down low."

"From us?"

"From everyone. Maybe he thought someone at Gagnon Lumber was compromised or leaking information. Or maybe he hadn't confirmed anything and wanted to be sure first. But the maps are just a small portion of what he collected, and I'm working on trying to understand it all."

"You think someone betrayed Dad?" Adele asked.

"We should talk to Richard. See if he suspected anything," Henri added. He was probably right. Richard was an asshole, but he and Dad had been lifelong friends and worked together for decades. If anything had been happening under the radar, he'd probably know.

"This." Paz slammed his hand on the door frame. "This is why we need a PI. Someone to dig and let us keep our hands clean. We can't go around accusing and interrogating people."

Adele stood, her face red and her shoulders squared. "We can. I'll start a list. We won't stop until we get answers."

"Adele." Henri sighed. "You can't torture confessions out of our employees. It's bad for business and it won't stand up in court."

"I don't give a fuck about court."

Hazel stepped close to Adele, putting a hand on her forearm. They were physical opposites, but both women were fierce in their own ways. "Give me some more time. There is a lot more to look into. And I think I need to go up to camp, see how things work, how everything is laid out. Maybe talk to some folks. I can ask questions that the rest of you can't in the name of research."

My brothers nodded, but Adele still looked dubious. "Take her to camp," Henri said, his hands on his hips. "Give her whatever she needs." He turned to Paz. "And you work on finding someone to investigate. We'll find out what happened to Dad. And we'll make sure whoever is responsible gets justice."

Chapter 31
Hazel

"We should get out of bed," Remy rasped, burying his face in my hair.

"Oh yes," I added, snuggling against his bare chest, eyes closed. "Definitely. We should go be productive."

We lay like that for a long moment, soaking in the feel of one another's warm skin. Finally forcing my eyes open, I peeked up at him, taking in his scruffy beard and wild hair. He was so absurdly sexy. How on earth had I resisted him for so long? Being in his proximity had me fighting the urge to switch the topic of my dissertation and instead focus on the science behind how even the most superhumanly self-controlled woman is no match for the raw masculine appeal of Remy Gagnon.

He pulled me to his chest again and kissed me, morning breath be damned. "Shit, you are gorgeous." His hoarse morning voice sent bolts of desire arcing through me. "Like Snow White with glasses and a genius IQ."

With that, I pushed him away. "Ugh. That's my problem. Cute and sweet and harmless." I crossed my arms over my naked chest. Story of my life. Always the character who's seen as weak, who needs to be saved. Never the one doing the saving.

"You, my sweet wife, are completely missing the point. Snow White is *hot*. Smoking hot." He sat up and pulled me on top of him, his desire poking my thigh. "That little dress. Sexy as fuck. And the headband?" He threw his head back. "Unreal."

My husband was ridiculous, but the way he palmed my breast, brushing back and forth across the nipple, had desire pooling in my core, despite our discussion about a 1930s Disney princess.

"You're beautiful and playful and so fucking sexy," he whispered, nipping at my earlobe. "So beautiful. Like birds and forest creatures help you get ready in the morning."

I giggled. "I'm sure as shit not doing laundry for a bunch of creepy men who live in the woods."

"I'm a creepy man who lives in the woods," he quipped, kissing my neck.

"But I don't do your laundry anymore."

"Thank God. I'd have no clothes left. We both know your talents are not in the domestic arts, wife."

"I have many skills," I argued, relishing the feel of his lips on my skin as he worked his way down my chest.

"Mm-hmm," he agreed, gently biting my nipple and tugging.

I moaned, getting more and more worked up by the minute. "Data analysis."

"And building statistical models."

"And blow jobs."

He pulled back and raised one eyebrow. "Is that right?" He rubbed his chin. "I may require a demonstration of your skills."

I pushed at his shoulders until he was resting against the pillows, then shimmied my way down his body and settled between his legs. His erection strained as I ghosted my lips over the tip. "I'd be happy to oblige."

<hr>

My life had changed in so many ways over the last several weeks. Living with Remy and sleeping with Remy. And not the platonic, opposite sides of the bed sleepovers we'd had before. Naked snuggles and orgasms and late-night snacks and waking up every morning to his handsome face smiling at me.

It was intoxicating. Remy had been part of my life for twenty-eight years, and I'd thought I knew everything about him. But he continued to surprise and delight me.

And I'd never seen him this focused. He trained nonstop, working with Henri late at night and getting up early to run before work. I had even learned to cook. Well, sort of. I had perfected his favorite post-workout protein shake, and it made me feel like Goddamn June Cleaver to hand it to him after his run every morning.

Especially when he gulped it down, slapped my ass, and insisted I join him in the shower after.

I was beginning to see what all the fuss over marriage was about. Over the years, I had dated a few guys I was attracted to but didn't actually like very much. And other times, I'd had relationships with guys I adored and admired, but had zero chemistry with. With Remy, I had the best of both worlds. Friendship and emotional support. Not to mention red-hot sex. The kind of thing I never knew existed in real life.

But it was becoming increasingly difficult to remember that what we had was only temporary. That eventually, we had to move on. And as sobering as that fact was, I couldn't avoid it. I couldn't hole up in this love shack in the woods of Lovewell with him forever. We each had our own lives and goals and things to do.

Remy had selflessly given me my health back. For that, I would owe him forever. I cared about him too much to drag this out and hurt us both. He deserved everything he wanted in life and more. And although it might hurt me, I would cheer him on every step of the way.

So I forced myself to think only of the present. Lovewell, research, Remy, and helping the Gagnons.

Next week, we'd head up to camp. Henri had a list of things he needed Remy to take care of up there—it would make our presence more plausible since he hadn't been there in months—and I'd have two days to poke around, ask questions, and get the lay of the land. I wasn't sure what I would find, or if there was anything to find, but we still had so many questions. What was Mr. Gagnon working on? And did it have anything to do with his death? The family was still grieving. Every day without answers only compounded the pain they felt. I wasn't a cop or an investigator, but I would do what I could to help.

. . .

"Are you sure you're okay with this?" I asked. He had never given me his side of the story. Granted, I'd heard recitations from everyone else in town, but I wanted him to trust me with all his secrets, even the messy ones.

He was cutting up a rotisserie chicken we had purchased at the grocery store. Protein shakes were still the extent of the cooking skills either of us possessed, but he was getting good at preparing precooked food.

I watched as he sliced the chicken and laid it on the salad mix. Compared to me, he was Jamie Oliver, only hotter. After arranging everything just right and adding a handful of cherry tomatoes, my newly discovered favorite food, he carried the plates to the table, ignoring my question.

We sat across from one another and chewed silently. Letting the question hang in the air.

After a few minutes, he put his fork down and cleared his throat. "I'm not, really. But I've got to be. I haven't been up north since last fall. And I gotta face what happened."

"Can you tell me about it?" I asked gently.

"Over the past few years, I drank a lot. Way more than usual. Crystal and I were on, and then we were off. We were engaged one day, and the next, she was throwing things at me. I wasn't progressing as an athlete, and I felt useless at work."

I nodded, hoping to encourage him.

"My dad had sent me up to camp a few years earlier, to learn the ropes from Richard, who is the foreman up there. With Henri in line to take over for my dad and Adele running the machine shop, it was the natural place to put me. I love the woods and I've got all my heavy machinery licenses. I grew up out there and had a good rapport with the crew.

"But Richard hates me. Always called me stupid and undermined me. I was miserable. And after Dad died, I just stagnated. My relationship was a mess, my career was going nowhere, and I felt so trapped. So I was drinking and not training and fighting with Crystal a lot. But then she confronted me. Told me she was leaving me. Threw the ring I had spent a year saving for at me and called me a loser. Said she had been seeing other guys behind my back."

"Oh my God," I said. "Sorry. I shouldn't have interrupted."

He gave me a weak smile. "It's okay. We had this ugly fight, and she kicked me out of the house. And I left, even though I was the one paying the rent.

"I left a bunch of stuff at my mom's and headed up to camp. It was the start of the season, and I was scheduled to be out there for a week, getting a new crew trained and operational. But I couldn't do it. Instead, I holed up in my room and got really stinking drunk. For a few days straight. Then I decided to take one of the trucks out and crashed it, totaling the truck and destroying a cold deck."

"What's that?"

"A cold deck is a carefully arranged pile of cut trees that are waiting for transport to the mill. Each one contains thousands of dollars in lumber."

"Oh no."

"Yeah. And sending heavy trees in all directions is incredibly dangerous. So not only did I cost the company tons of money, but I could have killed someone. Including myself."

He ran his hands through his hair. "Everything felt so out of control, and I missed my dad and felt so stuck and miserable. The thought of going up there and facing the guys who have seen me at my worst makes me want to throw up."

"We don't have to go," I said, placing my hand on his forearm. "It's fine."

"No." He pinned me with a sharp glare. "I've spent months trying to make amends to my family, trying to make things right. And maybe we can figure out what happened to Dad while we're up there. Or Henri. Anything really. This is an opportunity to help, to contribute. They haven't forgiven me."

"Maybe you need to forgive yourself."

"That's impossible." His dark eyes swam with vulnerability. "I'm so ashamed. There is no excuse for how I acted. I put people in danger and our family business at risk with my selfishness and stupidity."

He folded and unfolded his napkin, pushing down hard on the creases. "And Henri's accident. He wouldn't have been behind the wheel of that truck if it hadn't been for—"

"He's fine," I interrupted.

"By pure fucking luck. Very few people have ever jumped out of a moving truck carrying a hundred thousand pounds of timber and lived. He could have died, and it would have been my fault."

"But he didn't die."

"That's not the point. I haven't shown my face up there since. I'm a disgrace to my family and the code we follow in the woods. Everyone knows it. Henri and Paz and Adele. They bust their asses every day for the company, the family, and my dad. And I don't measure up."

He violently speared a cucumber and put it in his mouth, the tines of his fork scraping against his teeth.

"Are you done?" I asked softly.

He shrugged, staring at his plate.

"At some point, you have to forgive yourself and accept who you are and who you are not. You're not Henri. And you're not Paz. Or Adele."

He snorted.

"You don't have to be anyone but yourself. Stop trying to live up to other people's standards. Set some of your own."

"I'm not even sure how to do that."

"You've spent almost thirty years trying to be like them. Trying to be someone that maybe you weren't meant to be."

"I'm a Gagnon. We cut down trees."

"You are so much more than that, and you know it. I'm your goddamn wife. Listen to me when I say you can do anything and be anything you want. You have so much raw talent and potential. You can sit here and beat yourself up, or you can learn from your mistakes and do better."

He reached across the table and grabbed my hand. "You make me want to do better."

My heart swelled, and that tiny part of my brain that believed in fairy tales and happily ever afters ran wild. Clenching my jaw, I locked down those thoughts and mentally chided myself. We'd agreed no future talk. Not even when he was vulnerable and sharing his feelings, which was hotter than watching him do thousands of shirtless push-ups.

Because every day, that part of my brain grew, getting bigger and wilder and more imaginative. I was beginning to want things I couldn't have. A future that wasn't mine. I owed it to us both to keep myself in check.

"That's why I'm here," I said, affecting calm in hopes that my outward demeanor could reflect on my wild emotions. "Because we're a team. I'll keep pushing you and you keep pushing me. And together, we'll figure our shit out."

Chapter 32
Remy

"Mom," I called, walking through the front door. Hazel trailed behind me with a bouquet of flowers she had insisted we pick up on the way. My mother had invited us over for dinner, and while we both knew better than to bring food to Loraine Gagnon's house, Hazel didn't want to show up empty-handed. So I had indulged my sweet wife, even though Mama G required no formality.

The house was mostly dark and eerily quiet. For as long as I could remember, it had been filled with music, either from my grandma's piano in the front room or the Bluetooth speaker in the kitchen that blasted Mom's seventies disco.

My childhood home was large and chaotic and filled with love. After Dad died, we'd all urged Mom to sell and move, but she refused. The house was too big, and the yard, which was a couple of acres and backed up to the river, was a lot to maintain. But she'd raised her family here and refused to leave behind the decades of memories written on every inch of the place. Instead, she'd gone on massive redecorating and decluttering binges and was constantly texting us photos of her meticulously organized closets.

"Mom," I called again, passing through the kitchen.

The flood lights at the back of the house were on, so I grabbed Hazel's hand and tugged her along with me onto the back deck.

"Surprise!" came a cacophony of voices, then the deck was lit up like Christmas. I had to shield my eyes against the glare as I adjusted to the shock. It took me a minute, but then I pulled Hazel close and scanned the yard. It was filled with string lights, picnic tables, and balloons. And a *Just Married* banner hung across the back of the house.

My mother rushed up to us, a plastic flute of champagne in her hand. "Happy wedding party," she cried, giving us both kisses on the cheeks.

"What is this?" Hazel asked, her eyes still wide behind her glasses.

"Since you guys had that quickie wedding at city hall, we decided it was time to throw you a little party."

"And this being Lovewell," Lydia appeared, wearing several sets of Mardi Gras beads that said *Just Married* on them, "everyone wanted in. So we crowd sourced it."

She held an arm out, her palm open, to the yard, where a makeshift dance floor had been set up and the Timber Trio, Lovewell's local band, was setting up, plugging their equipment into a generator Henri was tinkering with.

There were tables heaped with food, and most of the town was here, mingling and cheering as we made our way through the crowd.

"Mom," I chided, turning back to her. "I told you we didn't want to do anything."

She patted my cheek. "That's nice. But you're my son and Hazel is my daughter-in-law, and there's no way I was going to let you get away without celebrating."

Lydia nodded, looping her arm through my mom's. "It's not worth fighting us, especially when we've teamed up."

Next to me, Hazel shrugged. "Is that why you forced me to borrow this dress?" she asked Lydia, gesturing to the off-the-shoulder sundress she was wearing. She looked both innocent and devastatingly sexy at the same time—again, she was my Snow White—and I was mentally calculating how long we'd have to stay at this party. I couldn't wait to take her back to the cabin and peel it off.

"Yup. Wanted you to look good for the photo booth."

"There's a photo booth?" I asked, scanning the yard.

"Catch up, Remy. Lovewell knows how to party. And pretty much everyone here owed your mom a favor, so it was time to collect."

Hazel and I wandered around the gathering, hand in hand, accepting congratulations from what felt like every citizen of Lovewell. My high school track coach, the owner of the service station, and almost every lunch lady we'd ever had was there, ready to celebrate us.

It felt amazing and overwhelmingly shitty all at the same time.

Because, despite my very real feelings and my ever-present, insatiable desire, this marriage wasn't built to last. We'd agreed to one year, and no matter how amazing it felt right not, I could not hold her back. She was focused and determined and excited about her future. I wouldn't take that away from her.

I would honor our commitment to the one-year marriage gig. But I was determined to soak up every moment I had with her until then.

And tonight, I'd work extra hard to honor her. Because she was glowing. Hazel wasn't used to attention or being showered with love. Her whole life, she hadn't felt like she mattered to anyone but her brother. But she mattered to me. And with Lovewell's help, I thought she might be convinced.

I headed over to where my brothers were manning the fire pit and Goldie and Tucker were roasting marshmallows. Paz was wearing shiny shoes and sporting a close shave, as usual, but pulled me in for a man hug and uttered a quiet congratulations.

Part of me wanted to punch him for the way he had talked about my wife and the way he had been treating me for the last few months. But my mother would skin me alive with a rusty axe if I dared disrupt her lovely party. So I returned the hug and thanked him for his well wishes.

"Uncle Remy!" Goldie squealed, jumping into my arms. She had melted marshmallow all over her face and stuck in her blond pigtails. "Summer vacation is awesome! Alice takes me to camp, and we made friendship bracelets." She held up a tiny arm wrapped in at least a dozen of them in every color of the rainbow. "Can I make one for you and for Auntie Hazel?"

I gave her a squeeze. "We would love that so much."

Henri snorted and held up an arm covered in bracelets made with glittery beads and what looked like a princess crown charm.

Chuckling, I set Goldie on her feet and tugged on a sticky pigtail. "I'm so glad you're here to celebrate with us, kid."

"Uncle Remy," she said, tugging on my arm, "when did you know that you loved Auntie Hazel and wanted to marry her?"

I squatted so I was eye level with her and scratched my beard, searching for a child-appropriate answer. "Hmm. I guess it was when she threw a blueberry pie in my face," I said, and in that moment, I realized that was the truth. "She threw one of Miss Bernice's famous pies at me. It was an accident, or at least I think it was. Covered in crumbling crust, I looked down at her, blueberry goo stinging my eyes, and realized I had to marry her."

"Aww," Goldie said, clasping her hands over her heart like a miniature version of a swooning woman. "That is so romantic."

"You deserved it. The pie in the face," Henri clarified.

I shrugged and stood, taking a sip of water. "Probably."

"Training hard?" he asked, his usual gruff manner melting in the presence of his almost adopted daughter. Henri and Alice had been working through the process of formally adopting Goldie and Tucker, and we were counting the days until they were legally a family.

I nodded. "Nonstop. Lift, chop, protein shake, sleep, and repeat."

"Good man." He clapped me on the shoulder. "I wish I had known. That you were planning to marry Hazel. I would have taken you out. We could have talked, man to man."

I turned toward my brother, the most silent of the strong and silent variety. "Really? Talk? You?"

He punched my shoulder. "Not too much talking. We could have grilled steaks. Lit a huge fire and burned shit. And then, you know, talked about life or some shit."

"We can still do that," I said. "Especially since I'm a married man now. I could give you some tips." I lifted my chin, gesturing to where Alice sat on the other side of the fire, chatting animatedly with some of the teachers from school. "You ever gonna make it legal?"

Henri took off his hat and ran a hand through his hair. "Jesus, dude. I'm working on it. It's gotta be just right. I can't fuck it up."

I patted him on the shoulder. "After national's, we'll go camping, like old times. We can burn shit and work on the perfect proposal."

He grunted, which was a more enthusiastic response than I had anticipated, and then took off to intercept Goldie, who had found a fresh bag of marshmallows and was stuffing them into her mouth like a chipmunk.

I wandered the yard, stopping every two feet to chat with guests and accept hugs and congratulations. Despite the guilt eating at me over the party they'd thrown for my fake marriage, it was humbling to have the town here. All these people, who had been important to both Hazel and me throughout life, had come together to honor us.

I finally found my wife, who was in the photo booth with Lydia, making silly faces. Dylan was there as well, sipping a beer and hovering in the background. He'd been quieter than usual tonight, his shoulders slumped and his eyes downcast every time I caught sight of him.

I gave him a nudge. "Hey, man."

He threw an arm around my shoulder, perking up a little

and making my stomach sink. How could I stare at my beautiful wife, feeling like the luckiest guy on earth, and then lie to my best friend's face about it?

"Everything okay?" I asked, trying to deflect my guilt.

He shrugged, taking another sip. "Things are weird with Lydia."

I raised one eyebrow and steered him off toward a vacant picnic table. We did not talk about Lydia. In all the years we'd been friends, we had never spoken aloud about his feelings for her. It was obvious to everyone on earth that he was in love with her. The two of them lived in separate bubbles of delusion, not understanding how perfect they were for each other. But we all knew and held out hope that one of them would finally come to their senses and make a move.

"What happened?" I asked, dropping to the picnic table bench so I faced the fire.

Frowning, he scanned the crowd, then sat beside me, his elbows on his knees and his beer dangling from his hand between them. "Nothing. I don't want to ruin your party."

"You can tell me anything, man," I said, hating myself a little more for keeping secrets from him while encouraging him to share his.

He ran his hands through his hair, leaning closer. "I kissed her. And then everything got weird. I'd give anything to just go back in time and take it back. I'm such an idiot."

Before I could respond, Hazel came bouncing toward us with a huge smile on her face. "Dylan," she said, throwing her arms around his neck. "This is so much fun."

His face morphed into a smile. "You deserve a party. I don't care if the marriage is fake. I'm proud of you. You're healthy and on your way to being a goddamn doctor. And you," he turned to me, "are going to nationals. Finally. After all these years, you made it. Clearly, this marriage was a genius idea." He puffed up his chest. "Since I came up with it, I'll accept your gratitude in the form of imported beer and pizza."

I punched him in the shoulder. "Thanks, man."

"There's no one I would trust with my sister, but you're doing a stand-up job."

My heart squeezed. Coming from Dylan, that meant a lot. Hazel caught my eye, and I raised one brow. It was time to tell him. We couldn't keep him in the dark. There was something real here, and even if it was only temporary, telling him felt like an important step.

Hazel gave me a slight nod, and I cleared my throat. But before I could speak, my mother hurried over. "Kids," she said, grabbing Hazel's hand. "No one is dancing. Come on, newlyweds, get things started for us."

"Okay, okay," I said to my mother, giving Dylan a nod. Hopefully we could catch him later.

I turned to Hazel and held out my hand. "Care to dance, Mrs. Gagnon?" My heart soared when she nodded enthusiastically and practically jumped into my arms like Goldie had earlier.

The crowd gathered around to watch us when we stepped onto the dance floor, their scrutiny wreaking havoc on my nerves. But as I scanned our friends and family, I locked eyes with Jasper, who I'd cut trees with every winter since high school. He was watching us from the makeshift stage, and with a wink at me, he strummed the opening bars to "More of You" by Chris Stapleton.

I made a mental note to thank him for the perfect

romantic but not sappy song, then I pulled Hazel tight against me and closed my eyes.

"This is technically our first dance," Hazel said, resting her chin against my chest, her face pink from all the attention.

"Then we best make it a good one," I said, twirling her while our audience *oohed* and *ahhed*.

"I can't believe they did this." She bit her lip and looked at the folks circled around us. "We just got married. It's not that big of a deal."

I pulled her closer as other couples joined us. "Not that big of a deal? Lovewell throws parties for far less, and it's a sticky July night filled with stars and fireflies. It's perfect for a little backyard wedding shindig."

She rested her cheek on my chest, the scent of her shampoo floating around me. "It's so kind. People cooked and planned and set up. It's a lot of work."

I took her hands and pulled back. "When are you gonna realize how fucking special you are? That you deserve all the good things?" I twirled her again, then pulled her flush against me when she returned.

We danced through three more songs, her head on my chest and Jasper providing the perfect soundtrack on his guitar.

I held her as close as I could, memorizing every moment with her. I wanted to ask her for more. More than a year, more than convenience. A chance for something real and lasting. I wanted to tell Dylan and shout it from the rooftops. I wanted to be with her. For as long as she would have me.

And under the stars, to the soft sounds of Jasper's guitar, the timing was perfect.

But then I dipped my chin and studied her beautiful face, her closed eyes and wide smile, soaking up the love and kindness of this place.

And I couldn't do it. I couldn't ruin her perfect night. Because Hazel, the kid who'd never had a birthday party, deserved to absorb every moment of this without me complicating it. And as much as I wanted to ask, I was afraid of the answer. So I squeezed her just a little tighter and rested my cheek against the crown of her head.

"Thank you," she said into my shirt as the song ended. "For marrying me."

I tipped her chin up and kissed her softly. "It is my absolute pleasure to be your husband."

Chapter 33
Hazel

I woke up with the best kind of hangover.

An orgasm and happiness hangover.

I had gorged on fun last night, dancing and celebrating with half the town, and then Remy had taken me home, climbed under the skirt of my party dress, and kept me up way too late.

I had overindulged on friendship and support.

And it felt amazing.

Sitting up, I stretched, blinded by the light streaming in through the massive windows.

Remy was gone, probably in the kitchen making a protein shake or out training already. We were three weeks from nationals, and he'd ramped up his training schedule over the last few days.

In the evenings, we had taken to analyzing YouTube videos of other competitors and past champions, looking for special techniques or tweaks he could use for a leg up.

Having never been into sports, I was surprised at how

much I enjoyed the process. But because I was a data person, analyzing times and angles and swing speed came naturally. Those were all data points ripe for my brain to wrestle with.

I got up and threw on a sports bra and a pair of shorts, already feeling the July humidity creeping in. After filling a glass of water, I headed to the living room, where we had our training schedules planned out on whiteboards.

I ran a finger down the list, searching for today's schedule. Remy was set to chop wood, so he was probably practicing up at Henri's house. Needing to get a short jog in—because my time with my husband had helped me realize that I didn't mind running so much—before I sat in front of my computer for the day, I figured I could go surprise him there.

I grabbed a hair tie and a water bottle and headed out into the sunshine in search of my lumberjack.

My heart was pounding as I hoofed it up the hill to Henri's house. My trail running route was only two miles, but it kicked my ass every time.

As I crested the hill, a low whistle echoed against the trees. And there was Remy, legs planted wide, maul resting on his shoulder, with his shirt off, watching me plod up the hill.

"Looking good," he hollered.

"You're not the only athlete in the family." Panting, I slowed to a walk, then tipped my water bottle and guzzled half its contents. "It's getting a tiny bit easier every time."

He ambled over and kissed the top of my sweaty head. "That's my girl." Slapping my ass, he waggled his brows. "And you look really cute in those shorts."

I rolled my eyes and found a stump to sit on while hydrating.

"Don't let me interrupt," I said, waving at the massive log he had on a metal stand. It was one of his weakest events, the standing block chop. It involved a piece of white pine, and the objective was to drive the top off the wood block as quickly as possible, striking it with the axe on both sides. It was a test of accuracy and power and required short, strong strokes mixed with deadly accuracy to weaken the wood in precisely the right spot.

I pulled my phone from the side pocket of my leggings and scrolled to the timer app. When I was ready, I gave him a nod, and he got into position.

"Go," I called, watching him swing with precision. I was supposed to be watching his form, but fuck, each swing caused his muscles to ripple and contract, showcasing the sheer power of his body and making my clit ache.

I had always gone for the nerdy guys. The smartest guys in any room, but who probably couldn't drive a stick or change a tire if their lives depended on it.

Men who wanted to debate philosophy, not go for a hike.

And before now, that type of guy had been right for me. I certainly didn't have any regrets.

But Remy? He was all man. And he did something to me no guy had ever done.

And it wasn't just the muscles.

It was the way he protected and cared for me. The little things that showed he was paying attention. His body was impressive, sure, but not as impressive as his heart.

Last night, I had lain in bed, sated after multiple orgasms, and watched him sleep. Maybe it was a bit creepy, but Remy was in perpetual motion. The only time he was still was when he was sleeping. So, after one of the happiest and most memorable nights of my life, I examined my husband. I took a moment to appreciate the messy hair, the muscles, and the big, kind heart.

He was so much more than met the eye. He was vulnerable and strong. Possessive and permissive.

I could be me. All the time. In all my messy glory. And he was okay with that. He *liked* that. Showing up every day and surprising me with how much he cared.

This was so much more than a marriage of convenience. This was so much more than friends with benefits. How much more? I had no idea. All I knew was that he made me a better person. Reminded me of my value and encouraged me at every turn.

After I'd ogled my husband swinging an axe for an uncomfortable amount of time, he raised one eyebrow. I sat up on my stump, hoping he was going to suggest a shower where I could soap up all those glorious muscles.

"Hop on," he said, walking toward me. "We should get some more carrying practice in."

I would much rather have hopped onto another part of his impressive anatomy, but I agreed. I was the one who had written the damn training plan after all.

"Okay," I said. "I guess we do need to practice."

"Good girl," he said, picking me up and managing to slap my ass in the process before taking off at high speed down the hill.

We collapsed, sweaty and exhausted, under our favorite tree.

"That creek looks really good right now," I said, tipping my head in the direction of the crisp, clear water that ran along the back of Henri's acreage. This spot was so peaceful. There were so many things I'd forgotten over the years. For years, I had been desperate to get out of this town and live my life in the city, and after a decade of basement apartments, traffic, and constant noise, I was developing a newfound love for the tranquility of rural Maine.

Remy was reclined against the trunk beside me. "I could be persuaded to skinny dip," he said, giving me a wink.

"The water's probably freezing!"

"It's July. Warmest it's gonna get." He bit his lip, his eyes alight as he regarded me. "Come on, I'll race you."

Then he was jumping up, kicking off his shoes, and peeling off his shorts, all the while running toward the water. His glutes looked extra delectable as he jumped into the creek. It was only a few feet deep, but he plunged down dramatically, splashing and throwing his arms up.

I toed off my own shoes, padding slowly toward him, watching the droplets of cool water slide down his chest.

I gathered up his shorts and boxers and folded them neatly, placing them on a nearby rock. Then, after scanning our surroundings to make sure we were alone, I added my own sports bra and shorts to the pile.

Dipping a toe into the water, I shuddered, an icy zing coursing through my veins. It was freezing, but my sweaty skin and aching muscles craved it. Almost as much as I craved my smoking hot husband, who was floating, buck naked, on his back.

I waded in, enjoying the sting of the cold water. When

I was waist deep, Remy wrapped his arms around me and kissed me fiercely. "I could not ask for a better training partner. How'd I get so lucky? You're always up for anything."

"I'd follow your fine ass anywhere. Including an icy body of water."

He ran his cold fingertips down either side of my ribcage, making my entire body shiver and need pulse in my core. I kissed him again, urgently, letting the cold of the water and the heat of his mouth drive me wild. I was lost for this man, my temporary husband.

Picking me up, he gripped my ass with one hand while he guided one leg around his waist. I followed suit and wound the other around him as well. His erection was nestled perfectly between our bodies, and we rubbed against one another, eager and hungry.

"Fuck." He groaned, angling me back so I was hovering over the water while he bit at my nipples. "I need to be inside you."

Pulling me closer and banding an arm around my back for support, he found my clit and rubbed furiously. I gasped, desperate for all of him, as he slipped a finger inside me.

We were in the woods, in broad daylight, humping each other like wild animals. It was the most exhilarating thing I'd ever done.

But before I could get the relief I desperately needed, Remy shouted, the sound startling me, and I tore my eyes open.

"Fuck," he hollered, his arm slipping.

Without his support, I dropped into the water. It took me a minute to find my bearings, and when I stood, I saw it. A moose at the water's edge only yards from us, staring right at us.

"Get out of here!" he yelled, waving at the massive creature.

In response, the moose turned and nudged at the pile of clothes stacked neatly on the rock nearby.

"Is that...?" I said, trying to get a look at the giant animal's flank.

It turned farther, revealing a large scar. "It's fucking Clive," Remy hissed. "Asshole moose."

He splashed water at him and shouted in hopes of scaring him away. Clive was blocking the smooth creek bank where we had climbed in and, although he wasn't known to be aggressive, everyone in Maine knew it wasn't wise to get too close to a bull moose.

Clive took a step back, clearly unhappy with being yelled at. But instead of walking away, he bared his teeth and chomped down on the pile of clothes on the rock. Then he backed up and wandered away with them, my sports bra hanging out of the side of his mouth.

"What the fuck, Clive?" I called.

He moseyed toward the deeper forest, unbothered by our yelling, probably getting a kick out of leaving us naked in the middle of the creek.

"Cock-blocking son of a bitch," Remy muttered under his breath.

I elbowed him, shivering as the temperature of the water finally registered. "I'm a little more concerned about getting back to our cabin. We've got to get over the hill and pass Henri and Alice's house. And we've got no clothes."

Remy scratched his beard. "Okay. I could carry you."

"Naked me mounted on your naked back would be so much worse!"

"Yeah. Okay. I think our best bet is to grab our sneakers and jog home."

"Naked?"

"Yeah, we'll hustle and keep an eye out. I'm sure it'll be fine."

I trudged to the bank, shivering, regretting stripping naked and following my hot husband into a creek.

Remy climbed out after me and shook himself off like one of Henri's dogs. Then he stuck his feet in his shoes and laced them up, ass in the air, giving me a wink.

Meanwhile, I had my arms wrapped tightly across my chest. "How are you so cool about this?"

"Because a vindictive moose stole our clothes. That's the equivalent of a lightning strike. No way we could predict it or prevent it. May as well laugh about it and go home."

"But what if people see us?" I hissed, shuffling toward my shoes.

"This is rural Maine, and we live on the side of a mountain. How often do you see people around the cabin? Less than never, that's how much."

"But with my luck, there will be a parade and a presidential visit and a bus of school kids on a field trip."

He rolled his eyes and took a step closer. "It's summer vacation, so no school kids. And last I checked, there are no town festivals scheduled for this weekend, so we're in the clear. Just put your shoes on." He nodded at where they sat at my feet. "The faster we jog home, the faster I can get you in a hot shower and finish what we started before we were rudely interrupted."

"Fine," I huffed, slipping my feet in without bothering to untie my shoes.

"Let's go."

I followed Remy's light jog up the hill back toward the cabin with one forearm banded across my boobs the whole way. They weren't big by any means, but jogging naked sans bra was probably the most uncomfortable thing I'd ever done. What a pair we made, jogging up a hill with our bits swinging around in the sunshine.

We made it up the ridge and headed toward the trail that ran behind Henri's house unseen. Now all we had to do was loop around the property. At least on the trail, we had good coverage, then we'd head down toward the cabin. Once we did that, we'd be home free.

If only we were so lucky. Because at that moment, the stars aligned to ensure maximum humiliation. As we circled Henri and Alice's house so we could hit the trail, what should appear, but a truck. Filled with Henri, Alice, Tucker, and Goldie, the last of whom rolled down her window to wave hello to her aunt and uncle.

I screamed. Full-on screamed, diving behind a massive pile of split logs. Inside the house, the dogs were howling, probably worried a murder was taking place. I crouched down, praying that this was all a hallucination due to too much time in front of my computer, or maybe too much of Loraine's banana bread. *Please, God,* I thought to myself, *please do not let my brother- and sister-in-law, who I really respect, have seen me naked. And please do not let me have traumatized their children with my nudity and bad judgment.*

Tires came to an abrupt stop on gravel, and then a car door slammed.

"What the fuck?"

"Henri. Language." Alice's principal voice was terrifying.

"Sorry. Remy, what the fudge are you doing jogging down my driveway naked?"

From my vantage point behind the log pile, I could see Remy standing in front of Henri with his hands in front of him, probably to cover himself, while Alice hustled the kids into the house.

"It's a long story."

"And did I see Hazel?"

Like the complete and total coward I was, I remained hidden and didn't make a peep, knowing Remy, wonderful husband that he was, wouldn't sell me out. I'd just wait here until Henri left so I could sprint home, or until I died of shame, whichever happened first. Good plan. Solid work, Hazel.

A door creaked open, then the dogs were running, collars jangling. And then they were on me, licking me and making this entire situation even more awkward.

"She is here," Henri said, turning around like a gentleman.

"Here." Alice chortled, handing Remy a towel. "Cover up. And I'll leave this bathrobe on top of the woodpile. Just in case anyone needs it," she said loudly as I cowered in shame.

Alice was the kind of woman I looked up to. Fun and mature and hilarious, with a giant heart. I desperately wanted to be her friend, and right now, it was not looking so good.

"Thank you," I squeaked, pulling the robe down and

wrapping it around myself. Of course it was buttery soft and probably expensive. Alice had fantastic style.

Standing, I straightened the belt and lifted my chin, mustering the courage to act like an adult, and came face to face with my sheepish husband, sporting a pink towel around his waist, and Alice and Henri, laughing hysterically.

"This was Clive's fault," Remy said.

"An elderly moose ate your clothes off your body? Both of you? And you lived to tell the tale?" Normally serious Henri wiped tears from his eyes.

Alice was slapping her leg and practically hyperventilating. "He's a bastard, but you seriously expect us to believe that? Were you fooling around in the woods? I get it. Henri and I—"

Henri wrapped an arm around her shoulders and put one of his massive hands over her mouth, shutting her up before she could dish the details. "That's enough outta you," he said, dragging her toward the house. "We've got to go try and explain this to our kids. Please go home and put clothes on."

I nodded, mentally preparing to never look either of them in the eye again for as long as I lived. We said our good-byes and walked back to the cabin in silence.

"I am going to murder that moose," I finally said as we climbed the porch steps. "Make him into jerky and chew on him just for fun."

"Nah. This is one of those stories we'll laugh about forever and tell our grandkids someday."

We both froze, side by side on the front porch. Remy's eyes were wide with panic. We had made a firm pact not to talk about the future. Not to put pressure on whatever this was. To enjoy the now.

Which hadn't been a problem for Remy. He was Mr. Happy-Go-Lucky who lived in the present. And apparently, while I tiptoed around thinking about what would happen after next year, making light of the future wasn't an issue for him.

"Sorry," he said. "Bad joke."

I nodded, feeling more naked than I had behind that woodpile. But I'd have to shake it off. Because for the first time in my life, I was focusing on my needs and having fun. I didn't want this to end.

But as fun as it was to live in denial, I knew the hurt would come. Because I was so deeply attached to him already. But I had no choice. A deal was a deal.

Chapter 34
Remy

The truck rumbled up the wide road, through the trees and into a vast open expanse. A creek ran along the north side, flanking the boxy wooden buildings. Each sported a new metal roof, courtesy of a nasty blizzard in 2019.

"Are you okay?" she asked, her voice soft.

I nodded. I hadn't been up here since Henri's accident months ago. Back when I went off the rails.

I had deliberately stayed away. Mostly because I was embarrassed. Still was. But I had to man up at some point. I had taken responsibility, and I'd already apologized to each person on the crew. Since the incident, I'd been doing shit work for all three of my siblings. Spending my days in the office and breathing stale air was the harshest kind of punishment for someone like me, who needed to be on the move at all times.

"It means a lot to me. Getting perspectives from the folks

up here, seeing how it all works for myself. It will really help my research."

And that there was reason enough. "We got married to help each other. So that's what I'm gonna do. Help you like you help me."

"But I already had the surgery," she said.

"And? You're my wife. We're a team. You're gonna get that PhD, and you're going to crush it. Being your chauffeur and tour guide? Those things are insignificant, and it's not like I'm good for much else."

"Don't you dare say that. You're good for many things."

I put the truck in park and shifted in my seat, raising one eyebrow. "Oh babe, I know that. I know I was real good to you last night."

She froze, her face going pink, and I loved it. Getting under her skin, making her body respond to me. It was a rush better than climbing even the tallest trees.

Without waiting for a response, I jumped out of the truck and rounded the hood so I could open the passenger door for Hazel.

She took a few steps away and turned in a slow circle, her eyes wide behind the lenses of her glasses.

"Wow. This is not what I expected."

With a grin, I teased, "What did you expect? A bunch of dwarves singing and whistling while marching around with chainsaws?"

She giggled. "No, just... I don't know. We're really out in the woods."

I nodded. "This is God's country, babe."

Gagnon camp was our main outpost in the north woods. It was outfitted with dorms, houses, an office, and a small shop for repairs, along with a couple of pole barns and storage structures that housed materials and fuel. The main dormitory was a charmless squat building that my grandfather had built in the 1960s.

"Everything is pristine right now because the major logging season is over. You should see this place in winter. Equipment everywhere, guys playing flag football in the snow, pancakes on the griddle at midnight. There's a lot of life here in our little corner of nowhere."

"Did you come up here as kids?"

"Oh yeah. All the time. It was a great privilege. Hang out with the guys and stay up late. I'd climb the tallest trees and throw snowballs down at my brothers."

"So what's happening right now?"

"Road work, forest management, planning for the upcoming year. And selective cutting; mostly in challenging places like on hillsides or hard to reach areas. We do that stuff in the summer so we're ready come fall."

She snapped photos with her phone, fascinated.

"But if it's really rainy, we can't do much of anything. Roads wash out, machinery can get stuck in the mud. And Adele gets really angry if we ruin her cranes."

"I can imagine. I wouldn't cross her."

I pulled her close and kissed the top of her head. "That's a lot coming from you. My wife is pretty fierce."

"Oh, stop." Her face was pink again, and she was biting her lip in that sexy way I loved.

"My wife is hot and kinda scary. I dig it," I said, seeing if I could make that blush darken. Tugging her closer, I dropped my lips to hers. The kiss started out chaste, but then I was turning her and licking across the seam of her lips, and that quick peck became a long, languid, lust-filled kiss. I couldn't help myself. Her lips were just too fucking perfect.

I was mentally strategizing where we could find some privacy when a throat cleared behind me.

When we broke apart, I spun, finding Richard standing several yards away, arms crossed, his usual scowl in place. He had been my dad's right-hand man for decades. A grouchy bachelor, he loved being in the woods and ran a tight ship up here. After proving myself to be useless at the business and technical sides of the operations—unlike my siblings—I was sent up here to learn the ropes from Richard and help oversee the cutting and hauling operations at camp.

He hadn't cut me a single break in the nine years I'd been working up here. Usually, he treated me like an annoyance instead of a colleague. But while he was one mean son of a bitch, he knew his stuff, and my dad had trusted him completely.

I gave him a smile and draped an arm over Hazel's shoulders. "Richard. Meet my wife, Hazel Markey-Gagnon."

Hazel peeked up at me from under my arm, her face turning beet red.

Taking a step away, I gave her a nudge. She wanted to come up here, so she would have to accept that I was going to kiss her silly any chance I got.

Clearing her throat, she pulled her shoulders back. Then she strode over to him, offering her hand. "It's a pleasure to finally meet you. Remy speaks so highly of you."

His face softened. Only slightly, but more than I'd seen in the decades I'd known him. Hazel had that effect on people.

"Why'd you marry this bozo?" Richard teased, returning

the handshake. "Is he blackmailing you?" With that question, the man smirked. I'd known the guy for thirty years and had never seen him smirk. Mostly, he just yelled and told me what I was doing was wrong.

"Blink twice if this is a hostage thing. I know an escape route through the woods." And was that a *joke?*

Hazel laughed and turned to me. "Remy, you didn't tell me he was funny." When she turned back to him, she broke out her most charming smile. "I'm sure you're very busy, but I'd love a tour when you have a chance. I'm a student doing research, and I'd love to know more about how things work up here."

"Yeah. You are the expert," I added.

Richard narrowed his eyes and scowled at me, then schooled his expression and nodded at my wife. "Sure thing, Miss Hazel."

Hazel spent the day taking photos and chatting with the crew while I hauled our bags to the private cabin. My dad had built it when he and my mom were newlyweds. Having his own space away from his crew was important to him, and my mom loved to come up here and cook for all the guys.

As newlyweds ourselves, it was fitting that we were staying here now.

"It's like a honeymoon," she said, taking in the tiny space. A bed in one corner and a wood stove and a loveseat on the other side.

"The guys keep it clean. In case my mom comes up. Mama Gagnon still commands a lot of respect up here."

"I don't doubt that."

"But she hasn't been up. Not since Dad died."

Hazel squeezed my hand. "Maybe one day she'll come back."

Dinner was served in the mess hall. Ace, one of the crane operators, was cooking, and Matt was playing guitar. This time of year, we only kept a skeleton crew at camp, but they were having a good time.

We wandered the halls of the large building so Hazel could look at the old photos on the walls. It never failed to hit me, the history of my family and our ties to this land. Men in hats and collared shirts standing proudly with axes next to massive felled trees. Photos of logs floating down the river to the mill, of horses pulling loads of lumber. Hazel stopped in front of each one and studied it carefully, a small smile on her face the entire time.

"This," I said, pointing at a black and white photo that was dated 1925, "was my great-grandfather, Pierre."

Her face lit up. "He looks like Henri without the beard."

I laughed. He did. Barrel chested and tall, with a serious demeanor. I had never met him, but my grandparents had told story after story about him when I was a kid. "That's him. And the first Gagnon lumber crew."

She stepped closer and pushed her glasses up her nose, studying the grainy photograph for a long moment.

"And this," I steered her further down the hall, "was my great grandma, Celine. The love of his life and spirit of this place."

It was a formal portrait, taken in her finery. Her hair was cropped short, and she wore a small hat and a fancy dress with a collar. Around her neck, displayed proudly, was the compass.

Hazel's hand went immediately to the compass pendant she wore. She squeezed it, then rubbed her thumb over the smooth brass as she examined the photo of Celine.

I put my arms around her, kissing the top of her head. "She'd be proud to see you wear it."

She wiped a tear away and pulled free of my hold. "Show me more," she ordered quietly, wandering down the hallway.

After the tour, we returned to the cabin, where Hazel sat on the bed, typing furiously. In the center of the room, I stretched, basking in the effects of being out in the woods. It had been so long since I'd been up here, so long since I'd felt the freedom of the wilderness. And I was in the honeymoon cabin with my wife.

Who was now pulling papers out of her bag and furiously spreading them across the quilt. Hmm. Not the sexy fantasy I had envisioned.

"I have this feeling," she said, pushing up her glasses. "It's probably nothing."

I dropped to the mattress beside her and scanned the array of papers, feeling totally useless. "Explain."

"The photo we saw. That old outpost."

She squinted at her computer screen, moving her finger along the track pad, then turned the whole thing so we could both see the documents on the screen.

"It's Sinistre Nord. Look at this map."

She'd pulled up a map from the seventies that was covered in scribbles in what looked like my dad's handwriting.

"This." She poked her finger at a spot. "That's what your dad was talking about. What he was researching."

"That whole area was destroyed in a massive wildfire decades ago."

"Have you been out there, seen it for yourself?" she asked, tapping her temple with a pencil and squinting at the screen.

"No. I've flown over it with Walt. There's a wildflower meadow and some new growth, but it's in no-man's-land. An area we don't cut anymore. It's technically owned by the state."

"But that area used to be logged, right?"

"Yeah, that whole section was used. There used to be trails and everything. Before we built the roads."

"Great, so we can go see it," she chirped, sitting up straight.

"Hold up." I put a palm on her knee. "Just because there were trails forty years ago does not mean there are any left. No one goes up there."

"Okay," she pouted, shoulders slumping. "I guess you're right."

Blowing out a long breath, I shook my head and grinned. "You want me to drive you up there, don't you?"

She nodded. "I have a weird feeling. I promised Henri I'd help figure out what your dad was working on."

Of course I'd take her. There was nothing I wouldn't do for my wife, and I wouldn't pass up an opportunity to understand more about my dad.

"Is it close by?"

I pulled her laptop closer. "Let's map it out." I was a decent navigator, having spent so much time up here. "We can drive this far." I pointed at a spot where the most passable road disappeared. "And then we'll have to take one of the ATVs up the dirt trails."

She studied the map. "Is it safe?"

"Sure. Most of the trails are probably grown over, but with an ATV, they're passable. Adele will only kick my ass a little if we borrow one."

With a little more plotting, we worked out where to leave my truck and which paths to try.

"It'll probably take an hour to get to the drop-off point, and then another hour on the ATV. Obviously, if we can't find a trail, we'll have to turn around."

She bit her lip and studied the map on the screen. "It may be nothing."

"If we leave early, we can be back by midafternoon. There won't be much to see, but I'll take you. It's been a while since I've been out to the backcountry. I'll pack supplies, and you can take photos or notes or whatever you need."

"Okay. Thank you so much for doing this for me, Remy."

The way her face lit up made my heart dance. God, she was beautiful.

"Do you have boots? Bear spray?" I asked.

She frowned. "You know me. Bear spray comes in real handy in the libraries and universities I hang out in."

"Yeah, yeah." I bumped my shoulder against hers. "I'll hit the supply shed. Pack what you need. Wear good shoes and lots of layers. And I'll sign out a radio so we can reach camp."

She threw her arms around me and squeezed, her face pressed to my shoulder. "You are the best husband ever."

"You know," I said, holding her tight, letting my body respond to the way she felt in my arms, "most wives want jewelry and flowers." With that, I pinched her nipple just the way she liked it.

She squeaked and startled, but she didn't pull away. "Oh Remy, we both know I'm not most wives."

I rolled her onto her back and hovered over her, kissing her neck as she wiggled beneath me. "True. You are one of a kind. And you're all mine."

Chapter 35
Hazel

We set off early, packs ready and a charged radio in tow. We rumbled up the dirt roads in Remy's truck until we reached the end of the old road. Just as we suspected, there wasn't much here.

Except for two trails. One heading west and the other north. No markings, but they were cleared and moderately wide.

I consulted the map and the route we had found while Remy unloaded the ATV. "We're definitely in the right place."

He nodded, strapping his pack of supplies behind the ATV's seat. "Don't get your hopes up, okay? This very well could be a long, bumpy ride to nowhere."

I took the helmet he held out to me. "Aren't you the pessimist? I'm going on an adventure with my sexy, mountain-man husband. I'm good, no matter what we find."

I had never ridden an ATV before, so I clung to Remy's back with all my might and tried not to fall off. He went fairly slowly, given how bumpy, narrow, and tricky the trail was. Very quickly, I realized this was not my preferred mode of transportation, no matter how hot Remy looked driving. It didn't take long for nausea to take over, so I spent most of the trip willing my body to keep it together. All the while, my stomach roiled and I broke out into a cold sweat.

After about half an hour, Remy came to a stop. When he cut the engine, I finally peered over his shoulder. Five minutes in, I'd grown tired of holding my breath and tensing my shoulders each time we came close to a tree stump or the ATV wobbled its way over ruts, so I had been hiding behind him.

He killed the engine and pulled off his helmet, then worked to unbuckle mine. I, on the other hand, was awestruck.

"What is this?" I asked, finally hopping down and spinning in a slow circle, marveling at the scene before me.

Between walls of towering pines was a lush, colorful meadow. Waist-high flowers. Long grass and small trees. Birds chirping and insects buzzing. What had to be three or football fields of life spread out far and wide, then tapered back into the forest at the edges.

I walked out of the tree canopy, tilting my head and closing my eyes, soaking in the sunlight warming my face.

"This is what happens after a wildfire," Remy explained. He pointed out some of the plants. "I don't know all of these, but that's hawkweed, and that over there is devil's paintbrush."

I marveled at the beauty before me, taking in the sounds and smells.

"Nature has a way of fixing itself. After a fire, certain

species take root, returning nitrogen to the soil and making the ecosystem even stronger."

"It's breathtaking."

"I'm glad you like it. Usually, the wildflowers do their job and the trees grow back. Like that. See the immature trees over there?" He pointed to the far end, where a mini forest had sprung up. "But in this patch here, the flowers took root and never left."

My heart beating wildly, I turned and threw my arms around his neck. "Thank you for showing me this."

"We've still got a ways to go. Let's see if your hunch is correct."

After consulting the map, we took off again, eager for the surprises the wilderness held for us. We edged around the wildflower field, up a steep hill, and back through the dense forest. It was darker beneath the canopy, and there was a chill in the air.

The terrain was even more rugged out here, so I buried my face in Remy's shirt once again and held on tight. When he slowed, I craned my neck to see around his helmet. Before us was another clearing, this one decorated with moss-covered rocks, a scattering of tree stumps, and a small log cabin.

Remy cut the engine and jumped up. "Holy shit."

I followed, then scrambled to open my backpack.

"This is it!" I held up the photos, which I had stashed in plastic bags for the trip, comparing the scene in front of me to the one in print I'd studied so thoroughly.

It was ramshackle at best. A tiny box with a big stone chimney and a small porch.

Several tree stumps were arranged around an overgrown

stone fire pit that obviously hadn't been used in a long time. But this was it.

Remy threw his arms around my waist and lifted me off my feet. "You are kind of amazing. I can't believe you sleuthed your way into finding this place."

He caught my mouth in a kiss, and I sank into him, grateful to be off that ungodly ATV.

And then we heard it.

A massive crack of thunder.

Above us, the formerly sunny sky was now blocked out by dark, thick clouds.

"Oh shit," Remy said, grabbing our bags off the back of the ATV. "Let's see if we can get inside."

The door stuck but wasn't locked. Remy pushed his way in just as the drops began to fall, and I scurried after him. He pulled a tarp out of his backpack and ran back out to cover the ATV, anchoring it with a few large stones we rolled from near the porch.

"This is nuts. How long do you think this has been here?" I asked, taking in every detail. The faded plaid curtains, the large fieldstone fireplace, and the dusty shelves filled with chipped blue plates.

Remy walked the perimeter of the room, admiring the ancient wood stove and pine slab table. "A long time. I can't believe my dad never told us about this place."

As I spun, taking in the rough-hewn walls, my eye caught something above the door. "Look up here," I called to Remy, striding over to it. Above the door frame was a thick slab of wood with dozens of names and dates carved into it.

Remy shone his flashlight on it. "This was my grandfather." He pointed to a carving that said *Louis Gagnon, 1957.*

I turned on my phone, which had been completely useless since we'd left Lovewell, and snapped a few photos before turning it off to avoid draining the battery. "Your siblings will love to see this."

He ran his hands through his hair, which was mussed from wearing the helmet. "They're not gonna believe we found this place."

"I wonder how it survived the fire."

He pointed out the window at the skinny trees on the west side of the clearing. "See the difference in the tree growth over there? It doesn't look like it traveled this far over. The pines on this side of the ridge are hundreds of years old. We've thought this was no-man's-land for years."

"And you've got a sea of wildflowers and a very old cabin."

He stalked over and dipped his head to give me a delicious kiss. "And a wife who surprises me every single day."

Spinning me to face the window again, he looped his arms around my waist and rested his chin on my shoulder. And there we stood, looking through the grimy window as rain poured down.

"We should check in," Remy said, heading for the pack just inside the door.

I wandered around, scanning every inch of the space more closely as he radioed the team at camp to update them on where we were and get a weather update from Richard. The vibe of this place was strange. It looked as though it had been forgotten about. Remote. But not totally untouched.

"Looks like we may be stuck here for a bit. The weather isn't supposed to clear until after midnight."

"Shit."

"It's July in Maine. Naturally, we were due for a random, biblical-level thunderstorm. We can wait it out." With one arm, he snagged my belt loop and pulled me closer, trailing the fingers of his other hand across my collarbone. "I can certainly think of a few ways to pass the time."

He looked all scruffy and delicious. There was no way I was keeping my panties on if we were going to be stuck here for hours. But there was an uncomfortable nagging in the back of my brain.

"Don't you think it would be dirtier?" I asked. I ran a finger over one of the shelves that held plates and mugs. "It's not that dusty. And the door opened after a bit of a push. If this really hasn't been used in decades, wouldn't it be in worse shape?"

Remy shrugged. "No one comes out here anymore. The trail we took isn't even on our maps."

I picked up a ceramic mug. It was white with small blue flowers. "These mugs don't look all that old." I turned it upside down, noting the brand name written in flowing script on the bottom. "I wonder what Zellers is."

Remy stepped up beside me for a closer look. "I've been to Zellers before. It's kind of like Target or Walmart in Canada. They sell everything. Tires, baby gear, clothing, and some groceries..."

"And mugs?"

"Yeah."

"Do you think Zellers was manufacturing mugs back in '57 when Louis came here?"

"I don't know. Possibly."

"And what about those keys?" I pointed to a keyring

hanging from a rusty nail next to the door frame. "There isn't a lock on the door here, so what are those for?"

He shrugged again, still unperturbed. "I've spent a lot of time out in the woods. You find the weirdest things. One time, we found a VW Beetle with a tree growing out of the hood. It was miles from the nearest road. It's part of what makes the wilderness so fun. There's so much to discover. Don't overthink it."

I put the mug back and continued my inspection. The space was tiny, and it was humid, given all the rain. It beat down on the roof, a loud pitter-patter that kept pulling me from my thoughts.

He wrapped his arms around me from behind and nuzzled into my hair. "You gotta admit, it's kind of romantic."

It was a tiny outpost in the middle of the wilderness. Generations of names carved into a rough slab of wood, chipped coffee mugs and a tiny cot. It was cozy and desolate, and the rain only added to the ambiance.

And then I did something truly stupid.

"It's a good thing we found it. It's a good place to impress your next wife." As soon as the words left my mouth, I regretted them. It was the sort of offhanded, boneheaded thing I said occasionally. Usually, I was quiet and controlled and strategic, but with Remy, I could let my guard down. Unfortunately, in doing so, it allowed my crazy insecurities to slip through and bubble to the surface.

He froze, his body rigid behind mine and his chin resting on top of my head, but he didn't speak.

I needed to say something. To take it back. Things had been so incredible, and we were enjoying our time together, as fleeting as it was. From the beginning, we had agreed not to talk about the future. And then I had to go and shove my size-seven foot right into my mouth.

"Don't talk about my next wife," he growled, his voice strained.

I pulled away and turned to face him. Shit. He was angry. I expected awkwardness, not anger.

"Remy," I said, sliding a hand up his chest.

"Do not speak." He stepped out of my hold and ran a hand through his hair, his brow furrowed. Remy rarely got mad, and never at me.

I'd messed up big time. "It was a stupid comment," I insisted, trying to rescue the situation. "Sometimes my mouth gets ahead of my brain. I know we agreed not to talk about the future, but, honestly, it's hard to keep myself from fast-forwarding in time and imagining you happily married to someone else."

His eye twitched, and he balled his hands into fists. "Stop it, Hazel."

Finally, he took a step toward me. All I could do was watch him. I swallowed thickly as he loomed over me, feeling intrigued, uncertain, and a little turned on by his anger.

"You are my wife," he said slowly, his jaw still tight and his dark eyes an inferno. "There is no one else. And every single day I wake up next to you, I'm more convinced there will never be anyone else," he confessed, searching my face.

I froze, my mouth agape. "Remy."

He crowded my space, pushing me against the wall, his hungry eyes devouring me. "You're it for me, Hazel. My desire for you grows every day. The urge to talk to you, to touch you, and to be with you? It consumes me."

"Stop," I said, panic rising in my chest. We had an agreement. This wasn't part of the plan. "I can't hear this right now."

"Why not?" he scoffed. "Because it's the truth?"

I shook my head. Damn it, why did I have to poke this bear? We had been dancing around our feelings for weeks, living in denial and having a blast.

"Remy," I pleaded. "We had an agreement. I had the surgery I needed. You're going to nationals in a few weeks, and we're working our asses off to be the best wife carrying team there."

"I don't give a shit about our agreement. The reasons we got married in the first place don't matter anymore. You are my wife, in body and spirit. This is a real marriage, whether you want to admit it or not."

His face was inches away from mine, and his chest was heaving so violently it brushed against mine with every inhale. It would be so easy to let go. To free fall into his arms, just like I had into his bed. But I knew better. I owed it to myself and to Remy to keep some boundaries in place.

"Tell me," he growled. "Tell me you don't have feelings for me."

"My feelings are irrelevant."

His fist connected with the wall next to me, making me flinch. "They are not. Tell me, Hazel."

I regarded his pained expression, the fire in his eyes that had shifted, now fueled by anguish rather than desire. So badly, I wished I could tell him what he wanted to hear, to smooth things over and reassure him. But that wouldn't be fair. I had no idea what the future held, and I had been the recipient of too many broken promises in my life to make any of my own.

He caressed my face. "I know you're scared. It's fine. I'll be brave for both of us. Hazel, my friend, my wife, the person who makes me want to be better every day of my damn life. I love you."

He leaned forward and pressed a gentle kiss to my forehead. At the contact, I closed my eyes, giving myself a few seconds to soak this in, to enjoy it.

"You don't have to say or do anything," he rasped. "But I can't hold this in anymore. You have knocked me straight onto my ass, and I feel so fucking lucky to be your husband, even for a short time."

I threw my arms around his neck, clinging to him. I wanted to say it. Tell him that I loved him and that I cherished every second with him.

But I had been on my own my entire life. During so many lonely days, I had dreams of being that girl. The girl who fell in love, who got the doting husband and the kids and the summer cookouts and the happily ever afters. But that's all they were. Dreams. Because I was not and would never be that girl.

"I want to be yours," I said into his chest, greedily taking the warmth and comfort his body so readily gave.

"You *are* mine," he replied, his hands roving down my sides and gripping my hips hard. "I know what's at stake, but I'm not losing you. Get used to it, babe. Because you might not be ready yet, but I'm warning you now—I'm making you mine forever."

Chapter 36
Remy

Being stuck in a torrential downpour in a remote mountain cabin was kind of hot.

Both literally and figuratively.

We passed the hours playing hangman and tic-tac-toe in the notebook Hazel had packed and reminiscing about our childhoods.

But I was growing restless. I had laid it all out there. Told her how I felt. And she had reciprocated... sort of. Hazel had always struggled to be vulnerable, to trust anyone. So when she'd told me she wanted to be mine? Well, my brain went wild. We had officially crossed the line into something more, something lasting. It would take time and a lot of patience to get her to where I was, but it was a start. And I'd take it.

A lifetime of friendship plus a couple of months of marriage had taught me a few things about my wife. And I'd use that knowledge to the best of my ability.

So I dropped to the floor and started doing pushups. There wasn't much else to do here anyway, and I needed my body in top form. Plus, I had to burn off the wild energy coursing through my veins.

I paused between sets and looked up at her. She was staring, biting the pen. Her eyes were wide, and her chest was rising and falling rapidly.

With a wink, I started my next set. Because my self-control was fading and I needed the outlet. My feelings and my need for her threatened to overtake me, and the last thing I wanted was for her to retreat after such a major victory.

"Do you have to do that right now?" she asked.

I sat back on my knees, using the hem of my T-shirt to mop the sweat off my face, catching the moment her eyes widened. Jackpot.

"While I admire your dedication to training, being stuck in a tiny cabin in a lightning storm is hard enough. You know watching you knock out pushups like a Navy freaking SEAL gives me a throbbing lady boner."

I laughed. "Lady boner?"

She covered her face with her hands. "Ugh. That's a gross expression. I don't know. Stop being so manly and hot. I'm trying to process over here."

She got up off the cot and stood over where I was kneeling on the hardwood floor.

I hauled myself to my feet and stripped off my shirt, then tossed it over the back of an old wooden chair. I stretched out and gave her a smile. "That's much better. You're always making me wear shirts."

She pushed her glasses up, then trailed her fingers down my chest. "It's for your own protection. Every time you whip out those lumberjack arms, I lose all sense of control." Her hands stopped at the top of my jeans, her fingers resting on my belt buckle.

Angling in, I nipped at her earlobe, and in return, she deftly undid my belt buckle.

"Mrs. Gagnon, are you trying to seduce me?" I asked, watching as she pushed my jeans over my hips.

She peered up at me, biting her lip. "Oh, Mr. Gagnon, we both know you started it."

Then she dropped to her knees, the move almost making me pass out. Hazel on her knees in front of me was one of my favorite sights.

I gasped as she slid me into her mouth, and it took all my strength to keep my knees from buckling beneath me. With one hand, she gripped my shaft hard, just like I liked, then her mouth got to work.

When I hit the back of her throat, I threw my head back and moaned. I had to suck in a sharp breath and grit my teeth to keep from losing consciousness. My vision went blurry, and every encouragement I murmured to her was unintelligible. "You are so amazing... can't keep going..."

It only took a matter of seconds to realize I had to slow this down. So using every ounce of blood left in my brain, I shook myself out of my delirium and hauled her to her feet. Once she was in my arms, I carried her over to the wooden table and put my hand between her shoulder blades, pushing until she was tilted forward and braced on her hands.

I let my fingers travel down her spine until they landed on the waistband of her leggings, which I pulled down and let pool at her feet.

I smacked her ass hard, the crack echoing through the

small space. "That's for trying to distract me with a blow job," I said as she wiggled her ass in front of me.

"And this," I said, slapping the other cheek, "is for almost getting away with it."

I ran my fingers along her seam, feeling how wet and ready she was. "You're drenched." I grabbed her hips from behind. "Now spread those legs for your husband."

When she obeyed, I pushed inside her, rough and already throbbing. Every cell in my body was on fire for her. "You thought you could distract me," I growled, holding her hips so firmly my fingertips would probably leave bruises. "But this conversation is not over. I want you, Hazel. Forever."

She cried out, gripping the table and bucking against me as I moved faster and faster, my movements becoming wild.

With one arm, I reached around her and found her clit, pinching it hard.

"Yes. Remy. Yes," she cried, her walls tightening around me.

"Does my wife need to come?" I asked, holding on for dear life. She was clenching and gripping me so tight my peripheral vision was blurring.

"Yes. Please."

I rubbed her clit hard, just the way she liked it. She arched her back and cried out as the first wave of her orgasm took over.

I didn't let up. I thrust into her over and over, rubbing and cursing and reveling at the sight of her coming undone.

"Who gives you what you need?" I asked as my own orgasm swept over me.

"My husband." She sighed, collapsing onto the table, sweaty and spent.

I rolled over on the tiny cot, the springs screaming beneath me. My shoulder ached and my body hurt from sleeping on the ancient thing, but I pulled Hazel closer.

"I would kill for some coffee right now."

"Me too. Next time we come up to the sexy cabin, I'll make sure to pack instant coffee."

She snuggled closer and planted a kiss on my lips, then pulled back. "I'm sorry. About what I said."

"Nope." Shaking my head, I tugged her to my chest again, taking her lips with mine and showing her I meant business. "Don't apologize. I needed to get some things off my chest. And, as always, you pushed me to be my best."

"But—"

I held a finger up to her lips and growled. "I love you. That's it."

She bit her lip and rolled her eyes, but she wasn't fooling me. She liked it when I got a little bossy.

"Let's walk a bit. Check out how muddy the trail is."

When we exited the cabin, the sun was creeping up over the horizon, dappling through the trees, and the air was far cooler than yesterday. We admired the old stone fire circle, the rotting stumps that had been used as chairs, and the stack of old firewood that was probably home to hundreds of mice and snakes.

"What is that?" Hazel asked, removing her glasses and squinting.

One area of the clearing was devoid of the pine needles, tree branches, and the moss that carpeted the forest floor all around it.

"Shit," I cursed, brushing at the dirt with one boot and uncovering what looked like a large piece of metal. "Back up."

"Is that a lock?"

Sure enough, a huge silver padlock had been covered by a pile of leaves. We used our feet to work at clearing the space further, revealing what looked to be a metal door in the ground. It was probably eight or nine feet long and six feet wide, with a large handle that was secured with the lock.

The door had been painted green, but the paint was flaking, and spots of rust had broken through.

"The keys," Hazel said, running back toward the cabin while I was still trying to wrap my mind around what something like this could be.

She returned quickly, jangling the key ring. "It's gotta be one of these."

"Wait. We shouldn't open it."

"Are you nuts? We found a hidden door in the ground in the middle of the woods! We're opening it."

"But what if it's dangerous?"

"It's not a viper pit, Indiana Jones. This is Maine. Probably old moonshine from back in the bootlegging days."

Even when confronted with a random bunker in the middle of the woods, Hazel remained logical. Just another reason I was crazy about her.

"Okay, okay. I'll open it. Back up."

It took several tries, but once I found the key that released the padlock, I removed it and set it in the dirt beside the door. Then I yanked on the thick metal handle. It creaked loudly before opening like a hatch, dirt and leaves sliding down as I propped it open.

"What the fuck?" Hazel said, peering in.

I pulled a flashlight out of my back pocket and shined it around the space. A step stool was propped against one metal wall, and against the others were dozens of guns, some big, and some small. Boxes of ammunition were stacked up neatly on wire shelving units.

I stepped onto the stool, lowering myself halfway inside, baffled by the discovery and what it could mean.

"Move over," Hazel said, stepping down next to me.

"Stop." My pulse was racing. Who the hell was stashing an arsenal of weapons out here? "Don't go in."

She pushed up her glasses and grabbed the flashlight. "Just let me peek." And before I could react, she jumped down and scanned the cramped space, illuminating rows of weapons.

With her free hand, she dug her phone out of her pocket and powered it on. She took photo after photo, stepping farther into the dank room. When I lost sight of her, my heart rate skyrocketed and my hands trembled, so I ducked low, needing to keep her in my line of vision.

"Motherfucker," she shouted.

I jumped down the steps and rushed toward her. I had to crouch. This storage container, whatever it was, was tight.

When I got my hands on her, I blew out a long breath. She was fine. But she was standing in front of dozens of heavy-duty clear plastic storage totes stacked along one wall.

But instead of sports equipment or gardening tools most

people stored in these types of things, the bins were filled with plastic bags.

She snapped open the closest one and plucked a baggie out of it.

My lungs seized when she held it up between us. "Is that what I think it is?" I croaked.

"Look," she said, shuffling so we were side by side and using the flashlight to study the contents of the bag. "See the imprint on the pill? The *M* with a square around it? That's Fentanyl."

What the fuck? What were massive boxes of pills doing hiding in the woods? "Are you sure?"

Hazel was obviously an expert in the opioid epidemic, but these could be anything, right?

She gave me a wary look. "I wish I didn't know these things. But I am 100 percent sure." She put the bag back and replaced the lid on the storage tote. "We gotta call the police." Nudging me toward the stairs, she surveyed the space around us. "Don't touch anything. We've got to get out of here and call for help." She snapped a few more photos with her phone before powering it off again.

I helped her out, then closed the heavy door with a clang. We left the lock in the dirt and jogged back to the cabin, hearts and minds racing. For years, we had known opioids were coming in from Canada. Was this where people had been stashing drugs? No wonder the trails were in such good condition.

I turned on the radio I'd set on the counter the previous night. "Base camp, this is Remy Gagnon," I said into the microphone. I waited for a response, clasping Hazel's hand, unable to fathom not keeping a hold on her right now. "Do you read me?"

Seconds later, it crackled to life. Gagnon Lumber had someone scheduled to monitor our set radio frequency twenty-four hours a day. With no cell phones and no internet out here, it was a safety precaution we took seriously.

"Read you, Remy. This is Richard. Over."

"I need you to contact Henri and law enforcement ASAP. Hazel and I found a storage compartment filled with guns and pills. Over."

"What the fuck?"

I laughed. Of course that would be Richard's response.

"This place is impossible to find. Call Henri now. I'll wait for instructions. Over."

"Copy that. Calling Henri."

I paced around the cabin for a few minutes, processing everything we'd discovered. A secret cabin? Unmapped trails? Guns and drugs? Hazel and I had just stumbled into something huge. Had this been what my dad was working on before he died?

Hazel, who'd managed to escape my hold, had been meticulously reviewing his research. She'd found the photos of the cabin and the maps of this area mixed in with stacks of paperwork he'd collected.

Before I could ask her to walk me through the clues, the radio crackled and Henri's annoyed voice came through.

"Remy. This is Henri. Over."

"Go for Remy. Over."

"What the fuck is going on up there? Over."

"Using maps Hazel got from Dad's notes, we found a

remote cabin off some trails from the Nowhere Road past mile marker 111. While we were checking things out, we found a hidden bunker filled with guns and drugs. You gotta get the police up here ASAP. Over."

"Copy that. I'm with Paz. He's on the phone with our state police contact. Are you safe? Over."

"Yes. This place is remote, and it doesn't look like anyone has been up here in ages. Even the firewood is old. We were going to take the ATV back to camp. Over."

"Don't. Stand by. Over."

Through the crackling and static of the radio, other voices echoed. Paz, definitely, and maybe one more.

"Remy. The staties have a unit up near Baxter State Park that can meet you in an hour or two. Can you take the ATV back to the Nowhere Road? Over."

"Wilco. Tell them I'll meet them at mile marker 111. They'll need ATVs. Trucks won't fit on this trail. Over."

"Got it. Over."

With an arm around Hazel, I kissed the top of her head and inhaled her scent. None of this would have been possible without her. Traffickers had been running wild in our woods for years. And finally, we had something. Because my tenacious, genius wife convinced me to take her into the woods.

"They're en route. I'm going to head to camp and meet the DEA guys there. They need a few hours. You go meet the state police. I'll be in touch. Stay on the radio. Over."

"Copy that. Over and out."

Chapter 37
Hazel

"You should get going," I told Remy when he clipped the radio to his belt. "It's going to take even longer because of all the mud."

"Pack up your research, and we'll head out."

"Someone needs to stay here and keep watch," I said, crossing my arms. "And you had to drive so slowly yesterday so I wouldn't get sick. You'll be faster on your own. I'll stay here and take photos and be ready to show the police everything."

He ran his hands through his hair, a pained look on his face. "I can't leave you here. What if they come back?"

My heart clenched at his concern. Every day I spent with Remy, I fell in love with him a little more. The way he wanted to protect me only compounded those feelings. It was so silly to deny it. Of course I loved him. The problem was that love was big and scary and overwhelming. I couldn't figure out how to convince my brain it was okay to tell him. I'd kept my heart closed off from anyone but Dylan my whole life, and though logic was my thing, reconciling that with what my heart wanted was difficult.

I pulled him close, resting my head on his chest. "It takes forever to get up here. The good guys are already on the way. You know where the roads are now, so you can show them. And this place has been empty for a long time. You'll be faster without me."

He squeezed me tighter. "I don't want to leave you."

"It's only for a few hours. Now get going. The police will be waiting for you."

He huffed and pulled back. "Keep the radio?"

I nodded and took it from him when he unclipped it from his belt. "Of course."

"I don't like this."

Patting his cheek, I gave him a weak smile. "I'm fine. And when we get back to camp—after really long showers— we can celebrate our inadvertent drug bust properly."

He winked. "Or we could shower together."

"Even better."

He ran his knuckles along my jawline, sending a shiver through my body, then tilted my chin up for a kiss.

"I'll be back soon. Stay safe."

I sank onto the cot, the intensity of the morning already exhausting me. What were the odds? I pulled a notebook out of my backpack and flipped to a new page so I could document every detail of the cabin and the surrounding area. This way, I'd hopefully unearth more clues about who had been here.

It would take Remy about an hour to get back to the main road where we had left the truck, then the police would follow him back, so I had a few hours of quiet to work.

Remy's words from the previous night washed over me. All this time, I had thought it was impossible to let someone in, to accept help. But the truth was, I had been doing it since the day I came back to Lovewell. What we had was real. Had always been that way. Partnership, passion, and a deep commitment to one another.

Long term, we had a lot to figure out. But I wanted to try. I rarely did anything without devising a careful plan, usually overthinking things and creating unnecessary anxiety in the process. But my survival instincts were well honed after a lifetime of disappointments. My walls were high, but I had built them brick by brick over the past twenty-eight years to shield me from each bad experience, heartbreak, and missed opportunity I had lived through.

And here was Remy, breaking through. Climbing up and chipping away and helping me lower my defenses. And making me question my priorities in the process.

For so long, I had put my achievements first and my happiness second. But right now, with my heart full of love and my lungs full of mountain air, I knew I could have both. That I had met my person. Someone I could depend on. A man who would support my endeavors.

It would take time to break old habits and unwind patterns I'd followed for so long. But I wanted this. Wanted him.

I closed my eyes, visualizing what we'd done on that old table last night. A low commotion outside pulled me out of my thoughts quickly, though. Engines—several of them—and shouting.

But Remy had been gone for less than an hour.

I rolled over on the bed and shimmied to the dirty window to peer out. In the clearing were half a dozen ATVs, some pulling trailers. I ducked quickly, my mind whirling. This couldn't be. Remy hadn't been gone long enough. And Henri said it would take the state police at least an hour to make it to their designated meet-up location.

Another quick look revealed the guns. Lots of them. Strapped to backs, in holsters, and in the hands of several menacing-looking men. A few had masks pulled up past their noses, but I could make out a few faces. No one I recognized, but from my vantage point, I watched, waiting for the rest to reveal themselves. There had to be seven or eight of them, spreading out around the area where we had found the stash.

Slowly, I shifted on the cot. The rusty springs creaked, making my heart seize. The men outside didn't seem to notice, though. They looked far more concerned with checking the perimeter of the clearing.

My hands shook as I pulled on my hoodie. I needed to get out of here before they made their way inside. I crouched down and slipped my shoes on, then slid my backpack over my shoulders. My phone had some battery left. I just needed to get to a place where I could get a signal and call for help.

And I had to get word to Remy so he wouldn't find himself wandering into a trap when he returned. These guys had enough firepower for a small special forces unit. I squeezed my eyes shut, pulling up images of the trail in my head. The rain had washed a lot of it out, but I was sure I could pick it up if I headed southeast.

Fumbling, I attempted to tie my shoes. When my fingers wouldn't cooperate, I took a moment to focus on my breathing. In and out. In and out. I could do this. I was small and quiet. I could escape and call for help. I just needed to stay calm.

Slowly, I crawled across the floor to the back of the cabin, hoping I could slide through the back door unnoticed. Outside, one of the men on the meadow side was speaking in a language that sounded like French. If I made for the trees as quickly as I could, I might go unnoticed.

Just as I made it to the door, I remembered the radio. It was still sitting on the wooden table where I'd left it when I kissed Remy goodbye. Could I risk going back for it? It was only ten feet or so—

The front door shook and scraped against its frame as someone worked to open it. Kicking myself for not thinking to grab the radio first, I slid out the back door and scurried behind the woodpile. Every few minutes, I peeked out from behind it, getting a sense of how many people there were and where they were located.

If I could make a break for it, the forest got really dense about thirty yards in. Right then, I was thankful for Remy's insistence that I take up running. Hopefully, that, along with my small size, would help keep me from being caught.

More shouting in French had me frustrated with myself for switching to Latin during sophomore year.

"Someone was here," a man with a Canadian accent shouted. "There's a glass of water and a radio on the table."

"It must be the woman," said another, the sound of his

boots on the plank flooring muffled from this distance. "Find her." *Woman? How would they know a detail like that?* Had they been watching us? At the thought, bile rose up in my throat, but I forced it back down, willing myself to concentrate.

I slumped against the woodpile and inhaled and exhaled deeply once, twice, and a third time, to get my breathing under control. The tree line was close, and I was wearing dark clothes. I could get there. I itched to stay and get more information. Figure out who they were and what they were doing. But I had to get word to Remy and the Gagnons.

The roar of another ATV approaching gave me cover, and I ran for it, sprinting as fast as I could. After several yards, I hid behind a copse of mature pines so I could consider my next move.

But as I settled low, I realized this was an opportunity. These guys had been running around these woods undetected for almost a decade. And now I was a stone's throw away from them.

I scanned the area, looking for a sturdy hardwood tree with low branches. A sprawling maple about ten yards from me looked perfect, so I crept toward it as quietly as possible. Then I grasped a low branch and pulled myself up.

My shoulder burned as I scrambled up onto the branch, keeping close to the trunk to conceal myself. I reached for the next one, using my feet to give me a boost.

I straddled the branch for a moment, peering over my shoulder at the men who were loading up their ATVs with the bins and boxes we had found. Another was patrolling the clearing with a rifle.

I was only ten or fifteen feet off the ground, but I had a

decent vantage point, so I swung my backpack off one shoulder and dug my phone out. I zoomed in as far as I could, snapping photos of the men and their vehicles. Then I switched to video mode and recorded footage of them carrying the bins to the ATVs, hoping the bags filled with white pills were recognizable, along with the rectangular packages of what I assumed was heroin.

Satisfied with my evidence collection, I turned my attention back to my escape. Climbing down would be more of a challenge than climbing up, especially as my stomach lurched when I saw just how far it was to the ground.

After I secured my phone, I clipped my backpack on and shimmied down the trunk, stretching my short legs out for the branch below me. As I moved, I planned out my route, looking beyond the trees to determine the fastest path away from these goons and their guns.

Just one more drop. Damn. At times like this, I hated being short.

Hanging from the branch, I gave myself a pep talk. I just had to let go and land. One, two, three—

"Hey," someone shouted behind me. "Quest-ce que c'est que ca?"

I froze, my legs dangling feet above the ground. They'd seen me. Shit. I dropped down, ignoring the searing pain in one ankle, and ran. Shouting and more garbled French erupted behind me as I pushed through the undergrowth, past a handful of boulders, and deep into the forest. After several minutes, I hid behind a fallen tree, taking advantage of my size, and caught my breath, peering above the trunk to be sure I was alone as I did.

But soon I heard footfalls. "Come out, come out," a burly

guy with a beard and a shaved head said. "Wouldn't want you getting lost in the woods." His Canadian accent was thick, and he had a large tattoo of a dragonfly on his neck.

My pulse was racing as I flipped through everything I knew about self-defense, which was functionally nothing. This man had a gun, and I had a water bottle, a cell phone, and a notebook.

My best bet would be to run. I'd gotten quicker over the last several weeks, and by the sheer size of this guy, odds were he was not super fast.

So I got to my feet and crouched low, grateful that I had been training with Remy. My short trail runs and pushups weren't much, but at least I had some stamina. I picked up a rock and threw it as far as I could. When it landed, the man spun toward the sound, which meant his back was turned toward me.

And then I ran. Ran as hard and fast as I could to the dense tree line, praying I'd get there. I knew where to head and where to step based on my tree planning, and I pushed myself harder than I ever had, elation bubbling up inside me. But as quickly as it came, it was gone. The bubble popped when he shouted, "Stop running, bitch. I've got a gun."

But I ignored his warning, instead jumping over a rotting tree and stumbling down a small hill. No way would I let that roided-out monster catch me. The trees here were dense, and there were rotting logs and boulders everywhere. I turned hard, banking around a cluster of birch trees toward what looked like a small stream.

"Fuck," he yelled, still pursuing me on foot. "She's getting away."

There wasn't a rat's chance in hell they were good guys.

They'd evaded capture for years, and their gear was professional grade. Not to mention the menacing henchman vibes
they put off.

Zigzagging and jumping over tree roots, I forced myself
even deeper, searching for a place to hide as I went.

Over stumps and roots and through brambles, I ran,
while their voices got farther and farther away. Though I'd
put distance between us, I couldn't keep up this pace much
longer, so I scanned the area, looking for a large fallen tree
or a—

In an instant, I was flying through the air and landing on
my hip with a thud, my face slamming into the mud.

My left thigh was scraped and bleeding, but the true
issue was my throbbing right ankle. Wincing, I closed my
eyes, feeling the tears welling up. I wanted to cry out. But I
gritted my teeth and listened for any signs that the men were
approaching.

I could no longer see the cabin or the clearing, and the
dense growth out here was disorienting. Holding my breath
and biting back a scream of agony, I pushed myself up and
tested my ankle.

Putting pressure on it resulted in a shooting pain that
worked its way up my leg, but I'd have to push through. I
reached into my backpack for my phone and powered it on.
The battery was at 20 percent, and it still had no signal.

I looked around, taking in the cool, muddy forest,
listening for voices or movement close by. I wasn't sure how
far I'd gone, but it was not far enough. Blowing out a long
breath, I headed toward the stream, figuring I'd follow it
south until I could get my bearings.

Fuck. I was going to have to hike my way out of here.

Chapter 38
Remy

Passing the wildflower field and approaching the clearing, it was obvious something was wrong. As promised, a few guys from our team and the state police unit had met me at the main road, some with ATVs and some on horseback. They'd come equipped with satellite phones, so I'd called Henri before we set off for the cabin. He was headed our way with the DEA agent from Bangor who had been up our asses for months, and he expected to be about an hour behind us.

My heart dropped as we approached the clearing. There were dozens of sets of tracks in the mud, and the cabin door was wide open. Leaving my ATV running, I jumped off it and ran inside. The place had been ransacked. The furniture was in pieces, and a window was broken.

I slumped against the wall for support, choking back the bile rising in my throat. Someone had gotten here before we did.

And Hazel was nowhere to be found.

Calling her name, I stumbled out of the cabin and raced to where we had found the stash. Everything was gone—the drugs, the guns, and all the survival supplies. Completely cleaned out. The police crept through the woods, guns drawn, but it was no use.

"They're long gone." I croaked, my legs shaking.

Matt, one of our foremen and a prior service Army Ranger, put his arm around my shoulder. "What the fuck happened?"

I dropped my head, studying the tracks in front of the cabin. They were wider than my ATV tires and fresh. The mud hadn't dried despite the sunlight filtering through the trees.

"Remy, we should head back."

I shook him off and paced, terror flooding me. Hazel, my Hazel, was in danger, and my stupid brain couldn't even work. "Give me the phone," I growled.

Stalking toward a large maple, I shoved the phone in the waistband of my jeans and jumped, hauling myself onto a branch. Up and up and up I went until the branches were a little smaller. I stopped on one I knew would easily hold my weight and pulled out the antenna on the phone. Up here, I could at least get decent reception.

"Paz," I said as soon as he picked up the phone.

He was the last person I wanted to speak to right now. I flat-out hated him in this moment. But he was back in Lovewell with phones and computers and all our equipment, and I needed him, so I had to put aside my anger.

"She's gone." I sucked in a breath, hoping to slow my heart rate. "Someone came. There are tracks all over the place, and she's gone. Everything is gone."

"Fuck," he breathed out. "Henri is on his way. I'll alert forest services and the mountain search and rescue team." He was rattling things off in his usual businesslike manner, his tone devoid of any concern. I knew how strapped those agencies were right now, and we were on private land, so they'd be at a disadvantage.

"I don't want search and rescue. I want my wife," I growled, frustrated.

"Fuck off, Paz," Adele said in the background. "We'll find her, Remy. What do you need?"

I looked out at the dense forest, racking my brain.

Had she been taken? Had she run away? Was she lost in the woods? We were hours from any type of civilization. She was a decent navigator but not exactly experienced in the backcountry.

Had she heard them coming?

"I want a plane. A helicopter. Whatever. If she's in these woods, the best chance we have of finding her is from the air."

"Walt just had his hip replaced. He can't fly."

"Then find someone else. Call the Heberts. Those fuckers have planes."

"Okay, okay. Stay on the line with Adele. I'll call Mitch and see what we can do."

The surrounding forest, even from this vantage point, was too dense. My elevation did fuck-all to help me survey the land around us. Miles and miles of untouched forest with no trails, no roads. Nothing was all I could see.

"Breathe," Adele ordered.

"I shouldn't have left her," I whispered, shame and regret flooding me.

"Don't do that. You need to stay focused on the mission. We're going to find her. I'll get the entire town—the entire state—in those woods looking for her. You are not alone."

I closed my eyes. That's all I had ever wanted. To not be alone. To have my person by my side through the good and the bad and the hilarious. And I had found her. Finally. But now she was gone. Probably scared and hurt. And it was all my fault.

After a few moments of silence, a door creaked open. "The Heberts can't get a plane up today," Paz muttered.

"*What?*" I saw red.

"Mitch said it's a resource management issue, but they could maybe free one up tomorrow. Said they just couldn't spare it."

"That's bullshit," I spat, fury coursing through my veins. "Our families are supposed to be in this together. We've joined recovery efforts for lost men and damaged equipment how many times? This is my wife in the woods with fucking criminals."

"Wait," Adele said softly. "I think I can get a plane."

"How?"

She coughed. "Um. Someone owes me a favor. Let me make a few calls. I'll get eyes in the air."

"Good enough. I'm going to start looking for her. Call me on this number if you have news."

"Remy?"

I was already mentally climbing down this tree and working through how I would start my search. "Yeah?"

"Someone has to tell Dylan."

"Fuck."

"I'll do it," Paz said. "Adele will get a plane, and I'll get Dylan."

"Thanks," I said before hanging up and climbing down as quickly as I could.

I jogged back toward the cabin, snagging my backpack from the ATV and putting the phone inside. Henri had arrived and was striding toward me.

"Follow those tracks with the cops," I said. "Some of them are wider. Makes me think they had a side-by-side or an XTV."

"Where are you going?"

I straddled my ATV. "To find my wife."

He put his hand on the handlebar. "Stop. You're losing it. Take a minute to calm down."

I glared up at my big brother and resisted the urge to punch him. "Do *not* tell me to calm down. What if it was Alice out there? Or your kids?"

His face paled and he swallowed thickly. "You really love her, don't you?"

"Of course I fucking do. You're not the only one who gets to fall in love. The rest of us are allowed to have feelings too. I'm going to look for her. I'm going to find her."

"In 30,000 square miles of wilderness?" he protested.

I tugged my helmet down and secured the strap. "She couldn't have gone that far. She could be hurt. Or worse. I gotta go."

"But—"

I held a hand up. "Stay here. Do your CEO thing. Organize everyone. But I'm not standing around. Adele is getting me a plane."

I revved the engine. "At least one of my siblings is

useful," I muttered, peeling out. This area was filled with old trails and washed-out roads. I would drive every fucking one until I found my wife.

Over tree roots, through streams, and around boulders, I drove and drove, constantly calling out. If she'd run, she would have headed east. The wildflower meadow was west, and she would want cover. Plus, she was smart enough to know to head toward the main roads.

The forest was a blur as I drove through, each bump and jump jolting my racing heart. Fear gripped every cell in my body, but I didn't let it slow me down. She was here. I knew it.

My wife was smart and strategic. She wasn't the type to get caught by a bunch of goons. What would she do?

I followed a decent-sized stream for a while, hoping to find one of the main rivers, and came across a huge outcropping of rocks. I killed the engine and took a water break, then climbed onto one of the boulders to get a better look.

"Hazel," I bellowed, my voice carrying through the trees.

Again and again, I called, knowing it was fruitless but desperate to try anyway.

I dropped to the rock beneath me, wrapped my arms around my knees, and buried my head, fighting back tears. This is what true failure felt like. Letting the person I loved down. Not being there to protect her.

But then I heard it. A voice, a sound, in the distance.

I picked my head up and listened.

When I heard the faint sound again, I stood, calling her name over and over. And there it was. Closer. Clearer. "Remy!"

I jumped off the rocks and sprinted toward where the sound was coming from, yelling the entire time.

I followed the sound about a quarter of a mile until I saw her. She was standing on a tree stump, covered in dirt, but she was alive and staring right at me.

"Remy," she said softly as I raced for her.

"Are you hurt?" I asked, hauling her into my arms. "What happened? I'm so sorry. So fucking sorry," I said into her hair as I crushed her to my chest. Her tiny body clung to me, and relief washed through me. She was here. She was alive and hadn't been kidnapped. I may be a complete failure as a husband, but I had found her.

"You found me," she said.

With my hands on her upper arms, I pulled back and studied her. "I would never stop looking. Ever. I'd live in these woods and search every day until I found you."

"I love you," she rasped, burying her face in my chest.

My heart stuttered at her words. Words I had never known I needed so badly. They burrowed themselves deep inside my brain, and an awareness settled over me. She loved me. We loved each other.

It didn't matter that we were in the middle of the Maine wilderness and it would be dark in a couple of hours. All that mattered was that I'd found her. She'd found me. And we would get out of this together.

Chapter 39
Hazel

"My ATV is up there." He pointed upstream and tugged on my hand.

I followed, ready to get the hell out of these woods and doing my best not to limp, but it only took three or four steps for Remy to notice.

"What happened?" He pushed a strand of hair behind my ear.

I shrugged, looking down at my torn, bloody jeans. "This is just a scrape. But I think I sprained my ankle."

"I need to get you out of here. But first, tell me what happened."

I grimaced. He was not going to like this. And frankly, I was too tired and too scared to tiptoe through the details.

"After you left, men showed up with ATVs. They had guns."

Remy worked his jaw back and forth, his fists clenching. "Did they hurt you?"

I shook my head. "I got away. Slipped out the door. They wouldn't have seen me at all, but I went back."

His eyebrows shot up. *"You went back?"*

I pressed my lips together and shrugged. "Yeah. I climbed a tree and took some photos. Video too. They were loading up the stash and the supplies. But then I kind of fell out of the tree, and that got their attention."

He rubbed his face with both hands. "So you escaped undetected and then ran back toward the bad guys with the guns?"

"When you say it like that, it sounds stupid. But I was a safe distance away and in the tree."

"You climbed a tree?" he asked, his head cocked.

"You're not the only one who can do it, you know. Jesus. I was raised in Maine."

"But you did it with a sprained ankle?"

"No, the ankle sprain occurred after falling out of said tree."

He didn't respond, just stared at me, open-mouthed, before crushing me into a massive bear hug. "You are an infuriating, brave lunatic of a woman. Do you know that?"

I couldn't speak. He was still clutching me for dear life, with his massive arms locked tightly around me.

He finally let go, slinging my arm around his shoulders and supporting my weight. Then he led me toward the ATV. "So they saw you."

"Yes. So I ran like hell and hid in the forest. When they were gone, I headed southeast until I found a creek, figuring I'd hit Lake Millinocket sooner or later."

"How did you find your way?"

I tugged on his sleeve so he'd stop. Then I pulled the

compass pendant out of my shirt. "I used the compass. Since great-grandpa Pierre used it up in these parts, I figured it would help me too."

"God, I fucking love you," he said, dipping down and taking my lips with his.

Deepening the kiss, I sank into him, letting him support me for several moments. Then I pulled back and looked up at his beautiful, earnest face. We were lost in the woods and dirty and tired, but I couldn't hold it in any longer. This man was mine, and I was his, and there was no denying this.

"I love you too," I said softly, watching the smile spread across his face.

We made it back to the ATV, drank the last of the water he had in his backpack, and took a few deep breaths. He turned the key in the ignition and pushed the starter, but it sputtered and then died.

I took a step back as he climbed up and tried again.

"Fuck."

"What happened?"

He turned and to me, his shoulders slumped and his eyes dull. The look I had witnessed a few times after I'd first returned to Lovewell but hadn't seen in weeks. It was a look of failure.

"Out of gas. I've been driving around for hours, but I didn't think to bring a gas can."

He raked his fingers through his hair and gripped so tightly I thought he would tear the roots right out of his scalp. "God dammit. I'm such a fuck-up."

"Stop," I said, putting a hand to his chest, trying to deescalate his anger.

"I left you in the woods alone. Vulnerable. With bad

guys with guns driving around. And despite the tens of thousands of square miles of forest, I find you only to run out of gas?"

"We can hike it. Plus," I gave him a playful wink, "I got photos of the bad guys."

"When we get home, we're going to have a long conversation about unnecessary risk taking."

"And I'm going to roll my eyes because I do not need you to mansplain danger to me."

"Let me find you a walking stick first. There's a whole trail network up here. It's all connected to the streams that feed into the Penobscot River. Once we get in an open area, I can use the sat phone to call Henri."

We headed through the woods, me with one arm slung around his shoulders and the other clutching the tree branch he insisted I use. If not for the ankle sprain and the life-threatening danger of a few hours ago, this would actually be a pretty romantic moment. Hiking through the forest with my lumberjack husband. The two of us alone in nature. We stopped every several minutes to consult an old map he'd found in his backpack. Not that it made much difference. The trails we were following weren't even on the maps.

"I still can't believe you found me," I said as he lifted me off a boulder and set me on the ground.

His gaze was serious. "I wasn't going to stop looking. I would have wandered these woods for the rest of my life."

My face heated at his admission. "You can't stay that stuff to me when we're lost in the woods. Now I wanna jump your sexy, romantic bones. Not hobble to freedom."

He laughed. "There will be plenty of time for sex when

we get back to Lovewell. Especially since I'm not letting you out of my sight for the next twenty or so years."

We made it down the hill, falling into companionable silence and watching the stream widen. When we found a well-cut trail, we consulted the compass and decided to take it farther south, hoping to find the river.

Our silence was interrupted by the sound of engines. Remy froze, then whipped his head one way and then the other as the noise got louder. He picked me up and left the trail, then dropped low behind a felled tree.

"Do you think that's Henri and the police?" I asked optimistically. "Or—"

He put his hand over my mouth, silencing me as three ATVs drove slowly by. The men driving them scanned the woods as they went, wearing helmets and black clothing and bearing a distinct resemblance to the fuckers who'd chased me through the forest earlier.

I closed my eyes and held my breath, all the fear and terror coming back to me, immobilizing me. The sound of the engines faded, but not before we heard them speak to one another in French.

"They're looking for you," Remy said, pushing me farther down. "We gotta get out of here."

Now that we'd stopped moving, I started to shiver, likely due to shock. The realization only made me panic more. What if they came back for us? I couldn't run, and I couldn't risk Remy getting hurt, or worse. My breath was short, and my heart was racing. Beads of sweat broke out along my hairline and rolled down my spine. I needed to think, to formulate a plan and move, but I was frozen.

Remy crouched down, taking my face in his hands. "I

will not let anything happen to you. Once they get a little farther, we're gonna run for it."

I shook my head, but I couldn't form words.

"I'll carry you." He put his backpack on his chest and snapped it in place.

When the engines faded to a light rumble and their voices could no longer be heard, Remy stood.

"Get on my back. They're not looking."

His voice pulled me out of my panic, but my adrenaline was wearing off, and all I could do was stare.

"We gotta run, and you can't on the ankle." He bent over like he did when we practiced our wife carrying technique.

"Remy, what are you thinking?"

"Hazel, do it now. We've trained for this. You know how to be the jockey. Keep close, and I'll get us out of here."

"I don't know—"

He grabbed my shoulders and regarded me with more intensity than I'd ever seen from him. "I've got you. You're gonna hop on my back, and we'll put as much distance between us and the men with guns as we possibly can. Don't be afraid. I won't let anything happen to you."

His face was so earnest and determined. And for the first time in my life, I felt truly protected.

He bent down, and I grabbed his waist, letting my legs, including my swollen, throbbing ankle, rest on his shoulders.

And then he took off. Running faster than I had ever seen him run, through the forest, over tree roots and around brambles. He was so fast and so quiet.

Shouts echoed in the distance, and Remy picked up the pace. The distinct sound of shots rang out, startling me and sending my full body into panic mode.

"Stay focused, Hazel," Remy said, panting. "You need to hold on and work with me. We're getting out of here."

I tucked my head against his lower back, clinging to him with all my strength and focusing on his body, anticipating his movements and shifting my weight accordingly. When he prepared to jump over tree roots, I could feel it. Before he banked to veer around boulders or engaged his core to accelerate down hills, I could sense it. It was exactly as we practiced. Feeling his muscles move, feeling his body work.

I blocked out the sounds around us. The engines, the voices, and the gunshots. Instead focusing solely on my husband. We were a team. And we had to move as one.

Eventually, Remy slowed, and I took a few deep breaths, listening for any signs of danger.

But aside from bird calls and crunching leaves, it was quiet. We hit a few muddy spots, and some larger hills, but from what I could tell, we were alone. We had lost them.

When he finally put me down, pulling me close and kissing my head, my tears flowed freely.

"Remy," I cried, clutching his shirt.

"Not now, babe," he said, rubbing my arms. "Let's get the map and figure out where we are."

I got my compass, and he pulled the map from his pack. Together, we determined where we had been, the approximate distance we had traveled, and how far we were from the lake.

"Mathematically, we know you run at roughly a seven-minute mile pace, and we went due east off the trail and then south. So we should be about a mile from Lake Millinocket, if we continue."

He scrunched his nose up. "How are you this good at navigation?"

I shrugged. "It's just math, and I'm a Mainer. The woods have been my backyard for most of my life. I may not be a big tough lumberjack like you"—I smirked—"but I get by."

"Oh, you do more than get by."

We reached Lake Millinocket just as the sun touched the horizon. Remy used the sat phone to contact Henri, who promised they had a float plane coming to get us. Where they'd tracked down a plane was a mystery, but I wouldn't question my means of rescue.

There was a dock on the lake with the most gorgeous view of the sunset over the dark water and mountaintops. Remy and I sat shoulder to shoulder on the wood planks, our legs dangling and his arm around me, waiting for our ride home.

And I finally let out a breath. We were safe.

I examined his profile—his sharp jaw, his thick beard, and those cheekbones, tan with a few freckles from days spent in the sun—and I was done for.

He had saved me. Protected me. And right there on that dock, the last few bricks fell, my protective walls finally crumbling under the weight of my love for this man.

Chapter 40
Remy

We were met back in Lovewell by dozens of law enforcement officers and most of the town.

It was late, and I was dirty and exhausted and deeply confused as to why Finn Hebert had taken a company plane to pick us up after Mitch had specifically told Paz there wasn't one available.

What was even more confusing was my sister's presence in said plane. When we climbed into the tiny aircraft, she shot me a look that said, *do not ask questions*. And my life had already been in danger once today, so I wasn't about to cross Adele. Hell, I'd rather take on the ATV henchmen than my pissed-off sister.

We landed on South Birch Lake, just outside of town, where my mother was waiting at the end of the dock. I'd barely helped Hazel out of the plane before Loraine Gagnon's arms were around us both.

She led us to her truck, where, in the dark, Paz and Alice and dozens of others were waiting to see us.

Including Dylan.

Who strode right up to me and punched me in the face.

I buckled and grabbed my throbbing jaw, then found my balance.

"What the hell, Dylan?" Hazel snapped, slumping against the side of Paz's truck to keep from falling. "Get away from him, you psycho."

I shook my head, still reeling. Dylan ignored Hazel and charged toward me again. "You promised," he hissed, his face red and full of fury. "You promised to keep her safe."

Holding my hands up in surrender, I squinted, already feeling my face swell. "I also promised not to fall in love with her. So you can take another shot. 'Cause I'm a shit friend."

His eyes widened, and he reared back, probably stunned by my declaration. And I braced myself, sure that the next punch would hurt even more.

But Hazel hobbled between us, a hand on her hip. "Stop it, Dylan. You're acting like a damn caveman."

His face softened, and he dragged his sister in for a hug.

She pushed against his chest. "And I kept myself safe, thank you very much."

"She did," I admitted. "She's smarter than all of us combined."

Dylan wrapped her up again, squeezing tight while glaring at me. This wasn't over. And I had a lot of apologizing to do.

We were escorted back to Henri's house, where my mom and Alice took turns fussing over us, insisting we not get up for anything and offering far more food than a human could consume in a day while the state police set up a makeshift command center, interviewing us several times and poring over the photos Hazel had taken.

She was being questioned for at least the eleventh time when I spotted Finn Hebert standing on the front porch, speaking to my sister.

When my mom's back was turned, I snuck out, interrupting the hushed conversation they were having.

Adele glared at me, which I ignored.

"Thank you," I said to Finn, offering my hand. "I'm in your debt."

He gave me a friendly smile and took my hand. "Glad to help. I'm not my dad. If someone needs help, I'm there."

Finn Hebert could only be kindly described as a Viking. Tall—and not Gagnon tall; more like NBA tall—with blue eyes and dirty-blond hair that was shaved on the sides with a man bun on top. Tattoos snaked up both of his arms, and he had a scar across his left cheek.

Despite the comic book–villain appearance, he was friendly enough. And he had defied his father and taken a company plane to rescue us. That alone was reason enough to give him a chance.

"I mean it," I repeated. "I owe you."

He rubbed his chin and smirked. "Well," he hedged, "I'm a big fan, and my brothers are always busting my balls about what a slow climber I am. I'd love some training tips."

I laughed. I hadn't seen him on the circuit, but his four brothers dabbled in timbersports, like many guys in the logging business.

"I'd be happy to share a few of my secrets."

"After nationals," Hazel piped up from behind me. She limped through the doorway and immediately settled under my arm with one hand on my chest. I liked her there. And I had every intention of fulfilling my promise to keep her close forever. I breathed easier when she was near.

"Good luck, man," Finn said with a pat on my shoulder. "I'll be rooting for you. I gotta get home."

"I'll walk you to your truck," Adele said, leaving us on the porch without another word.

Hazel rested her head on my chest while I took in the view. It was getting cool and the stars were bright. After so many months of obsessing about all the things I didn't have, I was suddenly struck with just how much I did. My family, my town, my girl. Nothing else mattered.

"What the fuck are you doing palling around with a Hebert?" Paz called, rounding the side of the house.

Adele ignored him, instead taking the porch steps two at a time. "I got some good photos of the trails," Adele explained. "The canopy is dense in some areas, but I was able to get some GPS coordinates. They probably aren't exact, but it should help."

"Thanks." I hugged her, even though I knew she would hate it. "You tell the cops?"

She dipped her chin. "I did."

"I owe you, sis."

Before she could snap back with a sarcastic response, Paz interrupted.

"You didn't answer me." He was close now, his fancy cologne wafting around us. I closed my eyes, suddenly feeling way too tired for his shit.

But Adele, as always, had plenty of fight left in her. She wheeled around, pinning him with a glare. "He's prior service Navy and got us a plane," she said. "No further explanation needed." With that, she stomped into the house, leaving us alone with an angry Paz.

"Henri should be back soon." He had stayed at camp to deal with law enforcement up there and interview members of the crew. In the years that traffickers had used our forests to move their product, this was the closest we had ever come to actually catching them. And there was no way Henri would not let up now that we'd had a break.

"They haven't found them," he said. "They cleaned out everything."

"I still don't understand how they knew we were there. We radioed on our private channel," Hazel mused.

"Did someone intercept our radio frequency?"

"Bet they did," Paz snarled. "Which wouldn't have happened if you'd come back to camp and used an actual fucking phone to call the cops instead of broadcasting it over the radio."

I clenched my fists, itching to fight him. After what Hazel and I had been through, he had some goddamn audacity starting shit.

"Actually," I said, standing a little straighter, "aren't you the one in charge of working with law enforcement on keeping our land safe?"

"I've got a shit ton on my plate. I'm the CFO," he hissed. "You know, a real job?"

I cocked a brow. "You could have consented to let them search the old camps."

"We didn't even know this camp existed before today. Dad's chicken scratch Post-it notes aren't exactly official documents. We had no idea that any of those trails were even cleared. Besides," he took a step toward me, his eyes flashing, "you're the one who's lived up there for months at a time. You're supposed to know these woods like the back of your hand. You're the fucking forest child who climbs trees and skips out on real responsibility."

I gritted my teeth, silently chanting *I will not hit my brother*. Especially with my wife standing here.

Blowing out a breath, I shook my head. "You're a sad, angry person. And you know as well as I do that we're all doing a shit job living up to Dad's legacy. Maybe you should get your ass out of your cushy desk chair once in a while. Take off your thousand-dollar motherfucking loafers and get in the woods."

He sighed, staring down at his feet. I saw it then. He was tired and worried and defeated. The past few years had taken a lot out of all of us, and he was too pigheaded and stubborn to admit he had been worried about me.

"I'm okay," I said, trying to make peace. "And so is Hazel."

He stared at me with his jaw clenched and his eyes narrowed. I had no idea what was going on in his head, except that he was clearly in pain. I had been so obsessed with my own stuff, so focused on my pain and my losses, that I hadn't stopped to think about what he'd been through.

"Boys," my mother shouted, in her *I mean business* voice. She turned to Hazel. "I think we should get you home. You shouldn't be standing out here in the cold. The nice police officers are going to keep a patrol outside the cabin tonight, just in case."

She glared at me. "Let's get your wife home."

I stood up straight. "Yes, ma'am."

Chapter 41
Remy

The next day was more of the same. We were back at Henri's for more interviews with the police and now the DEA. As well as our company lawyers. It was endless. Answering the same questions over and over again, with few breaks. I wanted these guys caught and brought to justice, but I wanted to be with my wife more.

Midmorning, Henri showed up and pulled me into his study.

"Any updates?" I asked, studying his face.

Henri shook his head. "The police are still looking. The feds are taking over the investigation, which is good news. They have a lot more resources. Hazel's photos helped. They're flying drones to map out the old roads and trails, look for anything suspicious."

I crossed my arms. That wasn't good enough, and he knew it. My wife and I had been chased by armed drug traffickers in the Maine wilderness. They'd seen us, and clearly, they'd heard us on the radio. They could know our names and everything about us by now. "They promised we'd be safe," I said through gritted teeth.

"There's no reason to believe you're not safe. The operation appears to have gone underground. They haven't been this successful for this long by taking risks. No one is coming into a tiny town hours away."

"That you know of."

I stared at one another for a moment, anger churning in my gut. It wasn't his fault. I knew that. He wasn't a cop. But the lack of movement on this investigation was eating away at me. We needed answers.

I didn't want to say this out loud because I still hadn't forgiven my other brother for how he'd treated Hazel and me, but I blew out a breath and went for it anyway. "Paz is right." I said, shaking my head. "We need an investigator."

"Already on it. Paz has a contact from Portland. We're working it out now. It's going to be expensive, but at this point, we can't take any more chances."

I gritted my teeth. I wanted Paz as far away from this as possible. This was my wife's safety we were talking about, and I wasn't taking it lightly.

"He knows what he's doing," Henri said.

"How can you be sure?"

"Because I trust him. He's going through some shit. He's been an insufferable asshole, but he's committed to our family and the business. He'll deliver."

It didn't feel like enough. Nothing felt like enough. It was all connected—the drugs, Dad's death, Hazel's research. We had found so much, and yet we still didn't have any answers.

"I could have lost her," I muttered, hanging my head, still wrung out from the previous day's events.

"I know."

"And Dad."

"I know."

I slumped in a chair, my head in my hands, and concentrated on breathing. My mind continued to spin out every catastrophic possibility. This problem wasn't going away. How many members of my family would be hurt before we put a stop to it?

"I'm giving you my word," Henri said. "We'll devote everything we have to this. We'll work with law enforcement, force the other families to cooperate, hire investigators. I'll even get Hazel a bodyguard if you want."

"She'd hate that."

"Hazel's family. And I don't care if she likes it. We're taking care of her."

I looked up at my brother, the stoic CEO who had given his entire life to the land and the company. For whom nothing was more important than work. He had transformed so thoroughly he was almost unrecognizable in this moment. He had fallen in love and become a dad. He had opened himself up to all the possible hurt and heartbreak and pain that came with those roles.

A wave of overwhelming gratitude swept over me, so I stood and pulled him into a hug.

"Thank you," I said.

"I'm proud of you." He patted me on the back harder than was probably necessary. "And Dad would be proud too. Wherever you go and whatever you do, nothing will change that."

Henri's words swam through my head as I hiked down to the cabin a few hours later. Hazel had been questioned for most of the day, and I was missing her fiercely. I needed to be with her, needed to make sure she was okay.

But my stomach sank at the sight of Dylan's Jeep parked in front. Fuck. It was time to face the music. Hazel and I were moving forward, and I had to make amends with my best friend. I had lied to him, compromising one of the most important relationships in my life. And I had to do better.

I had to take responsibility for my choices.

Dylan was chatting with my mother, who was taking a loaf of banana bread out of the oven. I guessed it was a good thing. The cabin smelled amazing, and it wasn't like that oven ever got any use.

I gave them both a tense smile.

"Hazel's resting," my mother explained. "She's exhausted, and she needs to keep her ankle elevated."

I nodded and gave her a kiss on the cheek before dropping my keys on the island. She looked from Dylan's tense face to mine. "I'm going to run up to the big house to drop off some snacks." She untied her apron and draped it over one of the stools. "I'll be back later. I'm making a special dinner for everyone tonight."

Dylan gave her a pleasant smile, and we both stood in the kitchen, completely silent, until the door clicked shut.

I swallowed and turned toward him, ready to face the music.

"I'm sorry," I said, a preemptive strike. "I'm a horrible friend."

Dylan stared at me, and the silence stretched uncomfortably.

After several excruciating seconds, he finally spoke. "She told me she's in love with you," he said, shuffling over to the couch. He dropped onto the cushion and rested his head on the back. "She also told me if I ever punch her husband again, she'd kick my ass."

I laughed. That sounded like Hazel, and it felt good to know she had my back. "I'm in love with her too."

"I know." He tipped forward and dropped his head into hands, pulling at his longish hair. "I've been ignoring signs for a while. I just didn't want to see it."

I stood quietly, unsure of what to say to make him understand that this was forever. That I wasn't going to let his sister go, that I would love her and protect her and give her everything I could for as long as I lived. But I kept quiet, too overcome with exhaustion from the last few days to even begin to articulate my feelings.

"You don't understand. Hazel is all I've got. You've got this big, happy family. She and I, we've been a team since we were kids. And she's worked so hard for so long. She's got tons of potential, man. More than you and I can understand."

I clenched my fists. I knew how incredible my wife was, and she continued to impress me more and more every day. The woman had carefully studied wife carrying, applied physics, and had come up with a training plan in one day, for fuck's sake.

I chose my words carefully, not wanting to pick another fight. "I know. I will never hold her back. I will be her champion and make sure she understands how extraordinary she is every day." How could he think, knowing me for so many decades, that I would ever keep her from pursuing her dreams?

"I know that," he murmured, his eyes fixed on the floor in front of him. "Deep down I know that. But I'm scared. I'm scared she's going to end up like my mom."

"Dylan, with all due respect to your mom, Hazel is nothing like her. She dreams big and has the work ethic to do anything she wants. And we're in this together. I'll follow her wherever she wants to go. I'll do whatever she needs me too. I'm a simple guy. I don't need much."

He looked up at me, a look of anguish on his face. The pain of being kept in the dark about Hazel and me etched in every line.

"I know I'm not good enough. But I swear I'm working every single day to be better. To be the kind of man who deserves her."

"You do deserve her. I see it. How you've taken care of her. Protected her. Given her everything you can. Driving an hour to the health food store, building her bookshelves, helping her make connections for her research. I see it. I get it."

I sat down next to him on the couch. Letting the silence wash over us.

"So what's the problem?" I asked.

Dylan regarded me, his lips pressed together for a long moment. "The problem is, I don't want to lose you both. My sister and my best friend. I know you'll take care of her, and I have no doubt she'll keep you in line. But I've got no one else."

"We're not going anywhere." I put my arm around his

shoulder and pulled him in for a hug. "I'll always be your best friend."

Curled up in our bed, I stroked Hazel's hair. After long showers and my mother force-feeding us yet again, we climbed into bed under a mountain of blankets and held one another for a long time. I couldn't get close enough, even now.

I had almost lost her yesterday. The thought made my throat tighten and my stomach seize.

With a finger under her chin, I tipped her head so she was looking at me. "I'm never letting you out of my sight again."

She gave me a sleepy, peaceful smile. "That seems inconvenient."

I kissed her forehead. "I'm serious. We're getting married."

She rubbed her eyes and shot me an annoyed look. "Did you hit your head? We are married. Legally and everything."

That didn't count. We needed to make this commitment again. Circumstances had changed. I wanted another crack at the vows and the *till death do us part* bit. "Don't care. Let's get married again. That's how serious I am."

She burrowed into me. "Let's go to bed."

"Nope. I gotta get this off my chest now."

"Okay." She sat up, pulling the comforter around her. "I'm ready."

"I'll go anywhere. I'll do anything for you," I said. "All I want are a few trees to climb and my girl. I promise I won't ever get in your way. You're brilliant. You're going to change the world, and I'm the guy who gets to wake up next to you. If you'll have me."

She smiled and kissed me. "Of course I will."

"So you'll marry me."

"Again. I'll marry you again."

I crushed her in a hug. "I mean it. You're stuck with me. And probably a cat and a dog and a couple of rescue alpacas, and when you're ready, a whole bunch of kids."

"Remy, I'm already stuck with you. We already said *I do*."

"But that's the thing, babe. That wasn't good enough. Now I want *I do forever*."

Epilogue
Remy

"You're so freaking beautiful. But in this getup?" I waggled my brows. "Damn."

Propped against a railing, I took in Hazel's competition gear. Tiny spandex shorts, a sports bra, and a plaid shirt with the sleeves cut off and tied at the waist. I wore a matching shirt, sans sleeves as well. My mother had stitched custom *Team Gagnon* labels to the back of each one.

"You're one to talk. I'm about ready to take out all these lumberskanks who keep eyeing your arms. I should have known better than to let you show that shit off in public," she said, hopping from one foot to the other.

Hazel was buzzing with excitement. For the calm half of this marriage, she was damn near bouncing off the walls. "We're going to win," she whispered in my ear. "And then I'm taking you back to our hotel room and having my way with you."

"I have the first full day of events tomorrow," I reminded her.

"It's fine. You can lie back, and I'll do all the work." She pinched my ass and giggled. "I'll make sure not to tire you out too much."

More than three months into our marriage, Hazel continued to surprise and delight me. Not only had she insisted on continuing our training, but after recovering from our ordeal in the forest, we had stepped it up a notch. After our escape from the woods, a little obstacle course seemed silly.

Her ankle had mostly healed. She had it taped up today, just in case, but I could tell she was feeling good. Granted, the hot hotel sex we'd had the night before *and* that morning may have helped our nerves.

Nationals was unlike anything I had ever experienced before. Professional athletes—including some of my heroes— walking around and chatting. TV cameras, press, and tons of corporate sponsors. We would be competing in an honest-to-God stadium, something I couldn't even fathom. It was surreal. I had made it.

More importantly, I was finally beginning to feel like I deserved to be here. And it was all thanks to the gorgeous woman standing next to me. I had trained harder than I ever had in my life, pushing my body past what I thought were my limits. And Hazel had been my strategist—planning with me, taking videos, studying my technique, and using her genius brain to help me gain every possible advantage.

I had coasted through most of my life, never giving anything my all. But that changed when I married Hazel. She hustled harder than anyone I had ever met. And watching her made me realize how much I had been holding back. How many excuses I'd made throughout my life. All the years that I could have been chasing my dreams instead of self-sabotaging. But things were different now. I was focused and ready.

The first events began tomorrow. It didn't matter whether I came in first place or last, because I had done everything I could in service of this dream. And now it was time to enjoy it.

So I got to stand in this stadium with the love of my life, surrounded by professional and semi-professional athletes, corporate sponsors, and thousands of cheering fans. And this alone was worth all the sacrifice and hard work. To share this with her.

It was time to line up with the other couples, including Cedric and Crystal, who I couldn't even be bothered to look at. I just didn't care. Hazel was sizing everyone up, and I swore I could see mathematical equations dancing above her head as she took in each person's size and how the couples interacted. For someone who claimed not to be sporty, she had a hell of a competitive streak, and I was reveling in it.

I was here with my girl. My wife. And we had been through hell to get here. I was living my dream by competing at nationals, and that was more than enough for me.

Because I had realized that my real dream, the thing that sustained me and inspired me, was my wife. Was the life we shared and the future and family we would build together. That was so much more important than any competition or sponsorship or career.

Regardless of what happened, I was here with my person. And someday, when we were old and gray, we'd tell our grandkids about this day.

She stood up on her tiptoes and gave me a kiss. "Love you."

We still hadn't figured it all out. Where we would live, what we would do, but none of it mattered. Hazel and I were a team, and we would tackle these challenges together. Because I didn't need much, but I needed my wife.

Out in those woods, I think we'd both had that epiphany. That our love was so much bigger than any convenience or agreement. The endless interviews with law enforcement had confirmed just how dangerous these drug traffickers were and how badly things could have gone.

Lined up in a row, we got into position and waited for the starting gun. I had grown accustomed to the feel of her wrapped around me, the position of her legs and the way she tucked herself against me. I was more than familiar with every inch of her body, and while that was useful in many settings, it would be an advantage today.

Training for this race was fun and intense and silly all at the same time. And I had my wife to thank for volunteering us. Because regardless of whether we won, this event had brought us closer. Had helped us to learn to trust each other. And that was more valuable than any prize or corporate sponsorship.

The starting gun sounded, and we were off, heading down a hill and into our future.

Bonus Chapter

Want more Remy & Hazel?

Scan below to get the Bonus Chapter

Warning: it will make you laugh, cry and swoon!

Need More Lumberjacks?

You can find the entire Lovewell Lumberjacks Series on Amazon. Free to read in Kindle Unlimited

Book 1: **Wood You Be Mine?**
Book 2: **Wood You Marry Me?**
Book 3: **Wood You Rather?**
Book 4: **Wood Riddance!**

Also by Daphne Elliot

LOVEWELL

The Lovewell Lumberjacks Series

Wood You Be Mine?

Wood You Marry Me?

Wood You Rather?

Wood Riddance

The Maine Lumberjacks Series

Caught in the Axe

Pain in the Axe

Axe-identally Married

Axe Backwards

Axe-ing for Trouble

THE MOM COMS

Mother Hater

Also by Daphne Elliot

HAVENPORT

The Quinn Brothers Series

Trusting You

Finding You

Keeping You

The Rossi Family Series

Resisting You

Holding You

Embracing You

Acknowledgments

Thank you for taking this trip to Lovewell with me! This book would not have been possible without the help of so many talented and dedicated people. I can't believe this is my tenth book in two years.

This book would not exist without Erica Connors Walsh. Thank you for being my friend, my cheerleader, and the best PA ever. You read every single word I write, constantly giving feedback and pushing me to do better. I appreciate your honesty and support. We have cried and laughed and yelled together over the past two years, and I am a better person and writer because of you. When we needed a cover, you jumped right in and took care of it. I believe deeply that some divine cosmic power brought us together, and I'm so grateful to have you on my team.

To my writing sister Jenni Bara, who's encyclopedic knowledge of the brother's best friend trope helped this book come to life. Thank you for your kindness, your patience, and your motherhood solidarity. I appreciate the hell out of you and root for you every day.

Swati M.H., thank you for your friendship and your wit. Despite the continent that separates us, you make me feel seen and appreciated. You are amazing.

To my author squad, Brittanee Nicole, Elyse Kelly, and A.J. Ranney. I love you all and am so lucky to have met you. This can be such a lonely journey, but your friendship is such a gift.

To my beta readers, Amaryllis, Swati, Christina, Amy and Jenni, thank you all for helping me work through Remy & Hazel's journey and giving me helpful notes.

Beth, thank you for your thorough editing. I am amazed by your patience, professionalism, and kindness. I'm sorry I'm such a lazy writer and never put my quotation marks in the right place.

Jane, thank you for the gorgeous photos. Taking photos of shirtless men is a hard job, and I'm grateful you do it.

Dane and Maddi, thank you for the amazing cover photo. You are beautiful people, inside and out and I am honored to have you on my book.

Thank you to my mother, who always pushed me to do my best and believed in me even when I did not. I am the kind of person who decides to write books in my nonexistent free time because of you.

Thank you to my family for being hilarious and loving and silly. To my children, G & T, you push me and challenge me and surprise me every day. Thank you for never going easy on me.

And finally, thank you to my patient and devastatingly handsome husband. You are my original Alpha Roll.

About the Author

In High School, Daphne Elliot was voted "most likely to become a romance novelist." After spending the last decade as a corporate lawyer, she has finally embraced her destiny. Her steamy novels are filled with flirty banter, sexy hijinks, and lots and lots of heart.

Daphne is a coffee-drinking, hot-sauce loving introvert who spends her free time gardening and practicing yoga. She lives in Massachusetts with her husband, two kids, two dogs, two fish, and twelve backyard chickens.

Find Daphne Elliot At:

daphneelliotauthor@gmail.com

Stay in touch with Daphne:

Subscribe to Daphne's Newsletter
Join Daphne's Reader Group
Follow Daphne on TikTok
Like Daphne on Facebook
Follow Daphne on Instagram
Hang with Daphne on GoodReads
Follow Daphne on Amazon